D1175247

Torrents of Destruction

Center Point
Large Print

Also by Robin Caroll and available from
Center Point Large Print:

Justice Seeker Series
 To Write a Wrong
 Strand of Deception

Torrents of Destruction

ROBIN CAROLL

CENTER POINT LARGE PRINT
THORNDIKE, MAINE

This Center Point Large Print edition is published
in the year 2016 by arrangement with RC Productions Inc.

The text of this Large Print edition is unabridged.
In other aspects, this book may vary
from the original edition.
Printed in the United States of America
on permanent paper.
Set in 16-point Times New Roman type.

ISBN: 978-1-68324-002-0

Library of Congress Cataloging-in-Publication Data

Names: Caroll, Robin, author.
Title: Torrents of destruction / Robin Caroll.
Description: Center Point Large Print edition. | Thorndike, Maine :
Center Point Large Print, 2016. | ©2015
Identifiers: LCCN 2016009445 | ISBN 9781683240020
    (hardcover : alk. paper)
Subjects: LCSH: Large type books. | GSAFD: Suspense fiction.
Classification: LCC PS3603.A7673 T67 2016 | DDC 813/.6—dc23
LC record available at http://lccn.loc.gov/2016009445

For Casey

Because you inspire me
to be better than I am—
and love me even when I'm not

"The cords of death entangled me; the torrents of destruction overwhelmed me. The cords of the grave coiled around me; the snares of death confronted me. In my distress I called to the Lord; I cried to my God for help. From his temple he heard my voice; my cry came before him, into his ears."

PSALM 18:4–6 NIV

One

Thunder crashed over the West Virginia sky. Clouds cast eerie shadows, foreboding and ominous. Katie Gallagher quickened her pace down the gravel path. The approaching storm interfered with her determined strides. Shadow, her Blue Heeler and ever-present companion, trotted at her side.

She pushed into the store with Shadow on her heels, headed to the counter, and dropped onto the stool. She flipped to this evening's appointment log and grabbed a pencil from the holder, rolling it between her thumb and forefinger.

Her elder brother Gabe's soft smile enhanced his tanned face. "Your group should arrive after seven tonight. Ready?"

Katie's gaze moved to the bank of windows across the front of the store. Lightning flashed in the bright afternoon sky over the Gauley River. While no rain pelted the area yet, foul weather would arrive soon enough.

Gabe adjusted the display rack of wetsuits a fraction of an inch, then hobbled back to study his handiwork, dragging his walking cast.

She scuffed the toe of her sandal against the tile, letting the shoe slip to the floor. "I still don't see why Christian can't take this group. I need to run the projection numbers for next month." Seemed like as of late, their younger brother constantly shirked his duties.

"We've been over this." While Gabe didn't sigh aloud, the implication was clear.

"But you and I aren't the only Gallaghers working Gauley Guides. Dad left the business to all three of us." She let out an exaggerated breath and tapped her pencil against the cash register. "I hate baby-sitting power executives who think they can tame the river."

"It's not like I asked to have my leg broken, Katie. I'd do it if I could."

And he would. Gabe carried the brunt of the responsibility for the family business. Good thing he had such broad shoulders. Katie didn't envy his load.

Guilt circled her heart, but the tight knot of irritation wouldn't let loose of her nerves. She had a stack of bills she needed to figure out how they were going to pay, and she wanted to check out the new equipment they'd just received. Besides, she yearned for some solitude after last weekend's trip with a group of rowdy college kids. "Christian's better suited for these guys."

Gabe concentrated on re-arranging the rack holding the life jackets, but shot her a scowl as he straightened two hangers. "Maybe, but he's not as good as you. He's taking the group tomorrow."

A day trip. So easy she'd mastered those trips

when she was only fourteen. "True, but Christian always seems to squirm out of the hard work." Maybe it was time he accepted more responsibility. He was nineteen now, time to grow up and act like an adult. It wasn't right for the brunt of the work relating to the business to fall on Gabe and Katie. They'd sacrificed enough already. Especially Gabe.

Gabe shuffled to the wooden counter where she sat. Resting his elbow on the glass top, he clucked his tongue. "These men are pencil pushers, sis. Come on—they're going to need the best guide to get them through the Upper Gauley. And since I'm unavailable, you're the next best Gallagher."

Her eyes narrowed and she shoved his elbow. Hard.

His arm jarred out from under him. He tottered for a moment, then straightened and laughed.

Katie glared. "Second best, am I? Gabriel Gallagher, I'll take you on any day of the week and twice on Sunday."

"I know you would. Look, it's only a three-day trip." Thick brown curls brushed his forehead, just as their father's had. "How bad can it be?"

"Never ask a question like that. You know better. You'll jinx me for sure." She turned to the shelves and flipped on the radio set to the weather station.

Tropical depression Emily still fringes on the coast of North Carolina. It has not yet been upgraded to a hurricane. The National Weather Service estimates the storm will make landfall by midnight. Stay tuned for more after these announcements.

Katie raised an eyebrow. "Should we cancel our tours this weekend?"

He limped across the room to lean against the door and stare at the late afternoon sky. "Emily's been sitting on the coast for several hours—I have a feeling she'll lose strength."

No one could read clouds like Gabe.

Still . . . "The wind's picking up, and it looks like we'll be getting some rain."

"I know what you're saying, but we need these trips. Since we bought all the new equipment last month, I'm depending on the confirmed bookings to keep us in the black."

Should she tell him the bank had called earlier today? Katie scrutinized her brother. Years of worry and stress lined his face, and his skin took on a pallor like a person who'd been in the hospital too long. No, she needed to ease his burdens, not add to them.

Gabe shuffled by, then reached under the counter and pulled out a can of fresh linen–scented air freshener. No matter how much he sprayed and disinfected, the odor of mildew permeated the shop. "I honestly don't think Emily will turn inward, and I don't want to fall behind on the bank note. Do you think losing everything would honor what Dad worked for all his life?"

Playing the Dad-card, the cheat. Her heart twisted at the memory of their father's lecture on dependability. She'd probably have to step up to the plate more to help Gabe since Christian was no help. "You want me to risk being out on the river with a hurricane making landfall?"

"It's not a hurricane, Katie. It's a tropical depression."

"Which will still swirl some nasty weather our way."

He stowed the spray can back under the counter. "We don't have a choice. You know the numbers we're dealing with." He paused, tilting his head. "Are you really worried? If you are, just say so. I don't want a scaredy-cat guide out there with clients."

Gabe pushed the right button. Indignation reared its ugly head. "Puhleeze! You know better. I kayaked that river at thirteen, during flood stage."

"Then what's the problem?"

Katie slammed the appointment book shut and stabbed the chewed pencil into the holder on the desk. "No problem."

"That's the spirit. Dad would be proud."

She gave a long, labored sigh. "You know I'll take care of things. I'd better go make sure my little executives' cabin is ready." She eased her feet inside her sandals and gave Gabe a hug, snuggling her head against his solid chest. The physical contact warmed her to her toes. "At least we don't have to feed them tonight."

Katie pulled away and jerked the master key off the board, then slipped it into the pocket of her shorts. "Christian better have stocked the cabin, or I'll have his punkin-head on a platter."

"Where is he, anyway? I haven't seen him for a couple of hours."

"Who knows? He's never around when there's work to be done." She snapped her fingers. Shadow bounded to her. She bent to scratch beneath his chin.

"That's not nice, sis. Christian tries." The slight reproach fit Gabe, ever the peace-maker.

Katie reached into the pocket of her shorts and pulled out a peppermint, then unwrapped it and popped the swirl-colored candy into her mouth. "Not hard enough."

"He'll come around. It's just taking him a little longer, but what can we expect? He's the baby."

She snorted and snatched a stack of fluffy towels piled on the round table.

"It's partially our fault, Katie. We spoiled him."

She pushed the door. The tiny bell tinkled softly above her head. "Then we need to un-spoil him and make him grow up and face reality." She let the door whoosh closed behind her and Shadow, not allowing Gabe time to respond.

She trekked toward the lodging cabins, inhaling deeply. The fragrance of pure river mixed with earth settled over her like the comfortable memory of fishing with her father.

Unlike her brothers, Katie had never felt the pull to leave here. No college romps for her, no indeed. The clean, crisp air year-round, the crunch of oak leaves in the fall, the roar of the class-five rapids in September and October . . . that was enough to satisfy the longings of her soul.

Katie picked up her pace as she passed Gabe's cabin—once the family's home. A raw stab of grief knifed through her. Her father was gone, but this land still belonged to the remaining Gallaghers. She stiffened her shoulder muscles, resolving to not let the family business go down. Not if she could help it. If that meant she had to guide a bunch of suits, so be it.

Shadow barked and darted ahead in pursuit of a gray squirrel scampering up the trail. Katie headed for the third cabin in the row. The rentals rested back from the gravel access area to the river. Now, in the purple mist of dusk, the wind lifted to a gust. She stood, relishing the sensation as the breeze rushed over her face, and tucked loose strands of her hair behind her ears and pressed on.

She bounded up the stairs, then shoved the key into the lock and opened the door. Shadow emerged from the tree line and edged near the door.

She rubbed behind his ears. "No, boy. You have

to stay on the porch. Wouldn't do for our special guests to find your hair all over their linens." She pointed a finger at him. "Sit." Shadow dropped to his haunches. "Stay."

As soon as she stepped across the threshold, the stale stench of mustiness accosted her, making her eyes water. She blinked several times before glancing around the room. A fine layer of dust rested over the coffee table and magazines. No hum of the ceiling fan sounded, no welcome mat laid on the floor. Dirt littered the air—dancing on the breeze sneaking in from the open door.

Annoyance pulled in her chest as she surveyed the cabin. If Christian had actually prepared this place for rental, he'd done a poor job—he hadn't even bothered to air out the main living area. She carried the clean towels into the bathroom.

Ttsss-Ttss-Ttsss! Ttsssssssssssss!

Katie stared, frozen mid-step. A bed of Northern Copperheads lay curled in the middle of the bathroom floor, slithering and striking. She slowly lowered her foot, searching with her toe for the floor behind her. Hauling in a slow breath, she set the towels on the dusty counter, then took precise steps backward until she cleared the room. She shut the bathroom door tight before rushing out of the cabin.

She closed and locked the cabin. Oh, Christian would pay for slacking off. This was the last straw. He had one thing to do. One!

Shadow trotted to keep up with Katie as she stormed toward Christian's cabin. The fury swirling in her chest matched the tempering clouds settling over West Virginia.

She stomped up the stairs to Christian's cabin and thumped on the door. Before he had time to respond, she gripped the knob and pushed the door open.

Christian moved down the hall, sans shirt, his hair dripping. "Don't you ever wait to be invited in?" He yanked a tee off the back of the couch and tugged it over his wet head. His green eyes pierced hers, flashing sparks in anger or irritation —Katie couldn't tell which.

"Don't you ever do your job?" She stabbed back with her glare, her rising blood pressure causing her pulse to pound. "Something as simple as prepping a cabin for our guests?"

"What are you mouthing about?" He ran a hand through his shoulder-length, shaggy blond hair. "I have cabin four all nice and ready for the guests."

She shook her head. He couldn't even follow the simplest of directions. "We reserved cabin number three for them, Christian." She hissed air between her teeth. "Three."

He shrugged. "No big deal. Put them in four. They're about the same square footage." His wide, boyish smile could almost diffuse her temper.

Almost, but not quite. "I can't put them there

because your group arriving tomorrow has four reserved." The urge to throttle her brother boiled into her chest. Didn't he realize the dire situation the business was in? She kept her fists balled firmly on her hips, not trusting herself to change the pose.

Christian rubbed the stubble on his chin, the scuffing noise breaking the silence. "Well, then, I'll get three ready tonight." He met her gaze. "Come on, Katie-cat, don't be mad." He flashed another hundred-watt grin and looped an arm over her shoulders. "Trust me, I'll get it done. Not your problem."

His awkward embrace warmed her. Her anger slipped away like an untied boat in the current. Christian knew how to diffuse her wrath, the imp. She wrapped an arm around his waist, loving the outdoor smell clinging to his body despite the shower. "Don't call me that. And you're right, it's not my problem." She squeezed him into a sideways hug. "But when you go to cabin three tonight, be prepared. There's a family of copper-heads in the bathroom . . . and that is your problem."

Hunter Malone leaned back against the smooth, black leather seat of the chartered Gulfstream 100. The temperature remained comfortably cool in the cabin, yet a line of sweat trickled down his back, pasting his shirt to his body. Flying at

25,000 feet didn't cause his discomfort—he'd been in and out of planes since his early twenties. Even the sharp drops and pitches didn't worry him. No, his nerves twisted at the prospect of white-water rafting on the famous Gauley River.

He'd done his homework on the elements and knew what to expect—the unexpected. Mother Nature could be most volatile when the mood struck her. Hunter glanced at his waterproof watch. They'd land in Summersville within the hour, and he'd have to force himself to prepare for his first rafting trip. He grimaced. He didn't like adventures. Not ones he couldn't control.

Lord, give me the strength to endure this. You are my rock.

"You'll have fun." The older man sitting beside him smiled. "I've done the Gauley twice before and it's a thrill you'll never forget."

Carter James, CEO of Lassiter James Accounting Firm. Hunter had a hard time picturing the fifty-something executive enjoying any thrill but the excitement of making a tidy profit off another man's hard work. Apparently, the founding partner of the firm enjoyed a good adventure, but how close to the edge would the old codger go to experience the rush? Something illegal?

That's what Hunter was here to find out. He frowned, then switched to a smile in the space of a blink. "I'm sure I'll remember this trip forever."

The older man nodded before glancing out his

window, dismissing the conversation. His knobby knees bounced. Hunter couldn't recall a time in the past six months seeing Carter anything but stoic.

With his own nerves jumping with excitement, Hunter pushed to his feet. The jet bobbed and dipped, and he stumbled on his way to the bathroom. His elbow jabbed Walter Thompson, who sat across the carpeted aisle.

Glaring at Hunter, his grimace in perfect harmony with the familiar scowl etched into his face, Walter grunted. "Watch it, boy."

Hunter swallowed his irritation, a credit to his years of training. "Sorry. Turbulence." He stared hard at Walter, the man well into his late fifties. Hunter knew how deeply embedded in the company Walter must be—he'd held onto his top ranking for four years now. How far would Walter go to prove his loyalty?

Continuing up the aisle, Hunter wove his way into the bathroom, then turned and locked the door. He withdrew his cell phone from his pocket, then pressed in the numeric code 962 as a text message, and hit SEND. The confirmation came within seconds. He slipped the phone back in his pocket, then waited two more minutes before flushing the toilet and exiting the bathroom.

He crept back to his seat, marveling that he'd finagled an invitation to this trip. He'd only been on the firm's payroll for six months, but his ability increased the firm's profit figure by ten percent, thus one of the reasons for his being on the jet careening toward Gauley River.

Dropping into his seat, Hunter massaged his temples. A long weekend loomed before him, and if he couldn't get the information he needed in the next few days, he didn't know how much longer he could carry on this farce.

Katie sprawled out on the braided rug laid across the wooden floor in the main lodge, rubbing Shadow's belly. The dog's rear leg twitched. She laughed and scratched faster, giggling as his limb moved in time with her fingers. "Good boy." She rubbed noses with her best friend, then stared at the clock over the mantle. Her group should've arrived by now. Outside, the final rays of the sun had long disappeared. Cicadas chirped, announcing the coming rains. The air whipped around the lodge, whistling and whooshing like ghosts in the mist. An eerie sensation seeped over the dwelling—a tension building unforeseen and unexplainable.

Katie stood, shaking off her sudden unease and moved to the counter. She let her gaze flit back to the reservation log lying open on the gnarled oak tabletop. According to the notation Christian had scribbled, the plane should've landed at the small airstrip in Summersville an hour ago. What could be keeping the stiff-shirt desk jockeys?

Hopefully, they hadn't backed out because of the approaching storm. If Gabe said the business needed the income, then they really needed it. She still hadn't told him about the bank's call.

The phone rang. "Gauley Guides by Gallagher."

"Just thought you'd like to know the snake problem has been taken care of." Christian's voice held a hint of laughter.

She couldn't stay at odds with him long. His good humor always wrenched her heart, and the imp knew it. "Good. I'm sure your little co-ed group arriving in the morning will be pleased." Shifting the phone to wedge between her chin and shoulder, she re-secured her ponytail.

Christian chuckled. "Don't know how that mama got in there to have those little rascals."

"What'd you do with them?"

"Took them to the other side of Summersville Lake and let 'em loose."

She gave a snort. "I'm sure the park rangers over at the National Rec area will love you for that."

"Just doing my part to preserve the natural wildlife."

Katie laughed and shook her head, lifting the end of the pencil to her mouth again. Her gaze fell to the appointment book. "Hey, are you sure you wrote down this time of arrival right? They're running late."

"Maybe they decided to delay takeoff. Or they

could have re-routed because of the weather. Who knows with rich dudes?"

"Yeah." A gust of wind drew her attention to the windows. Leaves flew by the panes, flipping and twirling. "What's your take on Emily?"

"Gabe assured me we'll be fine to raft. He knows his stuff, Katie. We have to trust him." He paused, mumbled something, then returned to the conversation. "We'll get some rain from the storm, sure, but I think Gabe's right. Especially if Emily loses strength before making land."

Headlights pierced the darkness, reflecting in the large windows across the front of the main lodge. Shadow stood and barked twice, his alert notification.

"Looks like the group has arrived. I'll drop by your place on my way home." Katie pointed at the dog, who sat.

"Uh, I'm heading out, Katie."

She flipped the pencil onto the counter. "No you aren't—you're on call tonight."

"Come on, Katie. I have a date."

Even though her brother couldn't see her, she couldn't resist scrunching up her nose. "Too bad. I have to take these guys out at first light, so I need a guaranteed good night's rest. It's your turn."

Footsteps thundered on the lodge's front stairs, the wood creaked in objection. Shadow stood again, his canine body quivering as he stared at her with his imploring eyes. Katie shook her head and pointed to the floor. She gripped the receiver. "I'll be switching the calls to your house when I leave, Christian. You'd better stay home. I mean it."

"Fine. Ruin my evening."

"Someday, little brother, you'll understand." Hopefully, sooner rather than later.

Much sooner.

TWO

Chilly air forced itself into the lodge, hovering over the group like the invisible cape of the grim reaper. Hunter stood behind the other men, his arms crossed casually over his chest, taking stock of his surroundings. The lodge appeared basic, no frills, but clean and comfortable. No dead animal heads peered out from the walls. He let out a relieved sigh—he didn't like trophy sportsmen.

"Man, the wind's biting tonight." Steve Smith shuddered and rubbed his hands together.

What were Steve's ambitions? How had he maneuvered an invitation on this particular trip, after one year of employment? His numbers weren't even close to Hunter's.

Steve lifted his gaze to meet Hunter's scrutiny. "Aren't you a little bit cold?"

Shrugging, Hunter moved toward the stone

fireplace. An oversized, framed photo of a beautiful woman graced the space over the mantle. Her honey colored hair lay lush on her shoulders, her sharp blue eyes and intense stare could stir a man's emotions.

"Wow, check her out." Paul nodded toward the doorway. The business tycoon was Lassiter James' best client.

All eyes shifted. Jerry Sands jabbed Paul in the ribs and chortled as the hostess moved to greet them.

Hunter drank in the sight of such an exquisite woman planted in the middle of nowhere. Her hair hung down over her shoulder—its tawny color, with sun-kissed golden highlights glistened in the overhead brightness. He cut his gaze to the picture over the mantle, then back to the young woman walking closer. She bore a resemblance.

She extended her hand to Carter, and Hunter took in her lean, tanned legs. Toned and taut, her skin glistened over rippled muscles.

"Welcome to Gauley Guides by Gallagher, gentlemen." Her voice sounded as smooth as her skin looked.

She drew closer to meet each man in turn. Her tanned face held a spattering of freckles over the bridge of her nose. Angel kisses, Hunter's mother always called them. Her smile showed a straight row of white teeth, the kind no dentist would dare cap.

Something about her drew him nearer. Her eyes. Hunter leaned forward, then moved around the men who shoved and angled to introduce themselves to her. Amazing. Her eyes shimmered silvery as the lines spiking through her irises were black, enhancing the depth of crystal blue.

A dog matched her steps, and almost absent-mindedly, her hand stroked the animal's head—a sign this canine was more than just a pet to their hostess. His heart thumped at the sight of her gentleness. In his profession, he'd seen too many people who were just plain hard.

"I'm Katie Gallagher. I'll be your guide this weekend."

Taking in a quick breath, Hunter studied the young woman. Her voice came out throaty, husky, yet delicately feminine. Her gaze lit on each man individually, giving the impression of sincerity with each blink of her eyes.

He swallowed a groan and gave himself a mental shake. He'd come to do a job, and he had no time, nor business, entertaining such ideas of attraction. It was too bad Katie Gallagher had to be so intensely attractive. Hmm. It'd make for a most interesting weekend.

Katie shook Carter James's hand, his skin smooth as a placid lake. This man couldn't do much more than move a pencil around or stroke a keyboard. She gave a mental groan. Just as she suspected—

high-powered executives out for a thrill. Would they ever learn? She smiled and nodded at each man in turn, all the while remaining aware of the man brooding at the back of the crowd.

She gave silent appraisal. Taller than Christian, he had to stand over six feet, and his shoulders were wider than Gabe's. She pushed down a rush of unfamiliar attraction, nodded at a question from one of the men, then let her gaze discreetly slide to study the brooding man once more.

His strong jaw entertained a five o'clock shadow, and his head full of wavy, dark hair ended just short of his shoulders. A little too long for a regulation accountant hack job. Her heart raced to the speed of a class-five rapid when their gazes collided.

A shudder coursed through her body. Curbing her overactive emotions, she thrust out her hand to the handsome stranger with eyes dark as the river at midnight. "Katie Gallagher."

"Hunter Malone."

His calloused hand made contact. She'd never classify this man as a pencil-pusher, not by any definition. Sure, lots of executives spent many hours at a gym every week, but not this man. No, his hands screamed of working outdoors, of blending with nature. Her kind of guy. If this man was merely an accountant, she'd wash every wetsuit the Gallaghers owned by hand—twice.

"Are you an accountant as well, Mr. Malone?" She pinched her lips together and arched an eyebrow.

"An assistant, if you will." He smiled wide, nearly causing her to swoon with his disarming grin. "But the name's Hunter."

Gulping back her high-school-girl-infatuation, Katie nodded and tugged free from his grip. She slipped her hand into her shorts pocket, then addressed the group. "We've got your cabin ready. I'm sure you will be very comfortable. You'll need to get a good night's rest, as we head out at seven in the morning."

Katie grabbed the master key from its hanger, then snapped for Shadow. She snatched the flashlight from its place beside the phone before forwarding the calls to Christian's.

Slipping into guide mode, she began the spiel she'd memorized at the age of ten. "My father, the late Michael Gallagher, established Gauley Guides by Gallagher in 1972. Since that time, we've added several cozy cabins for our clients, as well as a main lodge." She smiled and tried to make eye-contact with each man. "One thing our father firmly believed, and a motto we still adhere to, is having a real Gallagher guide in every boat we put in the water."

The men mumbled, but no one spoke directly to her. Katie sighed. These guys weren't interested in anything but bragging about how they survived the Gauley. She clung to the familiarity of the surrounding nature as she led the group out of the lodge and down the gravel trail toward the row of cabins, the Blue Heeler matching her stride. Katie beamed the flashlight on the uneven path, even though the moon's soft glow peeked through the clouds now and again.

The familiar scent of wet dirt carried across the air. Katie deeply inhaled the odor she associated with home. She loved everything about the Gauley, even the smells that turned some city folks' stomachs.

Tree frogs sang a lullaby barely heard over the rush of the river. Wind gusted, sending dried leaves adrift in its wake. The moon hurried from one dark cloud to another. Her single beam of light shone farther down the trail. Choosing to enjoy the peace of the evening, Katie led the group in silence, not bothering to dispense any additional history. Tranquility laid over the land and water, as always.

Ka-Boom!

The sound of the gunshot echoed over the river. Katie froze. Shadow barked, then growled.

The hairs on the back of Katie's neck stood at attention as she dropped to a squat. The reverberations from the gunshot continued to ricochet in the woods, its echoes piercing over the continuous roar of the Gauley. Thunder rumbled high in the sky. She spun to face her guests and noticed the men in a crouching position. Mr. Malone crept up beside her.

"Is this common?" His tone carried authority. His scrutiny roamed the area.

"No." Like him, she kept her voice quiet. "We don't even get sportsmen around here because of the National Recreation area."

"Where's our cabin?"

Pointing at the structure nestled in the edge of the woods about two hundred yards up and to the right of their present location, Katie laid her other hand on Shadow's neck. The fur on his back bristled against her palm. "Something's wrong," she whispered. "Shadow can sense it."

"Let's get to the cabin." Hunter motioned for the others to follow, but to keep down. "Lead— I'll bring up the rear."

She made her way toward the building, crouching as she scurried. She reached the stairs, then lifted her foot to the bottom step. A cold hand grabbed her shoulder.

She whirled, prepared to strike. Hunter shook his head and tugged her back a step. "Give me the key and let me check it out first."

His chivalry made her face fan with heat, but she pushed him back with a firm hand. While she appreciated his attitude, she couldn't allow herself to show weakness in front of clients. "Thanks, but no. This is my property, and I'll check it out." Her glance darted over the group.

"Everyone stay here, as close to the building as possible, just to be on the safe side."

Keeping her fingers wrapped tight around the key, she climbed the stairs to the door. She disengaged the puny knob lock. The door slammed back against the wall. Once she crossed the threshold, Katie flipped on the light-switch next to the main entrance.

A golden hue of brightness flooded the room—light sprawled over the ceiling. She blinked several times, allowing her eyes to adjust. She snapped twice—the dog appeared at her side. She rubbed his chin and whispered in Shadow's perked up ears. "Go check it out, boy."

The Blue Heeler rushed into the cabin, racing from room to room, then returned to her side, accepting her rub behind his ears.

Katie faced Hunter, who loomed in the doorway. "All's fine."

He motioned for the others to enter, then followed them inside and shut the door. His hooded eyes studied her. The others in the party all spoke at once—

"What was that?"

"Who's shooting?"

"Goood night! Is it deer season?"

Holding up her hands in a gesture to stop their chatter, Katie plastered on a smile, even though her stomach rolled. "Just a minute. Let me try to answer your questions."

Silence filled the still cabin, as if the air had been recycled one too many times.

She drew in a deep breath and then let it out slowly. "Okay. It was a gunshot and no, it's not open season on anything right now. We're too close to the National Recreation area." One of the men opened his mouth, and she held up her hand again to cut him off. "But there are times when some outdoor enthusiasts don't abide by the posted signs. More than likely, that's what we heard."

"But it sounded so close." Orson—at least, Katie was pretty sure his name was Orson—said in a shaky voice.

"I know it did. But keep in mind that over a river, sound carries." She laid her hand on Shadow's head, drawing comfort from his muscular body. "I'm going to call the ranger at the recreational area and see what he can find out. I'm sure he'll know. He's probably found someone who wasn't aware he'd crossed onto posted land."

"Is it safe to stay here?" Hunter's eyebrows scrunched.

One minute this Hunter Malone guy came across as taking charge, and the next he asked if they were safe? He was an enigma. Great. Something else to deal with that she didn't have time for. If the family business weren't in such dire straits right now, she'd send them all back to their little private jet. Instead, she sucked in her irritation. "Of course it's safe."

The men grumbled, but lifted their bags and milled about, checking out their lodging. She turned to go.

Hunter tapped her arm. "Do you really believe it was a huntsman?" He showed no fear like he'd tried to display a moment ago. What was his game?

She lifted a casual shoulder, studying his face. "Probably. Or someone lost, who fired the gun to help someone locate him. It's happened before."

"Until you find out, is it safe for you to walk outside, alone?"

She cocked her head to the side. "I'm fine. My cabin is only a few paces down, and my brother's is right on the way. I'll stop and talk to Christian about it, and we'll call the ranger from his place."

"I'd feel better if you'd let me walk you home."

Katie stared into his eyes. She recognized nothing that revealed the real Hunter Malone, so she laughed. "Such a gentleman." Snapping for Shadow again, she grinned. "I appreciate the offer, I really do, but I have protection. Shadow will see me safely home."

At the door, she lifted her voice. "You gentlemen get a good night's rest. We leave shortly after daybreak. There's a list on the kitchen table of what you'll need to bring on the rafting trip. Be sure to abide by the rules as we won't have room for more than your bedroll. And remember, no cell phones or other electronics. We serve breakfast at six-thirty. Don't be late."

As she reached the bottom of the stairs, Katie had an awkward sensation that someone watched her. Shivering, she pressed her leg against Shadow, his presence strengthening her resolve.

A thought niggled against her mind as she quickened her pace toward Christian's cabin—from what she'd witnessed, Hunter Malone could be many things, but an accountant or an assistant to one wasn't one of them. His quick take-charge attitude came across as reflexive. Just who was Hunter Malone, and what business did he have here?

She pounded on Christian's door, then grabbed the knob and twisted, but the door didn't open. Her mouth gaped. Since when did Christian lock his door?

The sound of feet padded against the wood plank floor. "Who is it?" His voice came through the wood.

"It's Katie. Open up."

The lock disengaged with a click, then the door swung open. Christian loomed in the doorway, wearing a tee and sweat pants. His normally shaggy hair looked even more mussed than usual.

Katie pushed into the foyer and stared at her brother. "What's with the locked door?" Shadow burst through the opening, sliding on the polished plank floor as he raced around the cabin.

"Uh, I thought you were tucking in your executives." Christian pushed the door closed and then leaned against it.

"Didn't you hear the gunshot a little while ago?"

Confusion marched over his face. A thin layer of sweat covered his brow. Her brother's face flushed bright crimson. Something didn't feel right. Not at all. Her heart tightened—he could be sick or something and she'd been mean to him earlier. She took a step toward him, peering into his eyes. "Christian, what's wrong? You don't seem like yourself. Are you feeling okay?"

Shadow barked twice—he was on alert.

Widening her eyes, Katie fisted her hands on her hips, reading her brother's expression. "You have company?"

The crimson flush gave way to vivid red patches spreading over Christian's face. "I, uh, told you I had a . . . uh, a date tonight."

Shadow barked again from the back of the cabin. Muffled sounds of movement came from the den.

And she'd worried he was sick. Her protectiveness tasted like acid on her tongue. "And your date's here, isn't she?"

He gave a slow nod.

Katie pulled back her shoulders and stiffened. "You're on call tonight, Christian." She couldn't prevent her voice from rising on the last word. Because they didn't have direct phones in any of the cabins, all calls to guests would come through the main line and have to be patched through.

"And I'll answer anything that comes in."

Her heart kicked into overdrive, and she breathed hard through her nostrils. "You have a group arriving in the morning, and mine is expecting breakfast at six-thirty."

He lifted his hands in mock surrender. "Take it easy, Katie-cat. I'll have breakfast ready and on the buffet on time. It ain't a big deal."

Rolling her eyes skyward, she huffed. "Christian, you need to understand that the business is in financial trouble. Our business. You need to start doing more. Gabe's killing himself trying to keep up with everything, and I can only do so much to help him."

"I understand that."

"Do you? Really and truly?" She shook her head. Her brothers were the only family she had left, and she loved them dearly. Christian just didn't get it, and arguing about it tonight wouldn't help. "And don't call me Katie-cat. You know I hate it." Without another word, she curled her lips over her teeth and let out a piercing whistle.

Shadow scampered down the hall, skidding to a stop at her feet.

"Just have breakfast ready in the morning, okay?" She jerked open the front door, then stomped down the stairs. Shadow whimpered, but fell into step beside her.

As she made her way to her cabin, gravel

crunched under her sandals. Reaching into her pocket, she pulled out a peppermint and popped it in her mouth.

She pounded up to her cabin and pushed open the door. Shadow raced to his food bowl, prancing in place. Katie pressed the can of dog food to the can opener, mumbling. Her intent to call the ranger got lost in the storm of her emotions.

Hunter kept a careful eye on the men in the group after Katie left. Carter ambled to the table. His hand shook as he held the paper Katie had mentioned, whether from nerves or age, Hunter couldn't be sure. Carter perused the list with a scrunched forehead.

"What does it say?" Walter Thompson, an experienced kiss-up in Hunter's opinion, sauntered alongside the boss and glanced over Carter's shoulder. His stomach poked out in a paunch, his shadow almost reminiscent of a Hitchcock profile.

"Says here we'll need to repack our stuff to fit inside a rolled-up sleeping bag, no more than two feet in diameter." The old man huffed, then let the paper drift to the table. He lifted a gnarled hand to rub his chin. "Go-ood night! How am I supposed to get all my belongings rolled into a sleeping bag?

"I'll help you." Walter twisted to look at Carter, adulation shimmering in the eyes lurking behind the horned rims.

Paul snorted as he crossed the room and lifted the paper, but not before tossing Walter a scowl. "Looks pretty straightforward to me, Carter. Just jam your undies and toothbrush in the sleeping bag and roll it up." His full belly-laugh echoed across the cabin, the gunshot obviously not unnerving him.

Jerry Sands laughed, making little nasal sounds. No signs that the excitement affected him either.

Hunter caught Orson's wide-eyed stare, his weathered face wrinkled in concern. Hunter gave a slight shake of his head.

From the corner of the room, the quiet accountant, Steve, shuffled his feet. "Is anybody else concerned about that shot we heard?"

Everyone stared at the mousey little man. Pity for Steve washed over Hunter. Short and thin as an ice skate blade, Steve appeared to be easily, and often, overlooked. His Adam's apple bobbed up and down as he looked around the group. "You know, that was a gunshot we heard."

Carter let out a snicker. "Yes, boy, it was. Added a little excitement to the night, wouldn't you say?"

"Aren't you the slightest concerned about that, sir?" Steve shifted his weight from one leg to the other.

"Not really." Carter shrugged, his bony shoulders lifting. "That little lady said she'd check it out with the ranger, or whatever. I'm sure it's all fine."

"I guess so." Steve's chin lowered to his chest.

Hunter cleared his throat. "I suggest we follow Ms. Gallagher's advice and get settled for the night." He made a point of tapping his watch. "It's almost nine now. I don't know about you guys, but if I have to be packed and ready for breakfast at six-thirty, I need to hit the sack pretty soon."

Jerry narrowed his eyes, glaring at Hunter. "What's with this take-charge attitude of yours, man? We don't need a den mommy."

"Just commenting on what I need—sleep." Straightening to his full height, he crossed his arms over his chest, then relaxed and let his hands drop to his side. He couldn't take a chance on throwing his trump card this early in the game. "So, who's bunking in which room?"

Three

Katie stretched like a cat, the crisp cotton linens grazing her skin. The streaks of predawn shimmered through the window. A sharp breeze shot across the room, fluttering the edges of the antique lace curtains. She shoved the comforter off her legs, swinging her legs to the floor.

She opened her cabin's back door to let Shadow out and studied the weather. An almost purplish hue painted the darkened sky, casting shadows over the river. Thunder rumbled—positives and negatives of nature colliding. The river churned, pitched, then calmed. Katie exhaled forcefully, then whistled for the Blue Heeler. After giving Shadow fresh water and kibble, she trudged to the shower.

She quickly dried off and slipped into her bathing suit. She applied a generous amount of body powder to her legs and arms and then tugged a black Body Glove wetsuit over the modest bathing suit. She squatted and rose several times, garnering room in the unforgiving second skin. Once comfortable, she hopped up onto the counter, resting her feet in the sink.

Propping her elbows on her bent knees, Katie then pulled her wet hair into a long French braid down her back. She secured the ends, and then lifted the tube of sunblock and spread it over her face.

Shadow barked.

Looking at him in the mirror, Katie laughed. Every time he watched her don the wetsuit, his black and grey body trembled with excitement. She shook her head as she jumped back to the floor. The dog loved white-water rafting. Always had, ever since she got him as a pup. She took a moment to run a hand over his thick fur and nuzzle him.

She brushed her teeth, then grabbed Shadow's safety harness and reached for her fanny pack filled with peppermints. She pulled it around her waist and went to snap the closure, but the clasp shattered, littering the floor with tiny shards of black plastic. Great. Now she had to find her old one. She tapped a finger against her chin. Where had she put it?

Katie pushed into her room. She tugged open the bottom oak dresser drawer and rifled through the mass of clutter. Her hand grazed bonded leather. She pulled out the heavy book and laid the worn and tattered Bible into her lap. She gasped when her fingers, as if they had a mind of their own, caressed the weathered cover. She couldn't remember the last time she'd opened the Bible. Her heart raced as fast as the Gauley current. She hadn't bothered to read Scripture since her mother disappeared. Once a vital part of her daily routine, now something to avoid. God hadn't stepped in then, so she certainly wouldn't buy into the fairy-tale notion He would any time soon.

She shoved the Bible back into the mess, yanked out the old fanny pack, then slammed the rawer. The loud bang settled over the room. She shook her head, determined to keep the ghosts of her past locked in a drawer forever.

She stood and rushed back to the front of the cabin, eager to get away from the demons sitting on her back. Grabbing up the broken fanny pack, she then transferred the peppermint candies to the old one before zipping it shut and hooking it around her waist. Katie snapped for the dog, then shut the door behind her.

Once outside, the roar of the river shattered the serene setting. The crispness in the air made her breath visible, hanging like a puffy cloud out of her mouth. Strong gusts sent the autumn leaves adrift. She hauled in a deep breath, filling her lungs to capacity, then let it out in a rush.

The first glimpse of sunbeams shot across the sky. Maybe Gabe had been right—Emily would decrease in strength before she made landfall. Katie glanced down at her waterproof watch that had been her father's. Grief tugged at her heart. She swallowed back the sorrow, burying it deep as she strode toward the main lodge. If Christian didn't have coffee made and breakfast ready, she'd rip into him like nobody's business, boyish grin or not.

Hunter slung the bedroll over his shoulder and glared at the other men in the group. Paul and Jerry tried to roll their sleeping bags, bulging with clothes and who knew what else. A sheen of sweat glistened on Paul's bald spot. They laughed at themselves as they made attempt after attempt, but to no avail. Jerry's mustache twitched as he chuckled. Hunter glanced at his watch and sighed.

Setting down his neatly wrapped bedroll, Hunter moved Paul out of the way with a nudge from his elbow. He slammed his palms down on the sleeping bag, flattening and smoothing. He squished the end into itself, keeping the bundle tight as he rolled it up. Once finished, he tied it securely with the attached string.

"Hey, that's really good. Where'd you learn to do that?" Paul's eyes were as wide as paddles.

Hunter lifted a brow. "Scouting." Still on his knees, he wobbled beside Jerry, who grappled with his bag. He gave a slight shove on Jerry's arm.

Jerry stiffened under his touch, shrugging off Hunter's hand. "I can manage by myself."

Narrowing his eyes, Hunter studied the invest-ments man. Medium height, medium weight, with average brown hair and bushy moustache, Jerry defined normal to a T. That sent a red flag waving in Hunter's mind.

Hunter pushed himself off the floor, strode across the room, picked up his small bedroll, and then slung it over his shoulder again. He shrugged. "Suit yourself. I'm going to the lodge to eat breakfast. I'm not up to facing class-five rapids without a hearty meal first." He opened the cabin door. It barely took three seconds for Orson and Steve to grab their packs and step out into the morning.

Paul stood still, eyes darting from the group at the door to Jerry, then back to the other men. Hunter stepped across the threshold, pulling the door closed behind him.

The chill in the air nearly stole his breath. When they'd arrived last evening, it'd been warmer. Hunter glanced down at his jeans and wondered if he should've brought his personal wetsuit with him. Blowing into his hands, he studied the other two men over his tented fingers. No, he did the right thing. No need to tip off anyone that he was anything more than what they thought he was. At least, not yet.

He moved toward the stairs. The cabin door creaked open. Jerry and Paul must've finally finished packing and joined them. Good, always better to keep everyone together where he could keep track of them. Once they were in the boat, his job would be easier. Truly, keeping up with six men in a raft, how hard could it be?

Hunter led the way to the main lodge, enjoying the morning's peace as opposed to last night's ruckus. Had Ms. Gallagher discovered who'd fired the gun last night? More than anything, he wanted to believe her offhand explanation. His trained mind, however, suspected it'd been more than a lost hunter. Either way, he'd ask as soon as he saw her.

Katie sipped black coffee, letting its heat warm her body. She glanced over at the executives rushing to grab breakfast. True to his word, Christian had everything ready and set out in the lodge this morning.

The front door opened, letting in a gust of air along with the last two straggling men. Loose papers on the counter took flight.

She set down her mug, then leaned over and retrieved the sheets of paper. She straightened and settled them on the counter before lifting her gaze to meet that of Hunter Malone's. Her heart flipped and twisted like a deflated raft in the current.

"Good morning, Ms. Gallagher." His cheerful tone sounded too close to Christian's this morning for her liking.

She gave a curt nod. "Morning, Mr. Malone."

His eyes widened for a split second before the guarded look reappeared. The slip occurred so quickly, she wondered if she might have imagined it. He smiled. "Please, call me Hunter."

"Hunter." She lifted her mug and took a long sip, then cringed as the scalding liquid scorched her tongue.

"Hot?"

She stared into his mocking eyes before turning away. She headed toward the buffet line where Christian stood, filling the steaming pans with scrambled eggs, bacon, sausage, and biscuits. Hunter's hand on her forearm stopped her as she reached for a plate.

She lifted her gaze to his face. "May I help you?"

"Did you talk to the ranger last night?"

Heat spread up her neck to her face. She lowered her stare to the floor. "No, I didn't."

"So, you don't know where that gunshot came from?"

"No. But since there were no other outbursts last night, I'm sure it was nothing." Katie smiled. "Don't worry about it. You'll be safe and sound."

Christian introduced himself to the men and now engaged in a playful argument with Jerry Sands about imports and exports. Katie bit her tongue. Why couldn't her brother take her overnight group and let her guide the day-trip ones scheduled to arrive later this morning? The little voice inside her head answered—because Gabe was depending on this trip to keep the business afloat. She wouldn't let her brother down, not if she could help it.

Plopping a spoonful of eggs onto her plate, she sensed Hunter's presence in the buffet line behind her. She finished selecting her food, then sauntered to the long dining table where Carter and Walter already sat.

Katie set down her breakfast, and pulled out the chair next to Steve Smith, the quiet accountant. His shyness propelled her to make him feel welcome. The others in the group came across as so boisterous it would be easy to overlook this slight of a man. Even though she sometimes cursed her own stockiness, she secretly harbored gratitude for her hearty build. It helped secure the confidence of men who put their lives in her hands.

Steve smiled at her. "Good morning, Ms. Gallagher."

"Please, call me Katie."

Patches of crimson graced his cheeks.

How endearing. "So, is this your first white-water rafting adventure?"

"Yes. I mean, the company took us to float the Buffalo River in Arkansas last year, but I don't think it compares."

Katie nearly spit out the eggs she'd just shoveled into her mouth. The Buffalo River compared to the Gauley? Instead, she smiled gently. "No, it's not quite the same. We have several class-five rapids, some of the most vicious you'll ever find."

His mouth formed an "O."

She bit back a laugh, not wanting to insult the man.

"But the Royal Gorge in Colorado might compare." Hunter Malone's deep voice was felt rather than heard when he spoke . . . so close she could feel his breath against her neck.

"Have you rafted the Royal Gorge, Mr. Malone?" She allowed a teasing lilt to slip into her tone.

"No, ma'am. And it's Hunter, remember?" His eyes sparkled, hinting at the humor lurking in their depths.

"Right. Hunter." She lifted her mug. "So, how do you know about the Royal Gorge if you've never been?" Taking a sip of coffee, she studied him over the rim.

"Friends of mine went last year. On their honeymoon." His dark chocolate eyes sparkled even more.

"Really?" She set the mug down. "Sound like fun people."

"Oh, they are."

"I have to say, Ms. Gallagher, I'm a little surprised you're our guide." Walter's aristocratic nose lifted higher.

Steeling herself against the bristling rushing to her surface, Katie forced a smile at the man across the table. "Because I'm so young?"

Under his breath, Hunter chuckled. Beside her, Steve gasped softly.

"Because you're a woman." Walter's face twisted into an arrogant grimace.

"I assure you, sir, I'm quite competent to guide. I was born on this river and have rafted it since I could sit up by myself." Heat crept up the back of her neck. She sucked in air. Calm. Keep calm.

Carter let out a roar of laughter and clapped Walter on the back. "See, she's a professional." He gave a curt nod in her direction. "Besides, she looks like hearty stock to me. We'll be fine."

Heat fanned across her face.

"He meant that as a compliment," Hunter whispered in her ear. He opened his mouth to say something else, but the lodge door swung open, drawing Katie's attention.

A woman in a bright pink wetsuit waltzed through the door, making a beeline for Christian. "Hi, my name's Ariel. The man in the store said you were going to be my group's guide today." She glanced around the room. "I guess I'm a little early. The others won't be here for some time, but I thought I could get a cup of coffee from you."

Christian nearly fell over himself pouring a mug for the beautiful woman.

Katie clenched her cup's handle. What was her little brother doing? He'd just had a date last night with someone who had to be important to him. After all, she'd been in his cabin. Surely her brother wasn't some kind of player? That'd just make her sick.

Christian flirted shamelessly with the woman. Katie turned her head, not wanting to see this side of her brother anymore. Using more force than intended, she pushed her chair back from the table.

A loud grating sound shot through the room as wood scraped against wood.

Standing, Katie offered a smile to the men at the table. "We'd better get a move on, gentlemen." She pointed to the hall off one side of the fireplace. "Down there you will find all the wetsuits and four dressing rooms. Make sure you select a wetsuit that fits snugly."

The men stood and moved toward the changing area. All except Hunter. He continued to sip his coffee and stare at Katie.

She squirmed under his scrutiny. "Shouldn't you go get changed?" she asked, quirking an eyebrow at him.

The outer corners of his mouth lifted. "You said there were only four dressing rooms, right? There are six of us. I can wait."

Refusing to rise to the bait he seemed determined to dangle in front of her, Katie turned to glare at her brother. He appeared mighty cozy, with Ariel clinging to his arm and smiling up at him.

Katie straightened her back, squared her shoulders, and strode over to them. She held her hand out to Ariel. "Hi. I'm Katie Gallagher."

Ariel's smiled and shook her hand. "Nice to meet you. It's a lovely place you have here."

"Thank you." She turned to her brother. "Don't you think you should be getting to the shop?"

Christian tossed her a disdainful look. "Yeah, we were about to head that way after I cleared the kitchen."

She didn't have to reply as Carter sauntered out of the dressing area, clad in a black wetsuit with yellow stripes. The desire to laugh at the old man's appearance and his obvious pumped-up self-importance in the get-up made Katie press her knuckles to her mouth.

Hunter appeared at her elbow, his voice booming, saving her from making a huge faux pas. "Carter, you look quite comfortable in that second skin. Now I'm eager to get myself all gussied up."

The old man smiled, his chest puffing. "Then get on with it, Hunter, my boy. Time's a-wastin'. I'm sure Ms. Gallagher here is eager to get us on that river." He clapped his hands, then rubbed them together.

Hunter chuckled as he headed toward the dressing room.

For a moment, Katie forgot about the old man and his outrageous appearance, about Christian's attitude toward women, even about being a guide to the group—instead, her mind focused on Hunter Malone.

Four

Sixth sense working overtime, Hunter shook off the foreboding pinpricks of doom hovering in his head. Inside the stall, he coated his legs with powder from the bottle sitting on the tiny ledge. Clouds of talc rose and tickled his nostrils. He let out a loud sneeze, then sniffed. His eyes watered for a moment before he could inhale. The smell of Gold Bond filled the crowded area.

Sounds of frustration coming from the adjoining

stall indicated Walter didn't know to use the talc. Hunter bit back a chuckle. Let the chief accountant get his thighs chafed—he'd sure rubbed Hunter raw enough times in the past six months.

The spaces were only about two feet by four feet. Hunter's wide frame barely fit. He bent to slip his legs through the propene material and his elbows knocked against the sides. The green indoor-outdoor carpet dug into the soles of his feet as he changed. The curtain used for a privacy door hung lopsided, as if someone had hurriedly hemmed the rod stitching uneven. Hunter smiled, not quite able to conjure up the image of Katie Gallagher bent over a sewing machine.

He pulled up the wetsuit and situated it over his hips. Hunter couldn't stop thinking about Katie. Even though Carter seemed to have insulted her with his "stocky build" comment—he couldn't remember the last time he'd seen someone turn so blazing red so fast. Despite his attraction to her, Hunter couldn't help but chuckle. What she had planned to snap back before Ariel had entered, he'd love to know.

Zipping up the diver-black suit, Hunter then pushed aside the stall curtain and bent over to slip his feet into the water shoes he'd lugged into the room. Grunts and groans still emitted from Walter's changing area, growing in decibels. Hunter hung his faded jeans on a hook, then headed back to the main room of the lodge, leaving Walter to continue his vain attempts to dress.

Hunter strode across the main room to the area in front of the fireplace. All the members of the group, less Walter, converged on the sofas. Even though the seats offered cushy comfort, the men sat on the edge, as if in anticipation, or worse, trepidation.

Katie held the men spellbound as she went over last minute instructions, using her hands as well as her words to communicate. Her ever-present dog sat on his haunches at her feet, his gaze glued to his mistress.

"And remember to follow my commands at all times." Her facial expression left no doubt of her seriousness. "This can be a fun trip, gentlemen, but make no mistake, the Gauley River isn't some tame little run. The Upper Gauley, which we are about to do, contains several class-five rapids, as well as fours and threes. It is imperative each of you do your part. We are a team in the boat."

Her shimmering eyes lit on each man in turn. "And most importantly, whatever you do, don't lose your paddle. Our motto is 'paddle or die,' and I mean just that, gentlemen. Now, does anyone have any questions?"

"What about the weather report?" Steve shifted in his seat and kept his gaze pinned to the floor.

"We're monitoring the weather. We may experience some rain and wind, but that'll just add to the excitement, don't you think?" She flexed her hands. Was she nervous about something—the imposing weather, perhaps?—or did she itch to get on the water?

Walter finally staggered out from the dressing room, his suit not completely pulled into position. His weathered face flushed in alternating shades of pink and red. The gray, thinning hair stuck out at odd angles from his head.

Katie's eyes widened as she stared at the man, and she shook her head. "Mr. Thompson, you'll need to fix your wetsuit."

The red blush across his face deepened, etching into the wrinkles on his brow. "This is the best I can do, Ms. Gallagher."

Katie's expelled sigh lingered. In four strides, she stood before him, grabbed the wetsuit around Walter's bulging middle, and yanked upward. Forcefully.

Hunter glanced out the window to avoid laughing in the poor man's face.

"Now, is everyone ready? Remember, no cell phones or other electronics on this trip."

Hunter swallowed back his reaction to her silhouette as she stood in front of the fireplace. Unlike the lithe supermodels of today, Katie's figure had curves—in all the right places. Her upper arms, as well as her calves and thighs, were muscular with no sign of flab. The black Body Glove wetsuit looked as if it'd been sprayed on her body, ending just below her knees.

He clenched his jaw, struggling to keep his thoughts on his task—it'd be best for him to treat her as one of the guys. Hunter nearly snorted. As if he could think of the fiery woman as one of the guys.

He let out a long breath. This was his job, his career, and he couldn't afford any distractions.

No matter how much that distraction made him think of . . . of what he didn't want to analyze.

Katie, with Shadow darting ahead of her on the path, led the group toward the shop, anticipation building in her chest. Wind swirled, carrying the scent of rain in its breezes, beckoning to her heart. A chill hung over the river—a foretelling of the shift of weather. Katie lifted her head and felt the movement of the surrounding area, the life and breath of the Gauley. No matter how many years or how many trips she'd guided, stepping into the raft first thing in the morning always sent a thrill zipping through her, as if she and the raging river were one.

Shadow rushed back to her, leaping and barking as he pawed the ground. Katie smiled. He loved rafting almost as much as she did. She patted her leg and Shadow leaned against her. She rubbed the soft fur between his ears to calm him, but noted how his body tensed, as if he couldn't contain his excitement.

Once they'd reached the gravel put-in area beside the Gauley Guides by Gallagher shop, Katie caught sight of the burly man standing by the raft. A smile lifted to her mouth, as well as warmth spreading into her heart. His thick graying hair hung down his back. A bushy mustache complimented his mountain man look. He cocked out his hip, and squinted in the morning sun's sparse rays, appearing ominous in form.

Katie grinned wider and rushed up to hug him tight before turning to the men in her group. "Gentlemen, this is Rory Franklin. Rory is our videographer and photographer—he'll be filming our trip as well as taking still shots for your souvenirs."

The men introduced themselves to Rory while Katie checked the bedrolls the men dropped beside the raft. She ran a bungee cord through each of the strings tied around the bedrolls, then looped the end to the inside of the little ducky Rory would pull behind his kayak. The tarp encasing the little river craft would protect the bedrolls from the elements. Katie secured the tarp, taking into consideration the high probability of rains and wind. She tossed in the additional supply packs and hooked them to the bungee cords. Double-checking the knots and connec- tions, Katie pulled and tugged against the cords.

Hunter squatted down beside her, resting his elbows on his knees. "What are you doing?"

"Securing your gear to Rory's kayak."

He clutched his hands together and rocked back on his heels. "You mean our stuff won't be in the boat with us?"

"No way." She nodded toward the raft. "With eight adults and one dog, the stuff wouldn't fit. We only have the basics in our raft."

"The dog is coming with us?"

Now she let out a real laugh. "Yeah, Shadow goes on all my tours with me. He's my bodyguard as well as my best buddy."

At the mention of his name, Shadow nosed between Katie and Hunter, pushing his snout under Katie's hand. She chuckled and rubbed his head. "See." She narrowed her eyes and stared at the comical looking crew talking to Rory. "At least Shadow's experienced," she mumbled.

"Hey, I heard that."

She laughed again. "Sorry." Katie shook her head. "I just prefer more experienced rafters when tackling the Upper Gauley first thing in the morning." She lifted her head to stare into the gathering clouds threatening to block out the sun's dim rays. "And in rain."

"Why didn't another guide take our group?"

Letting out a long sigh, she shrugged. Even though she normally didn't talk one-on-one to members of a group, this Hunter Malone knew which questions to ask. "Well, Gabe has a broken leg, so he couldn't even if he'd wanted to."

"And your other brother, Christian?"

What was with all his questions? She inhaled deeply, letting the air whisper over her teeth. "He's got a group later to do the Lower Gauley."

"Another overnight one? So we'll meet up with them?"

"My, you sure ask a lot of questions. But, no, the next group is just a day trip." A couple of strands of hair slipped from her braid, gently brushing against her face. She tucked them behind her ear and stood. "You shouldn't worry, though. I'm a better guide than Christian." Katie chuckled as she stomped a couple of times, getting the blood moving down to her lower extremities again. She refused to meet Hunter's gaze, afraid of the judgments she'd find lurking behind his hypnotic eyes.

Hunter shrugged as he rose. "I don't know, though. I don't think I'd want my sister to hang with a bunch of men unchaperoned for a whole weekend." His eyes bored into her, a silent challenge for more information.

She shifted her weight from one foot to the other. "It's not like that. The river's busy this time of year—crowded almost. I have my own separate tent for me and Shadow, and Rory acts as a chaperone of sorts."

A water-pungent breeze tugged the strands of hair free once more. Hunter reached out and swept them behind her ear, his finger grazing her lobe.

The gesture felt intimate . . . too personal. She'd just met him. She took a step backward, her heart pounding as loud as Paddle Rock's rushing class-five rapid. She swallowed, choosing to stare at the river for a moment rather than meet Hunter's piercing stare. "Besides, a rafting excursion isn't exactly a romantic trip."

Hunter's glance caressed her face. "I'm not so sure about that. I think with the right person, any trip can be romantic."

Heat rushed up her neck and crossed her face. Confusion hit her like a tidal wave. Hunter Malone, while attractive and interesting, would be here for a weekend, and one weekend only. No sense wasting mental energy on even thinking about a possible relationship with someone who wouldn't be around long enough to get to know. Besides, she needed to concentrate on her job—the river demanded her undivided attention. Other people's lives depended on her.

She straightened her shoulders and snapped her fingers. Shadow wiggled on the ground beside her, bouncing on his paws. Katie's hands automatically slipped the harness over the Blue Heeler, as she spoke to the men, whose attention she now had. "Rory will be towing our gear in the ducky behind his kayak. He'll be ahead of us the entire trip, filming and photographing."

Once the harness was properly on Shadow, Katie popped her hands on her hips. "Now's the time to get your life jackets on, take last minute bathroom breaks, and get yourself ready." She glanced at her watch. "Be back out here in fifteen minutes, and we'll be on our way."

In the shop, Hunter watched the other men argue over which life jacket was the best brand. Didn't they realize it didn't matter? All the propene/nylon suits hanging on the hooks were good, even though the distinct odor of mildew infiltrated each one. Gauley Guides by Gallagher advertised being a top-notch service all the way around, and Hunter hadn't been disappointed yet. Sure, the place could use some updating, but the facilities were acceptable.

His fascination with Katie Gallagher kept derailing Hunter's train of thought. Attractive and intriguing, she awakened feelings in him that he'd thought were buried deep. Having been trained to discern between the way people presented themselves and the way they truly were, Hunter couldn't find any evidence of deception or falsehood on Katie's part. Rare to find someone truly open and honest, yet also comfortable in their own skin. And Katie Gallagher was definitely comfortable with her place in life. She blended into the nature surrounding her as if she truly belonged in the wild.

But, he argued with himself, didn't she realize the temptations men faced? And here she sat, on a weekend trip alone with seven men. He shook his head. Not that he thought her immoral, not by any means, but he couldn't ignore the attraction factor.

Orson bumped Hunter's shoulder. "What do you think?" His voice barely audible over the other men's wetsuit debate.

Hunter narrowed his eyes into slits. He, too, kept his voice low. "Not now, Orson." His gaze drifted over toward the other men. "Later," he mumbled out of the corner of his mouth before moving toward the counter.

Christian stood behind the cash register, laughing heartily at the group and joining in on the men's lively discussion. Ariel sat on the stool beside him, her gaze feasting on him. Her eyes twinkled under the blaring overhead lights, and her mouth seemed permanently curved into a seductive smile.

Using deliberate casualness, Hunter leaned nearer and made eye contact with Ariel. Her eyes were blue, but not nearly as striking as Katie's. She met his gaze, lifted a brow, then darted her stare toward Christian. Hunter rubbed the tip of his chin, then tugged on his right earlobe.

Ariel hopped off the stool and stretched. Clad in a second-skin wetsuit, she drew every man's appreciative glance. She bent toward Christian, whispered something in his ear, then strutted down the hall.

Hunter tapped the counter with his finger to get Christian's attention. "Where's the men's room? Your sister said I only had fifteen minutes to take care of business. It might take that long to get this wetsuit off."

Christian chuckled and pointed down the hall where Ariel had disappeared. "Down there to the left, man. Be sure and use powder on your body before you try to pull the wetsuit back up. Makes it much easier."

Hunter nodded, then turned and sauntered in that direction. The corridor, like the shop itself, boasted green Astro-Turf. The light brown paneling must keep the obvious wear and tear from showing as much. From the corner of his eye, Hunter made sure the other men in the party were still occupied with selecting life jackets. He passed the point where he couldn't be seen from the shop's main room, then picked up his pace to a slight jog.

At the end of the hall, there were doors on both the right and the left, politely marked MEN and WOMEN. He rapped twice on the WOMEN's with the back of his knuckles, then waited a second, and knocked twice more. The door pulled open.

Hunter glanced down the passageway. No one lurked in the corridor. He stepped across the threshold and pushed the door closed behind him.

Ariel turned the lock, then smiled at Hunter.

Five

The second hand on her watch spun. Katie made quick, short strides beside the raft. Her water shoes kicked gravel with each punctuated step, sending puffs of rock dust into the air. The few broken sunbeams glistened off the river, casting a shimmering glare. For the eighth time in the last five minutes, she glanced at her watch before shielding her eyes with her hand and glowering at the door to the shop. What could be keeping Hunter Malone?

Carter chuckled. "Maybe he has a nervous stomach or something." He did amateur knee bends.

"Or maybe his breakfast didn't agree with him," piped Jerry as he fingered his too-thick mustache. The way he leered at Katie made her flesh crawl, acutely aware of his gaze.

Katie opened her mouth to comment, but the door swung open and Hunter waltzed out. His loping gait delivered him to her side within moments. A reddish hue darkened his neck. "Sorry. Had a tough time getting the wetsuit back on."

Walter let out a roar of laughter. "Tell me about it, man. These things could easily be utilized in a torture setting." The more mature man clapped Hunter on the back.

The other men joined in on the laughter. Katie didn't see the humor. She also couldn't help but recall the few minutes it had taken Hunter to don the wetsuit earlier this morning. Why did it take him so long now? She popped a peppermint in her mouth before motioning for the men's attention.

Katie directed her group to don their helmets and life jackets, then pushed the raft into the river. Underlying currents tossed the boat around —drizzle fell against the inflated tubing. The remaining sunbeams hid behind the gathering clouds. The earthy, clean scent of rain hovered over the river, a premonition of things to come.

The men climbed into the boat, and Katie instructed each person where to sit before latching Shadow's harness to the long cord, affectionately called the chicken strap by river guides. She lifted her paddle and demonstrated a final time how to row the boat, then gave last minute instructions. The cool aluminum in her palm filled her with anticipation.

Hunter sat next to her on this leg of the journey —in the place she personally referred to as the "chicken seat." She reasoned that she'd selected him for this position due to his apparent upper body strength. His pull with the paddle would come in most useful as they made the first turn and battled Initiation, the first powerful class-five rapid.

Shadow barked as the raft cleared First Maneuver

and turned toward Initiation. The muscles in Katie's shoulders and back tensed. She braced her feet against the bottom and side of the raft, and hollered out to the men to get ready.

Paddles hit the water. Katie shouted out directions.

The level of the water rose and fell, pitching the boat up and down. Drizzle, carried on the wind, gusted against their faces.

The men struck the river with the oars. Water splashed into the boat, spraying everyone. Drizzle turned into sprinkles as the raft crew paddled furiously.

They passed through the first rapid, Initiation, no worse for wear. Katie studied each man's movements to see who the strongest were—the information would be most useful when they hit the class fives.

Nervous chuckles sounded over the raging river. Katie smiled. The men were pleased with themselves. She could practically see their chests puffing out. They'd get through five smaller rapids before they came to the first five-plus, Insignificant. Leaning to pet Shadow's water-sprayed fur, Katie let them enjoy their achievement. Soon enough, they'd face a serious rapid.

She used the lapse in intensity and concentration to study Hunter, doing so from the corner of her eye. Water sat on the curls snaking out from Hunter's helmet, making his hair look even darker. Blacker than black. His distinguished chin set firm. Minus sunglasses, the concentrated squint of his eyes made him more mysterious, more alluring. Katie jolted her gaze to the other men in the boat as her heart raced, and not from any adrenaline rush.

The good-natured ribbing among the men made Katie grin once more. There were some obvious lines on the social ladder, but overall, they got along well. Maybe they weren't so bad for a bunch of members of the pocket-protector club. Except for Hunter.

Katie cut her gaze over to him, watching as he stared at the others. His pectoral muscles glided in synchronized harmony with the movement of his arms as he paddled, pulling Katie's eyes to his chest. The infuriating inability to look away crawled between her shoulders blades and rested there. She closed her eyes to break free from the sight, imposing her ironclad control of will over her thoughts. Katie couldn't understand why the man got under her skin so easily. She opened her eyes, forcing herself to focus on the river, not the man beside her.

One thing bothered her—he didn't fit the accountant mold at all. Why was he with this geeky group of guys? He looked more like the adventure junkies who came to the Gauley every year. She'd bet her third of the business he was more than just a bean-counter with Lassiter James

Accounting Firm. Yeah, she'd stake the business that Hunter Malone had something to hide.

Instinct kicked in, pulling her back to the task at hand. She whipped her paddle into her lap. "We're approaching Collision Creek, which is a class-three rapid. Hold your paddles steady and let the current carry you," Katie commanded as she watched to make sure the men followed her orders.

They paddled through Collision Creek and French Kiss before entering a calm portion of the trip. Katie cleared her throat. "We've just passed through French Kiss." Her eyes shot unintentionally to Hunter, and she swallowed.

Hunter's brows shot up, crinkling his forehead into a furrow of tanned creases.

She froze as heat rose up the back of her neck. "Which is a . . . uh . . . also a class-three rapid." Katie licked her lips.

She needed to stop acting like a little schoolgirl with a crush. She took a deep breath before launching into her tour guide speech. "The US Army Corps of Engineers completed the Summersville Dam project in 1964. The Summersville Lake Dam sits three hundred and ninety feet above the Gauley, and has three discharge tubes. When released, the average discharge is about 624,000 pounds per second."

Katie made sure each man's full attention riveted on her as she spoke, then continued. "Now, the unique part of our dam is the name. The Corps of Engineers typically named dams after the closest town. In this case, the closest town was Gad." She chuckled. "They opted to name this the Summersville Lake Dam when they considered Gad Dam probably wouldn't be such a good idea."

The men hooted and hollered.

"Come on, you're pulling our leg, aren't you?" Carter asked.

She shook her head and held up her right hand, as if being sworn in at court. "Nope, true story. You can look it up when you get back."

She sobered and lifted her chin. "Okay, we're approaching Insignificant, the first five-plus rapid." She shifted in her seat, wrapping the cord around her wrist. "Insignificant has a big dip, then we'll go down the 'wave train.' This is a shallow rapid, so we need to avoid the rocks lining the edge of the river."

The first jolts of the rapids popped against the inflated raft. Katie planted her feet. "Everybody get in the ready position. Remember, don't lose your paddle!"

The raft lunged under Hunter's shoes. His heart pounded. River water splashed in his face— raindrops soaked him from above. His arms moved in reflex, paddling with the current, just as Katie instructed.

The current pulled the boat right. Another splash of the cold water hit his face. The raft twisted left. Hunter made long strokes with the paddle.

In twenty seconds, they passed the big dip and raced down the trail of continuous rapids.

Hunter sent up a silent prayer of thanks for being kept safe thus far.

And for protection for the rest of the trip.

Only the raging call of the river could be heard once the raft slowed. The wind picked up in intensity, pushing hard against the raft. Katie adjusted her sunglasses and laughed. "Gentlemen, you did good . . . for desk jockeys."

Tension seeped from the group like air hissing from a cut inner tube. Bursts of laughter shot from some of them. Jerry even pushed Steve's arm in jest.

Watching Katie pet her dog, Hunter experienced an unfamiliar sensation settle over him. The woman appeared peaceful, serene, and flawless in her environment. Her strong sense of self and her comfort with nature did strange things to Hunter's thoughts. He shook his head, water droplets splattering from his hair.

He hauled in a deep breath and observed the other members of the group. Carter seemed to be thoroughly enjoying himself, sitting in the first seat on the right. The old man's eyes twinkled. Across the boat from Carter, perched Orson, looking anything but happy. The man's forehead knitted and his brows slashed down, forming a gray uni-brow over his deep-set eyes. Hunter tossed Orson a quick smile, then diverted his gaze to the next row in the boat.

Jerry and Paul sat next to each other, ribbing in almost a callous manner. The boat shifted and lurched, causing a spew of profanity to erupt from Jerry's mouth. Hunter cringed. Although he couldn't say anything, he sent up silent prayers for the man's salvation. Right now, he studied the partners in the investment business.

Although they claimed to be friends from way back when, Jerry deferred to Paul. Hunter watched the two men jab each other and lift their paddles over their heads in a gesture of victory. Yes, beyond a doubt, Paul was the leader of the two.

Raindrops fell at random. Hunter glanced skyward. Clouds covered the sky, but no lightning flickered—no thunder roared—not a single legitimate reason to get off the river. He didn't know whether to be relieved or disappointed. Instead, he turned his attention back to the men in the boat.

Directly in front of Hunter sat Walter, and across from him, Steve. Neither man spoke. In fact, Steve's face looked etched in fear. Hunter leaned forward and tapped Steve's arm.

Steve jerked around and glared at Hunter. "What?"

Hunter shook his head. "Nothing. Just wanted to tell you—you did good."

The cynical smile that crossed the man's face screamed of needing grace. An uneasy feeling settled over Hunter. He gave back a smile of sincerity.

Feeling under scrutiny, Hunter turned, meeting Katie's stare. Her silvery eyes glistened with unshed tears. Why? Did she wonder about Steve, too? If her mind held thoughts of Steve, why did she look straight into his being?

Katie looked away and blinked. Why should she be touched by Hunter's attempt to be nice to his co-worker? She shouldn't, period. Yet, Steve's face had changed under Hunter's approval, so she couldn't help but appreciate Hunter Malone all the more. Whenever he'd met her gaze, funny tingles pulsed throughout her body. She needed to be more careful around Hunter. Especially until she figured out what secrets he harbored.

Shadow barked.

Moving to a semi-standing position in the raft, Katie gathered her bearings. She clenched her jaw and shouted out more instructions. "Once we make it through this one, we'll face another five-plus rapid. Pillow Rock is nothing to play around with. Remember what I told you earlier—paddle or die."

The men jostled around in the boat, preparing

for a bumpy ride. The wind would make the rapid even rougher. Katie watched their nervous moves and refrained from smiling. It never ceased to tickle her to see grown men so unsure of themselves. Except Hunter. He didn't appear rattled at all. Matter of fact, sheer determination engraved his expression.

The boat shifted as Pillow Rock came into view. Katie wedged her feet against the side and bottom of the raft, tensing her muscles as she gripped her paddle. They hit the inertia wave, the large rock looming in front of them. "Wild or mild, boys?" she yelled over the raging rapid.

"Wild."

"Wild."

"Wild."

"Mild."

Katie smiled as Steve yelled out his choice of mild. She stuck the face of her oar into the water and guided the raft toward the left, the wild choice.

The rapid pitched them forward. The raft spun around backward over the little boulder peaking out of the surge. A quick downward thrust of rushing water caused the boat to go up on its side.

The swirling river pushed them free of the rapid, jostling the crew against one another. Katie steadied herself, felt Shadow wedge against her leg, and worked to bring order back to the group.

A smaller wave crested against the raft. Carter lurched to the center.

Jerry leaned back, bumping into Steve, who teetered on the edge of the raft. Jerry reached out to him, but Steve lunged off the side, falling into the swift current.

Katie's heart flew to her throat. "Man in the drink!"

Whipping her paddle to the other side, Katie made long, hard strokes. Her stare fixed on the water, watching for Steve. He was her responsibility.

Steve's head bobbed up behind them and to the left.

Hunter reached, throwing his upper body across the lip of the raft. Utilizing his arms of corded muscles, he grabbed the neck of Steve's life jacket and hauled the sputtering man back into the boat.

Katie shifted forward and wiped at Steve's face with the palm of her hand.

He sputtered, then spat. Water—or possibly tears—pooled in the man's glaring eyes. He coughed and shook his head. He panted a few seconds before he caught his breath. Steve scowled at Jerry. "You pushed me in."

Jerry's brows shot up. "I didn't push you in, dude. You fell."

"I did not fall. You bumped me, then pushed me."

Katie felt rather than heard Shadow growl. She swallowed as both men's faces grew red. Not a good situation. She cleared her throat and stroked

Shadow's head. "Getting dunked is part of white-water rafting, guys. It happens." Settling her gaze on Steve, she smiled. "Accidents happen in rafts all the time."

"This wasn't an accident. I felt him push me."

She pressed her lips together. In all her years of guiding, she'd never had two clients lash out at one another. This could get ugly—real ugly and real fast. She steered the boat into calmer waters. "What do you want to do?" she asked Steve.

Steve, face now white, glared at Jerry. "I want an apology. He deliberately pushed me into that rapid. If he doesn't admit it, I want off."

Katie raised a brow at Jerry.

Shaking his head, Jerry set his jaw. "I didn't do any such thing. Stop being a baby. Get over it."

"I want off." Steve stared back at Katie.

She let out a long sigh and studied Steve's face. Fear cloaked his features. Her heart pounded in her chest. "Okay."

Katie turned to the side, stood, waved her paddle high over her head, and gave a shrill whistle.

From a high rock on the side of the river, Rory whistled back.

She returned her attention to Steve. "As soon as we put out for the day, Rory will take you back to the lodge."

Steve didn't reply, merely gave a curt nod.

Paddling, Katie felt the tension settle over the

raft's occupants. Four more five-plus rapids to go, and they'd be clear. She could do this—keep everyone calm. She let out another long breath. Could Steve be right? Had Jerry pushed him? If he had, was it a joke, or had malicious intent lurked behind Jerry's actions?

Six

Aware of the implications, Hunter concentrated on what he'd witnessed—an accident, or an attempted murder? He'd seen Jerry bump into Steve—seen Jerry's arm go out to Steve, but to regain balance, or had Jerry actually pushed the man into the river? It all happened so fast, Hunter couldn't make the determination. He couldn't chance making a mistake. Not again. Not like he did with Misty Mulligan. He shook his head, truly baffled.

He needed answers. Needed wisdom. Needed the truth. Lives were at stake.

With subtle glances, Hunter studied Steve's body language. The hands that held Steve's paddle turned white across the knuckles. His brow crinkled, carved in concentration. His eyes, steady and unwavering, watched the water, but darted to Jerry's back. Hunter sighed. Fear ate at Steve Smith. Justified or not, Steve was leery of Jerry Sands.

"What do you think?" Katie's voice carried so

low over the river and wind, Hunter nearly missed her question.

He lifted his gaze to meet hers. Concern and worry blinked in her silver-blue eyes. Hunter shrugged. "Steve believes Jerry pushed him in." Following Katie's lead, he kept his voice at whisper level as he answered her as honestly as he could. "Whether real or imagined, Steve's scared of Jerry."

She nodded, the braid snaking down her back bobbing with her movements. The itch to reach out and tug her wet locks caused him to freeze. He didn't have time for this attraction . . . infatuation . . . whatever he chose to call it. Hunter wiped the moisture from his face in vain—the rain continued to sprinkle down on them, clouding his vision. Much like his growing draw to Katie clouded his judgment.

"Rory will pick him up when we put out near Mason Branch." Her voice dropped even lower. "I'm wondering whether I should have Rory call someone when he gets back to the lodge."

Hunter's heartbeat picked up. "Call who?"

"I don't know." She shrugged as she moved. "Maybe the police."

His stomach clenched. Just what he needed—locals on the scene to mess up everything. "I don't think that's warranted yet, do you? I mean," he hitched a brow, "we don't even know for sure if it was a deliberate act or simply an accident. Right?"

Katie locked gazes with him. Several moments passed. Maybe she hadn't heard him clearly.

Finally, she shrugged. "You're right. But I still feel like something fishy is going on."

"Why don't we just wait and see what happens?'

Letting the water drip from the end of her paddle as she crossed it over to stroke on her other side, Katie nodded. "Guess that's the best thing to do." She stared at the men in the boat, then back to him. "How well do you know these guys?"

"I've been with the firm for about six months. I don't know many of them at all."

"Only six months, huh?" Her stare rendered him incapable of looking away. "When we made the reservations, I understood it to be for the executives, the firm's best clients, and a handful of key personnel."

He flashed a weak smile. "I've set some sales records in those six months." Ignoring the little urchin sitting on his shoulder who sang *Liar! Liar!* Hunter widened his smile. "They thought I should be rewarded for my efforts."

It wasn't really lying . . . he did increase the sales record.

"I see." Her tongue clucked against the roof of her mouth as she broke eye contact to check on the dog's harness.

Morality breathing deep into his entire being, Hunter detested being dishonest—hated deception of any kind. Still, he didn't have much of a choice. Not if he intended to succeed at what he'd set out to do. He could only hope the end justified the means. But the thought of Katie's disapproving look being shot his way sent shivers of appre-hension over him.

Shaking off the imposing thoughts, Hunter concentrated on the sounds of the river. The roar got louder and blended with the wind, blocking out all else. Another rapid must be right around the bend.

Katie squinted from behind her sunglasses and watched the river. Hungry Mother, a class-four rapid, would be next. She shifted her gaze to the members in the boat. No matter the dissention going on, they would have to pull together as a team to make it through the remaining rapids.

The boat picked up speed and volume, and the rushing water drowned out everything.

Katie centered herself in the middle of the back of the raft, spreading her legs wide, one grazing against Hunter's.

He looked over and smashed stares with her.

Time stood still. Her heart flipped. Her atten-tion shot to her leg, where his touched hers. Her mouth felt like someone dumped a load of sand inside.

Shadow barked, breaking the moment.

Katie returned her attention to the wild water forging around the raft, and the driving wind that forced the air from her lungs. The boat slipped down, carried by the fast current.

The raft spun, then hit an underwater boulder, kicking the boat back toward the center of the rapid. A quick burst of wind twisted the raft about.

Katie switched her paddle to the left side, making long, steady strokes. "Paddle hard!"

Water sprayed. They rubbed against the decision rock, jostling and pitching everyone. Everyone slipped around in the vessel.

Shoved out of the raging rapid, the boat slowed.

Katie hauled in a long breath. Her gaze drifted over the group. "Everybody okay?"

The men seemed to regain their composure at once.

"That was fun!"

"All clear, here."

"Yowsa."

"Goood night!"

Katie laughed. Finally, some sense of teamwork. Maybe they'd survive yet. She glanced over to Hunter, who smiled and winked at her.

Her heart pounded in response, warmth crept up the back of her neck. Still smiling, she looked back to the other members of the group. "You gentlemen did great. That's what I call teamwork. Good job."

The men clapped each other on the back and returned to their chatter. Steve didn't join in on the banter, but at least he didn't snarl at Jerry anymore. Maybe he'd decide to stay for the rest of the trip. No one waited at the lodge, which bothered her. Gabe would have to watch the store, and while Christian would return after his run today, until then, Rory would have to stay and keep an eye on their guest. Katie didn't like that scenario—it would put a definite kink in her timeline.

For now, peace and comradeship prevailed over the raft. A few more major rapids and they'd put out for the day. Katie sighed and rolled the tension from her shoulders.

Shadow shook, sending more water droplets all over Katie and Hunter. She laughed and scratched under his chin.

The boat drifted into much calmer waters, but a distinct hissing noise reached Katie's ears and her relief crumbled.

Spiders of disbelief swarmed her mind. Nothing, but nothing, sounded like air hissing from an inflatable raft. Her heart sank. Rubbing up against decision rock must have punctured the raft. Now she truly faced a dilemma—how to get the boat out of the water amid the elements before they reached Lost Paddle, which they were quickly boring down on.

Katie sliced the water on the right side of the boat. "Everybody on the right side, paddle hard. Those on the left, don't do anything." She continued to stroke fast, not looking up to see if the men followed her instructions—she'd have to trust them.

If they missed slipping into Meadow River, they'd be pulled right into Lost Paddle. No way could they make it through the class-five-plus rapid with a deflating boat. They had to skid into the off-shoot.

Keenly aware when Hunter moved next to her to help, Katie kept a steady pace of strokes. She squinted against the driving rain and caught sight of Meadow River up ahead. "Everybody work harder. We have to slip into that." She nodded toward the off-shoot.

Oars slapped the water. The hissing grew louder. The right side of the raft lost more air, its rounded edge becoming mushy to her touch.

"Paddle or die!" Her voice carried over the river.

The sound of aluminum cutting through water gained pitch. The raft's momentum increased.

Katie pulled hard. She gauged the distance to their destination—less than two hundred feet to go. Using longer, harder strokes, their efforts caused the raft to shift and move toward Meadow River.

Grunts and groans echoed in her ears. The men pulled their weight, possibly even understanding the severity of the situation. God, she hoped they did. For a nanosecond, she considered her choice of words in her thoughts. God? Where had that come from? Must have been seeing her Bible this morning. Katie gave herself a mental shake—she needed to concentrate—needed to get the boat into Meadow River. Now!

The nose of the raft turned to lead into the off-shoot, but an undercurrent jerked the boat out of the mouth of Meadow River.

Katie glanced to her left, into the mouth of the Gauley. A large hydraulic loomed, its swirling eye drawing everything toward it. Katie groaned, knowing the raft would be sucked into its swirling force if she didn't make this sharp right turn. She tossed her paddle into the boat, unhooked and tossed off both her helmet and life jacket, then jumped over the side.

Icy water stung her unprotected lower legs. Ignoring the numbing sensations, Katie pressed her feet against the bottom of the river and propelled herself upward.

Shadow whined from inside the boat, moving himself to be on the side of the raft closest to where she'd jumped overboard.

Small, jagged rocks on the river's bed jabbed into the soles of her water shoes. She threw her right arm over the quickly deflating rim of the raft and pushed with every ounce of strength she could muster. Wind whipped around her, pushing her off balance.

Deep undertows of water whished around her legs. Her footing faltered. She slipped and clung to the edge of the raft. Over her shoulder, she estimated the distance between the boat and the hydraulic—maybe twenty feet. Katie surged forward, all too aware of the death cave lurking under the water's surface.

Shadow whined.

Katie fought to regain her placement on the rocky bottom. Using her leg muscles, she wedged her feet against the bottom and pushed the raft again. It inched forward, toward the off-shoot.

A loud splash exploded next to her.

Hunter surfaced beside her. "Watch out for the death cave and hydraulic!" she yelled.

He nodded. His muscular arms grabbed the raft and pushed.

The raft shot forward.

Katie dug her toes in for traction, still clinging to the boat, propelling it with each push of her legs. The wind thrust up a notch, now feeling like gale force.

Hunter shoved the raft farther into Meadow River. The middle of the boat now cleared the Gauley.

Letting out a long breath, Katie smiled at Hunter. "Thanks. I think we've got it now." She flailed her right arm about until she caught hold of the chicken strap. She held tight and wedged her toe under the bottom of the raft, and hauled herself over the edge and into the boat. Shadow licked her cheek. Katie petted his head. Panting, she offered her hand to Hunter.

His eyes trained on her hand, then back to her gaze. A broad smile spread across his face. "I don't think you can pull me in." His words were smooth and unwinded. "I'll drift out here till we get to the bank."

She flashed a quick grin, then faced the men in the boat.

Steve's face was white against his red life jacket, his eyes wide.

Katie laid a hand on Steve's shoulder, but spoke to the whole group. "The boat's been punctured. We're going to bank up here until Rory catches up, and I can plug the hole." She lifted her paddle and made the few final strokes toward the bank, ignoring the screams from the muscles in her arm.

Once the tip of the raft touched dry land, the men leapt from the boat. Tugging it behind them, they then collapsed on the bank. Katie unhooked Shadow's safety harness, letting the dog run free, and yanked her feet from the water shoes.

She unzipped her waterproof fanny pack, pulled out a peppermint and popped it into her mouth. She shoved the empty wrapper back in and zipped the pack closed. "We'll be here for a while. Anybody up for a snack?"

"There's food?" Paul asked and nodded toward the deflating raft. "Where?"

Katie chuckled, then leaned over to the four large pockets on the inside back flap of the raft. She pulled out two small bag coolers from the two pockets on the right, set them on the ground, then pulled out two plastic bags from the remaining two pockets on the left. "Gatorade and granola bars, anyone?"

The group converged on her like water over the dam. She handed out the bars and bottles, feeling Hunter's stare on her back, nearly scorching her. Once she'd distributed the snacks, she straightened and unzipped the top of her wetsuit. The burst of air against her wet skin sent goosebumps popping up over her flesh. She turned to hand the last bottle to Hunter, and ran smack into a wall of muscle.

Hunter stood before her, the top of his wetsuit also unzipped. Drops of water beaded against his chest, sitting atop the curls of hair spread over his muscular torso.

Katie's mouth went dry, despite the mint she sucked on. Her gaze lifted to his face. His eyes were dark, clouded over, and heavy looking.

His breathing came in short gasps. He bent his head, almost leaning into her.

Shadow barked and jumped on Katie's thighs.

Shivering, she stepped back from Hunter, then handed him the Gatorade. "Here."

"Thanks." His voice came out husky, rough. He gripped the sweating bottle and took a long swig.

Katie turned, strode back to the now deflated raft. She pulled out a dog treat, tossed it to Shadow, then tugged a smaller plastic bag from another pocket. She popped open the seal and withdrew the clear plastic squares and tube of sealing glue. She set them on the ground before lifting the edge of the boat.

Hunter materialized at her side, helping her hold up the heavy deflated raft. "So, what's a death cave anyway?"

"It's a cave under the water's surface—made from the rapids running across the boulders underneath and eroding them." She shrugged. "If you get sucked into one of those, death is imminent—no chance of surviving. They'd have to shut off the dam and drag the Gauley with meat hooks to find your body."

He shuddered and hefted the edges of the deflated raft higher.

She smiled her thanks, then ran her hand over the bottom of the raft. A small hole would be hard to find, but find it she must. Scooting along, she continued to feel for the burst of air. Still not locating anything, she moved her hand toward the center of the boat. Her fingers grazed a rough edge. She sucked in her breath as she felt the shape of the rip.

"Help me raise this part."

Standing inside the middle of the raft, Hunter grasped the edge she nodded toward, and hoisted.

She peered at the underside. She ran her fingers the length of the tear. No puncture here—this cut measured at least three inches long. Nothing her patch kit could repair. How had it happened? Decision rock didn't have jagged edges. Not that could do this kind of damage.

Leaning forward, Katie studied the gaping rip. Her heart locked up. The tear was almost in a perfectly straight line, no serrated edges—nothing uneven.

"What is it?" Hunter's voice washed over her, drowning out the growls of Mother Nature.

She studied him. Worry and concern lay deep in his expression. Katie glanced over her shoulder at the men munching on the bank, then at the rocky ground. She had to trust someone. While she didn't have the whole story about Hunter and his so-called profession, she could believe him. She nodded toward the tear. "This wasn't an accident. No rock could have made this clean of a cut." She rocked back on her heels. "The raft's been sliced."

Hunter tore his gaze from Katie and looked at the raft where she'd indicated. Yanking the material to cover his legs, he then ran a finger over a good three-to-four-inch cut. Katie had called it—this was deliberate.

"What do you think?" she whispered, glancing over her shoulder toward the men.

He chewed the inside of his cheek. Should he tell her? No, that would only frighten her.

Her expression shrouded with an emotion he couldn't determine. "Well?"

"You're right—this is a cut made with a knife or something, not a rock."

She let out a long breath, then stood. Wrapping her arms across her chest, she hugged herself. "I know. Guess I didn't want to be right." Shadow must've sensed her emotions, because he appeared at her side, leaning against her leg. She ran an absentminded hand over his head.

"What do you want to do?" He couldn't resist laying a hand on her shoulder.

"I don't know. I've never had someone cut up one of my rafts before." She pressed her lips together until they turned white. "We'll have to wait for Rory to circle back around. When we don't make the next set of rapids, he'll come looking for us. He can dump all our stuff here, head back to the lodge, and bring us a new raft."

"Sounds like a plan." What could be running through her mind? She didn't appear frightened. She looked more annoyed than scared. "What else?"

"I want to know who cut my boat. Rafts are expensive and this one is new." Katie's gaze rested on the mound of the deflated raft. "Well, it was."

He let out a sigh. How much to bring to her attention? Should he risk filling her in?

Still standing alongside the raft, she moved toward the back end. Her dog pranced behind her. Using her feet as a measuring tool, Katie paced off the length until she stood parallel to the cut, then squatted. "Right here is about the second seat back." She ran a hand over her wet hair. "Where Jerry sat."

Seven

Indecision and worry complicated her life once again. Katie appreciated neither. Would they forever haunt her stability? Katie kneaded her stiff neck muscles while rolling her head in a circle.

Shadow pawed at the ground, looked back over toward the wooded area, then back at Katie, his body wiggling.

"Go ahead. I'll whistle when I need you," Katie told the dog.

Barking, Shadow raced off. Katie smiled—she'd always said her dog could understand English.

Popping another peppermint into her mouth, she shielded her eyes against the rain that now had the momentum of a shower. She stared out over the Gauley. Surely Rory would be along soon. In the meantime, she could only assume someone had set out to sabotage the trip.

A cold hand on her shoulder caused her to jump and spin around.

Hunter held up his hands in mock surrender. "Sorry. Just wondered what you wanted to do."

"I don't know right now." Wiping her face, she shook her head. "Someone cut the raft. I intend to find out who, and why." She took a step toward the men taking shelter under a tree.

Tugging on her forearm, Hunter shook his head. "Sure you want to tip your hand right now?"

"What do you mean?" She stopped and stared at him.

He took a step closer, inching into her private space. Heat rose to her face. Leaning toward her, he lowered his voice. "If someone did cut the raft on purpose, should you alert him that you're on to him? Do you think he'll stand up and take credit? Couldn't you let everyone assume you think it was an accident?"

Katie's breathing hitched. She pressed her fingers to her lips. "But I have to get some answers." Her voice cracked.

"I understand that. I want answers, too." He nodded. "But maybe if you play a little clueless, he'll think he's gotten away with cutting the raft. And he'll make a mistake."

She couldn't think in such close proximity to Hunter. His nearness did strange things to her, caused reactions Katie wasn't ready to deal with. She took a step back. "And if he makes a mistake? What could be worse than cutting my raft?"

His mouth pinched shut. The stare he tossed back in her face made her blood run cold.

A sudden bout of queasiness made her waver. His hand snaked out to hold her up.

"You mean . . . you think . . ." Was he really saying what she thought he was saying? No, couldn't be.

"Yes, Katie, whoever did this could have intentions to do much worse down the line."

Bile threatened to scorch the back of her throat. She swallowed, but the acidic taste crept up her tongue.

Hunter pressed a bottle of Gatorade into her trembling hands.

Katie forced the liquid past her lips. The cold drowned out the burning sensation. She sucked in a quick peppermint-laced breath, then took another drink. Her nausea subsided.

"Understand where I'm coming from?" His voice was soft, even more than the whispering.

Letting out a long breath, she nodded.

"So, let's form a game plan."

Katie stared at him. How could he be so calm? Shouldn't he be more concerned? Maybe Hunter cut the raft. She faltered in her position and glanced to the men sitting a good couple of hundred yards from them.

He kept his grip on her shoulders. He brushed back a lock of hair the wind had caressed out of her braid.

His touch sent fireballs bouncing around her stomach. The gesture portrayed an intimacy she hadn't expected, but one she reveled in anyway.

His eyes held no malicious intent, not that she could see. She searched for revelation of whatever secrets he harbored. A sudden darkness dropped over his orbs, giving them a glazed effect. Hunter lowered his head toward hers with the slowness of a man unhurried by time.

Closing her eyes, she waited for his lips to brush hers. They didn't, and bursts of heat shot from the center of her stomach out through her body. She snapped her lids open. What was she thinking?

He backed away, but kept his grip on her shoulders. His expression conveyed his emotions —yes, he wanted to kiss her—no, it wasn't the right time.

"So, Ms. Gallagher, what do we do now?" Carter's scratchy voice boomed over her shoulder.

Katie jumped away from Hunter, and faced the older man who'd just saved her from doing something incredibly stupid.

Carter stood with his gnarly hands on his protruding hips. "Well?"

She made a decision. Even though she didn't know Hunter Malone well, she felt she could trust him. "The rip in the boat is too large to patch. We'll wait for Rory to come, and I'll send him to fetch us a new raft."

The old man grunted and shifted his weight. "So what do we do in the meantime?"

If the situation weren't so dire, Katie would've

laughed at his expression. Brows furrowed together and lowered to almost the bridge of his nose, Carter looked like some mythical creature.

She bit back the snort of laughter bubbling in her chest. Marching with quick strides, she reached the old man and gently touched his upper arm. "We'll take shelter from the rain under those trees." She guided Carter toward where the others sat. Hunter followed right behind them, his attention trained on the group.

A sharp whistle penetrated the wailings of the Gauley.

She and Hunter spun simultaneously.

Rory, paddling furiously in his kayak with the inflated ducky floating behind, neared Meadow River.

Bursting into a jog, Katie headed for the off-shoot. Small bits of rock and twigs poked into the bottoms of her bare feet, but she didn't care. She pushed harder, ready to cling to Rory's presence like a drowning person to a life preserver.

Hunter kicked into a run as well. Within two paces, he passed her, but Shadow burst out of nowhere and reached the edge of the river first. Hunter came in a close second. He grabbed the nose of the kayak, then tugged it against the bank.

Rory stepped from the little boat, petting Shadow. "Thanks, man. 'Preciate it."

Having caught up, Katie wrapped her arms

around Rory in a big bear hug, then veiled her words carefully as she told him about the cut in the raft. She didn't want to alarm him, or alert him there might be a shady character in their midst. If he thought, even for a brief second, that she'd be in danger, he'd never leave. Then where would they be? No, she had to downplay the incident, which she did as they walked away from the river.

"So, I need you to go back to the lodge and bring me another boat." Katie finished speaking, then walked toward the group, Shadow on her heels. She snapped and pointed, and the Blue Heeler sat and stayed.

Rory took her hand in his, matching her steps. His calloused fingers rubbed her palm. "Are you sure? In this weather?" He nodded toward the sky, which grew darker by the minute. "I almost didn't make it over to you guys. Storm's a-comin', Katie."

"I know. That's why it's so important for you to hurry and get the raft back to us." She squeezed his hand, wishing she could hold on to him for dear life, yet knowing she had to take charge of the situation. She dropped his hand with a final press, and forced a smile. "So we can get to camp before the weather really hits."

Rory nodded toward the men. "I'm going to leave the ducky here. I'd suggest you get some food while you wait until I get back."

"I'm going with you," Steve said as he drew to his feet.

Rory looked at Katie.

She'd hoped Steve would be willing to stick it out. Although, even now, he looked like a petrified little boy. And she had told him Rory would come get him. She flashed him a weak smile, then turned to Rory and nodded. "He wants to go back."

"Okay. We'll unload your gear from the ducky, and he can ride in it back to the lodge."

"Gentlemen, head on down to the river and grab your rolls."

The men lumbered to their feet and shuffled toward the kayak. Hunter hovered next to her. Leaning so close, his breath kissed her ear. "I'll make sure they get everything. I'll be right back." He sprinted down the slick bank.

She felt Rory's stare. Meeting his eyes, Katie shook her head. "Don't go reading more into something that isn't there."

"Sure looks cozy to me."

Swatting his arm, warmth seeped into her cheeks. "While you're at the lodge, will you get the updated weather report for me?"

All remnants of teasing left his face. "Worried?"

Katie shrugged with one shoulder. "Just trying to think ahead. If Emily's coming ashore and we're going to get blasted, I want to get these guys back to the lodge for the night."

"I'll hurry." Rory's voice sounded thick.

"I'll keep 'em in line until you get back."

He tweaked her chin with his thumb and forefinger. "You keep yourself in line, Katie-my-girl."

The men trudged toward her in the driving rain, toting bedrolls and smaller supply cases. She slapped Rory's arm. "Get. I'll handle things here."

Rory, with a long stride, looped toward the kayak where Steve waited.

Katie swallowed hard. A sense of foreboding slithered up her spine and settled in her chest. Fighting against the strong urge to run and jump in the ducky with Steve, Katie turned and trekked up the slope to the small cluster of trees. Shadow moved alongside her.

What more could be in store for her?

Hunter's senses still reeled from the near-kiss. He'd never expected to be so attracted to someone so fast. Something strange had happened to him—something he couldn't name, and didn't honestly know if he wanted to. Control. He'd built his entire life around that one necessity. Now he sorely lacked in that department.

He'd watched her embrace Rory with enthusiasm, and having never experienced the pangs of jealousy before, he'd never understood those poor souls who did. Watching Katie bring Rory up to speed with a relaxed ease that bespoke of a close relationship, Hunter finally understood.

But he needed to concentrate on the job at hand. His focus couldn't be shifted. Hunter looked over Katie's shoulder to the rest of the group.

One of these men had sliced the raft. Someone intent on sabotage. Only because the cut was below water level, and the force of the river, did it take so long to deflate. But who—and more importantly, what did he have planned next?

Paul and Jerry huddled with their backs against each other. Neither of them looked frightened nor upset. Matter-of-fact, in Hunter's opinion, they appeared to be enjoying the new twist on the adventure. An old, familiar sensation twisted in Hunter's gut. He couldn't prove it, but he had a hunch one of those two was the culprit. Or maybe both of them were behind the incident.

Leaning against the tree, Orson Toliver stared into the ever-darkening sky, his face wreathed in worry. His gaze darted to Hunter, and he raised his bushy eyebrows. Hunter lifted his chin but a fraction. Orson wasn't behind any of this—no way, no how. He had too much to lose.

That left Walter. Hunter's attention focused on the chief accountant at the firm. Sitting so close to the tree he practically hugged it, the man looked like a drowned rat. Somehow, the idea of Walter being involved in anything sinister or under-handed made Hunter want to laugh. He'd still keep an eye on the man, but Hunter mentally scratched him off the list of suspects.

Katie issued instructions as Hunter walked up behind her. "Let's grab the raft and drag it up here. We can use the chicken strap to tie it to the tree and make a shelter until Rory gets back."

The men groaned.

Hunter dumped the load of supplies and clapped his hands. "You heard the lady, let's get busy."

Carter mumbled, "Who died and made you boss? I'm the boss here."

Shoving out his hand, Hunter stopped Carter. "Actually, Ms. Gallagher's the boss on this trip. Just as you expect your orders to be carried out, so does she. So, show her a little respect."

The old man's face puffed up like a blowfish. His jaw dropped, and he glared at Hunter. "When we get back, boy, we're going to have a discussion in my office."

Throwing his head back, Hunter laughed. "Well, until then, I suggest you show Ms. Gallagher the courtesy of your respect." He stopped laughing and glowered at his boss.

Carter harrumphed, but headed to join the others by the deflated raft.

"That was nice." Katie sidled up next to him. "But I don't need you to fight my battles for me."

Did she have any idea how cute she looked when perturbed? Probably not. Her brow puckered into a tight little knot and her freckles seemed to jump off the bridge of her nose. "Just wanted to make them pay attention. Carter stays on a power kick."

"If you take up for me like some playground hero, they'll never respect me."

"I'm sorry. I didn't think of it that way."

She smiled, her dog almost moving in unison with her movements. He sure had been aptly named since he was always in her shadow. "It's okay. Just remember, I'm a big girl and can take care of myself."

He held up his hands. "Yes, ma'am."

"So, if he's such an ogre, why work for him?"

"It pays the bills."

"So does digging ditches—what's your point?"

"Uh, I'd rather not discuss it right now." He nodded toward the men pulling the raft who were about to reach them.

"Saved by the bell, you think?"

Again, warmth spread throughout his body. What was it about this woman that made his knees buckle when she smiled at him? He winked. "Except in the twelfth and final round."

Her hearty chuckle soothed like a balm to his ragged core. She turned to direct the men's efforts in stringing up the raft, leaving him staring after her. She pointed and made hand motions, her words carrying away in the wind. The dog zipped around her legs. Katie moved with the sure grace of a forest nymph. The scene warmed him even though he stood on soggy ground.

Grabbing gear, Hunter trudged to the area with three trees planted close together. Lightning flickered across the sky, illuminating the thunderous clouds forming in the distance. He dumped his load at the base of the center tree, then bit back a chuckle as Jerry and Paul struggled to secure the raft.

He shoved Jerry out of the way, then reached above his head and grabbed hold of a limb. Using his upper body strength, Hunter hoisted himself to the top of the branch. He swung his leg over and heaved to a sitting position, straddling the bough. "Hand me the strap."

Jerry tossed the strap up with more force than necessary. It slapped Hunter across the leg. He grabbed it, but scowled at Jerry while he secured it around the tree. Once he tightened the strap, Hunter swung down and landed on the mushy ground with a splashing thud. He straightened, then pushed Jerry's shoulder.

"Hey, man, watch it." Jerry's face turned red.

"Don't be a jerk, Sands." Hunter clenched his jaw. He faced Katie. Her eyes widened, as if shocked by his anger.

"Where do you want the next one tied?" he asked, flashing a wink.

"Uh . . ." Her gaze darted to the other two trees. She gave a nod to the tree on his right. "That one would give us the most coverage."

Once in position, Hunter rested his palms on his thighs. "What do you want to use to secure it?"

She shook her head sharply, as if clearing her thoughts. "Uh, we can use one of the ties from a bedroll."

"Do any of you gentlemen have a pocketknife to cut the string off the bedroll?" Hunter asked.

Silence hovered over the men. Hunter pushed. "Come on. Surely one of you has a pocketknife? The sooner we get this situated, the sooner we can get out of this pouring rain."

Paul looked at Jerry who shook his head slightly. Hunter swallowed back a sigh. So, Jerry had cut the raft. Why?

Seeming to understand where Hunter headed, Katie spoke sharply. "Anybody have a pocket-knife? I lost mine when I went into the river. Come on, speak up. The temperature's dropping and the wind's picking up."

Jerry nudged Paul, then jabbed him in the arm.

A flash of metal, then Paul dug inside his wetsuit. "I think I have one in my shorts," Paul stammered.

Katie held out her hand. Hunter noticed it trembled somewhat as Paul laid a closed hunting knife in her outstretched palm. She moved to the pile of bedrolls at the base of the biggest tree, grabbed one at random, then opened the six-inch knife and cut one of the strings. She closed the knife and slipped it inside her fanny pack, then positioned herself directly under him. "Ready?"

"Fire away, madam."

101

She grinned and yelled out "catch" before tossing up the string.

He caught it and winked at her again. Did he detect a blush inching across her face? The idea that his wink could make her blush made his chest swell. Hunter shook his head and concentrated on securing the edge of the raft to the tree. He completed the task, and jumped to the ground.

"Thanks, Hunter. I think this'll work out quite nicely." Katie unrolled one of the bundles, unfurling the tarp once covering the ducky. She laid it under the raft-roof before returning to one of the supply bags. She pulled out sandwich makings, then elbowed the cooler beside her. "Somebody get these opened up and see what Christian packed for us."

They passed around peanut butter and jelly sandwiches and cans of soft drinks, then settled on the tarp to eat.

Katie leaned back against the tree, sharing her sandwich with the dog. Hunter made his plate. He stood on the edge of the tarp for a moment, considering his options. Katie looked up and grinned at him. He flashed a wide smile, then sat beside her. A lightning bolt flickered across the sky, followed by an immediate clap of thunder. A strong gust blew against their faces. The wind tickled the edges of the makeshift shelter, then ripped it from the branch.

Dark, dense clouds filled the sky.

An ashen pallor over her face, Katie stood and yelled for the men to move next to the trees. She took two paces toward the river. Winds, sweeping like a colony of lost souls, swarmed across the Gauley. She shielded her eyes against the blast. Shadow hopped up and barked.

Hunter stood beside her. Leaning over, he yelled into her ear, "What's going on?"

"Oh, no!" her voice a mix of fear and awe.

"What?" He kept his mouth close to her ear.

"Rain bands." She pointed across the river, then twisted her body. Her gaze tracked the terrain around them before meeting his stare. "We're in trouble."

She grimaced. "Big trouble."

Eight

Katie grabbed Hunter's arm, pulling him toward her. "Those rain bands are coming in from the tropical storm." She screamed to be heard over the sounds of nature's wrath.

"We're already getting rain." He yelled, lifting a single shoulder. "What's the difference?"

"Those bands will come in on forty-to-fifty-mile-per-hour winds." Her heart pounded.

He stared at the weather pattern moving across the Gauley River. "Can we hole up here until Rory gets back?"

She shook her head. "He won't be able to get back. Not today." Katie shivered. "We'll get about eight to ten inches of rainfall in the next hour."

Hunter stared at her.

"Which means the river will be at flood stage in an hour's time," she yelled louder.

Understanding lit in his eyes. His jaw set. "What should we do?"

"We move up."

"That?" He pointed toward the steep incline.

She grimaced and nodded.

Hunter leaned over her, shielding her from the onslaught of gale-force winds with his body. "Are you sure that's the only way?"

"Yes. Meadow River is going to converge with the Gauley at flood stage soon. We'll be wiped out if we stay here." Despite all the rain, her mouth went dry.

Their gazes met and held. The rain, wind, and storm lay forgotten. He was so kind, so gentle toward her, yet so fierce in his protection. She could see herself spending time with him cuddling on the sofa, staring into the dancing flames of a glowing fire, Shadow lying at their feet. How long had she ignored her loneliness?

Finally, he broke eye contact and glanced back to the huddle of men beneath the small clump of trees. "Let's do it then."

Taking long strides, Katie approached the men.

Shadow danced at her feet. "Okay, gentlemen, listen up—we're about to get some high winds and a lot of rain. I mean, a lot." She had their undivided attention. "Emily must've made landfall and is kicking us some nasty weather. We're going to have to climb up the terrain to get out of flood danger."

Carter hauled himself to his feet. "What do you mean, climb up?"

"The hill behind you."

He spun, stood for a moment, before facing her again. His features scrunched into a scowl. "Gooood night! That's not a hill, little lady, that's a mountain."

"Whatever it may be, we have to move higher. In a couple of hours, this is all going to be underwater." She rubbed her hands together. "Now, first we need to filter some of the lake water into our empty water bottles so we'll have something to drink."

"How exactly do we do that?" Walter piped up.

Jerry crossed his arms over his chest. "I thought we were waiting for the Roy guy."

Clenching her teeth, Katie hissed in air. "Rory won't be able to make it back today. Not with the rain bands coming in. The Gauley will be at flood stage soon." She needed to get the men up to safety. They were, after all, her responsibility.

"Is it safe for us to move?" Paul asked.

"It's safer than staying here." Katie nodded

toward the sack of trash. "Everybody grab as many water bottles as we have and follow me to the river."

Katie reached into her personal pouch and pulled out a plastic bottle before heading to her bedroll. She untied the strings and unrolled the sleeping bag, then snatched up the cotton T-shirt, re-rolled the bag, and secured it tightly once more. Lifting the shirt and bottle, she spun on her heel and headed to the river. Shadow barked and shot ahead of her.

At the water's edge, Katie kneeled in the soggy grass. Holding the T-shirt, she ripped it into long strips. She passed out the strips to the men before demonstrating what to do. "Hold the fabric over the mouth of the bottle tight, like this." She pulled the material taut over the bottle, then gripped around the edge tightly. "Hold it down into the river, then lift it. Repeat until the bottle is filled."

Each man dropped to his knees, mimicking her movements. Beside her, Hunter continued filtering the water into his bottle. She smiled when he nudged her. At least she didn't feel like she shouldered the responsibility for the group alone.

Cracking jokes, Jerry kneeled beside Walter, Paul hovering on his other side. Orson and Carter knelt a little more gingerly than the others. Old age had a way of making one move slower.

Taking in the horizon and the tree line, Katie calculated they didn't have a lot of time.

A loud splash caused Katie to jump to her feet as fast as her heart lunged to her throat.

Sputtering, Walter broke through the water's surface.

Katie leaned forward, reaching for him. The current had him in its grip. "Swim this way, Walter. Come on," she cried as her eyes locked on the direction of the current.

Walter's head disappeared. Ten seconds later, it bobbed back up, a good ten feet away. She watched as he flailed about, drifting right toward the hydraulic.

"NO!"

Mindless to the men's shouts around her, Katie dove into the river. She broke through the top of the water. She tried to get her bearings . . . get Walter in sight.

He made a muffled sound to her left. She shot her concentration in that direction, barely catching sight of the tip of his ruddy hair before he slipped below the foaming water.

Hauling in a deep breath, Katie plunged underwater. She pulled herself forward with strong, practiced movements. She continued to swim until her lungs burned, then she popped to the surface.

Barely making out Walter's hand waving erratically in the rapids, Katie watched him hit the edge of the hydraulic. The pit of her stomach turned to mush.

Taking in another lungful of air, Katie dove again.

A hand grabbed her leg, yanking her backward.

She broke through the water, spitting and swinging.

"Whoa!" Hunter wrapped his arms around her, pinning her arms to her sides.

"Let me go. I've got to get Walter." She thrashed against him and the undertow.

"He's gone, Katie. Gone."

"No. I can save him."

He shook his head. "He went into the hydraulic. You said yourself there's no chance of survival."

"But maybe the current kicked him out into the Gauley." She squirmed. "I have to check."

"No. It's not safe." Using his legs, Hunter propelled them backward, away from the main current.

"Let me go. This is my job. I have to," she spoke through clenched teeth. She couldn't lose a man on her watch.

"He's gone." His hold on her tightened as he planted his feet and gently pulled her toward the bank.

Tears burned her eyes. "He can't be." She thrashed against him.

He tucked her head under his chin. She could feel his throat pulsating. "Let him go, Katie. Let him go."

Despair tore through her body as she leaned on Hunter, letting him lead her out of the river.

• • •

The other men maintained a solemn silence, as if stunned by Walter's accident. Or maybe it was being smacked with their own morality that held their tongues hostage.

Hunter kept his arm around Katie as he guided her toward the gear. Her dejection practically ripped his heart from his chest. He stroked her hair, trying to absorb her grief and break in confidence. Although she didn't really know Walter, his loss seemed to devastate her. Then again, most people weren't accustomed to someone dying right in front of them. She blamed herself. Katie Gallagher could act a tough game, but his training taught him to look inside a person's psyche. What he discerned in her was pain, but gentleness, and a great deal of responsibility.

Oh, God, I pray You'll surround Katie and the rest of us with Your love and peace right now. Thank You for saving the rest of us from harm. I pray for the strength to continue to keep us all safe.

She took in a deep breath, vibrating in his embrace. Katie pushed back and looked up at him. Unshed tears made her eyes attain an even brighter shimmer. She blinked. "I'm okay. We have to keep moving." She hiccupped.

Shadow jumped against her, wedging himself between them. Had it not been for the severity of the moment, Hunter would've laughed. The dog proved himself loyal to his mistress once again.

She petted the dog's head and made soft sounds. Seemingly satisfied at his owner's soundness, Shadow bolted toward the gear—sniffing as the men silently hoisted their bedrolls onto their backs. The horror of Walter's death washed over them all.

Katie reached for her bedroll, while Hunter slung both supply bags over his shoulder along with his sleeping bag.

"I can get some of those." She situated her bag against her back.

"Yeah, but someone needs to carry both the tents, right?"

"Right." She leaned forward and lifted her small two-man tent. As she secured it over her bedroll, Hunter yelled out, "Jerry, how about toting our tent?"

The man's face twisted into a frown. "Why me? I'm the client here, remember?"

Hunter took a step toward him. He lowered his voice. "Yeah, well, we're running out of firm employees. The pecking order has changed."

"I'll carry it." Paul grabbed the tent and swung it onto his back.

Jerry tossed Hunter a told-you-so look.

Clenching his jaw, Hunter glanced over his shoulder to find Katie watching their exchange with interest. He hauled in a deep breath.

Without saying another word to Jerry, Hunter faced Katie. "Lead the way, madam."

"Hey, can we change into our jeans before our hike?" Paul's face resembled a pouting child's.

"You'll be thankful you stayed in your wetsuit when the rains hit. However, it might be a good idea for everyone to change into their other shoes." Having made the statement, Katie plopped on the ground and unrolled her bedroll again.

Hunter dropped beside her and did the same. Everyone else heeded her advice as well. Once they'd secured their shoes, each person readjusted their load, and stood. Shadow barked and pranced beside Katie, who slipped a peppermint into her mouth.

Katie shifted the packs on her back, glanced around at each man in turn, then nodded toward the steep incline. "This way."

Heart thudding, Hunter followed the group. His mind skirted around the idea that they were down to a party of six. At the rate they were going, there wouldn't be a party left to make it up the moun-tain. He shifted his pack and dug in his feet. He'd stop these accidents. Before they lost another life.

Katie led the men up the steep embankment. They'd made it about five hundred yards when the rains hit. The fat drops pelted Katie's upper arms and neck, driving into her flesh by the strong wind. She scrunched her shoulders, lowered her head, and trudged upward. Shadow ran ahead, disappeared for a few minutes, then ran back barking, almost as an encouragement.

She glanced over her shoulder. Paul tailed right behind her, then Carter, Jerry, Orson, and Hunter. Each man's face lined in concentration as they followed her lead.

Katie made the next step, and slipped. She fell to her knees, breaking her fall with her hands. Paul gripped her arm. "Are you okay?"

"Yeah, thanks. The ground's saturated and now that it's coming down in buckets, it's slick moving." Regaining her balance, she pivoted. "Be careful. It's really slippery."

Only grunts and groans reached her ears.

Katie grabbed an oak sapling to use as leverage and pulled.

The wind and rain fighting against them hindered their progress, and the water sluiced down the hillside. Katie shook her head, sending excess rivulets flying. Not that she could tell—the rain drove down so hard, visibility remained next to nil.

The air gust swept against her back, propelling her forward—the water rushed over her feet, shoving her backward. She'd take one step up, then be pushed two steps down. Katie used every tree and bush she could get her hands on to keep her footing. Her palms stung as bark, leaves, and thorns dug into her flesh. She didn't have time to consider the pain—she had to keep moving, leading the group to safety. She couldn't lose another person on her watch.

She. Would. Not. Lose. Anyone. Else.

Katie forged up the steep incline, her eyes trained on the rough terrain beneath. The tent slipped from her shoulder, catching on the edge of her wetsuit.

"Want me to carry that for you?" Paul asked.

"No, I'm good." She shifted the pack higher on her back and kept trudging.

Another strong gust blasted against her. Her feet were soaked.

A loud thump, then a splat sounded behind her.

"Aargh!"

Grabbing hold of a tree, Katie spun around. Orson slid down the hill on his stomach.

"Help!"

Orson bounced and thrashed. He stretched out his hands, grasping at every object going by. He only grabbed air. Hunter turned, dropped his packs, and slid after Orson.

As if in slow motion, Orson picked up momentum. Hunter followed.

Thud! Thump! Splat!

Katie laid a hand to her throat and swallowed back her horror.

Time stood still as Orson tossed onto his back, arms flying out. He skidded toward a massive oak.

Katie opened her mouth to scream, but no sound came out. Her vocal cords remained tangled into tight knots. She willed her legs to move, to follow, see if she could help, but they were rooted into the ground.

Orson hit the tree, feet first, at full speed. He slumped against bark and laid still.

Hunter slid sideways as he reached Orson. Catching hold of the oak, Hunter wrapped his arms around the trunk and stopped himself.

Finally, Katie's feet opted to follow her commands. She descended the hill, Shadow sliding behind her. "You guys hang tight here," she said as she passed the men on her way down.

She snapped her fingers and stared at Shadow. "Stay."

Shadow whimpered and pressed against her.

"No, boy." She made her voice firm. "Stay."

As she slipped past Jerry, she could've sworn she heard a snicker. Not taking the time to register the sound, or the reason behind it, Katie continued her descent until she caught the tree next to the one Orson still lay at the base of.

"How is he?" she asked, looking to Hunter for reassurance.

Orson tried to roll over and let out a loud moan. He gripped his right leg. "Aww."

"Don't move. Let me check you out." Hunter's hands flew over Orson's body. He reached the right leg, just below the knee, and Orson let out a scream. Hunter withdrew immediately and glanced at Katie. "I think his shin is broken."

"Argh." Orson moaned and writhed.

Hunter's hand dropped to Orson's shoulder. "Just be still. Moving will only make it hurt worse."

Katie blinked, working to get her mind to focus. How were they supposed to secure a broken shin? She laid a palm against her forehead. The rain pounded against her head, intensifying the headache forming at her temples.

"What's going on down there?" Jerry hollered.

She pinched the bridge of her nose. Hopelessness washed over her, and she slumped against the tree. Sense of responsibility threatened to overwhelm her, right on the spot. She forced herself to grip tightly to the sense of security of the familiar. Her fingers trembling, Katie unzipped her fanny pack and pulled out another peppermint.

Nine

Hunter longed to pull Katie close and comfort her. For all her spunky attitude, she hurt inside, and he knew it. Unfortunately, holding her wasn't possible. Right now, they needed to come up with an idea of how to get Orson secure and move him to higher ground.

From the sounds below, the rains washing down

the hillside had already merged with the flooding from the river, and soon the water level would creep up the edge of the hill. They needed a game plan, and needed it like yesterday.

He looked up at the rest of the group, a good quarter of a mile away. "Orson's got a broken leg. Stay there until we think of something."

Scanning the side of the incline, Hunter looked for something to use to stabilize Orson's protruding bone. Moving it without a splint of sorts could be extremely dangerous for the older man. He finally spied a tree limb lying right behind Katie, about twenty feet from him.

"Katie . . . behind you. The branch. Grab it and toss it over here."

She wiggled around and moved toward the stick. A blast of water splashed down on her. She slipped, her legs shooting out from under her. Katie reached out and grabbed a neighboring tree with her lightning fast reflexes.

He let out a heavy breath. "Be careful."

Her head jerked around. Those silver-blue eyes of hers stabbed daggers into him. "You think?"

Pressing his lips together, he watched her inch toward the limb. The torrential rains and wind hindered her progress, but she fought with determination. What seemed like a millennium later, her hand wrapped around the piece of wood.

Hunter let out a long sigh as Orson groaned. At least his screams had diminished to whimpers now. Katie crept toward Hunter, and he laid his hand on Orson's shoulder.

"Here." Katie tossed the branch to him. He caught it easily.

Holding it up against Orson's leg from the knee down, he estimated it'd be long enough to use as a splint. Now he needed to find something to secure the stick to the leg. Orson still wore his wetsuit.

"Orson. Orson. Look at me."

The old man's eyes, deep with pain, gazed at Hunter.

"Are you wearing an undershirt under your wetsuit?"

Orson blinked, but didn't focus.

"Orson!"

"It hurts so bad."

"I know it does. We're trying to get you some relief. So I need you to tell me—are you wearing an undershirt?"

Orson shook his head.

Hunter let out a sigh. What to use? He scanned the area again, seeking out vines or anything. Nothing.

"What?" Katie called over to him.

"I need something to tie the branch to his leg."

She chewed her bottom lip. "Like what?"

"A rope would be nice, but I don't think we're going to find one anyplace close by."

"Can't you find anything that'd work?"

"No. We can't move him without splinting his leg."

"What about my fanny pack?"

Hunter stared at the little purse hugging her waist. The nylon belting sat on her hips. Her waist couldn't be wide enough for him to use the belting. "Nope. I need two ties, or one long enough that I can rip into two pieces."

Katie's shoulders drooped, then she turned her back to him. She pulled down her wetsuit. He noted the straps of her bathing suit, realized what she intended, then quickly looked away, heat flaming his face.

"Here." She tossed him the top as she pulled her wetsuit back over her bare skin.

He caught it and swallowed hard.

"Just get it splinted and let's move on," she said. But he noticed her face blazed too, even as she gawked at the darkening skies.

Katie slid across the rough grassy knoll that was already drenched and holding water. Hunter ripped her cotton bikini top in two and tied the limb to Orson's lower leg. The older man cried out several times, only to be hushed by Hunter's low mumbles. She couldn't hear the words, but assumed they were soothing as Orson settled down each time Hunter spoke.

She'd only made it halfway to Hunter when the rush of water down the mountain pushed her farther along than she'd estimated. Gritting her teeth, Katie reached for rocks embedded into the terrain. Anything to keep from sliding down the hill.

Hunter glanced in her direction. "You okay?"

"Yeah. Just making my way to you." In the back of her mind, voices screamed at her to hurry—night would be upon them soon. How she'd accomplish getting everyone to safety, she hadn't a clue.

At last she grabbed the tree beside Orson. Using all the upper body strength she could muster, Katie pulled alongside Hunter.

"I think it's as secure as I can get it, considering the circumstances." Hunter lifted his head and stared up to where the other men waited. "Now, how do we get him up there?"

Katie chewed her bottom lip. "A sleeping bag!"

"What?"

"If they throw down a sleeping bag, we can spread it out and lay Orson on it to haul him up." Her words tumbled out on top of one another.

"That could work." His eyes sparkled, from the rain or could it be admiration? A warming sensation rushed through her.

"It'd be much easier than trying to get him to hobble. It's hard enough for me, and my leg isn't broken."

"We'll need some sort of safety rope or something." He looked at her. "In case we slip."

"Why couldn't we use the strings from the bedrolls?"

"I don't think they'd be strong enough."

Katie let out a long sigh. Desperation circled her heart. "Do you have any suggestions?"

"Actually, I do."

"Could you share, please? Dusk will settle over the ridge soon, and we need to be in a secure place. I don't like the thought of trying to climb in this mess after dark."

"A body chain."

"A what?"

"A body chain." He nodded as he spoke. "We have the guys up there spread out between here and the top. They secure themselves to trees and lend helping hands as we pass up beside them."

She shook her head. "Kind of risky, isn't it?" Images of the slit in the raft danced before her eyes.

"Do you have any other ideas? If so, I'm eager to hear them." His stare planted her to the spot.

Orson groaned. "No, Hunter. Don't trust them."

Hunter lowered his head beside the hurting man, whispering.

Katie snaked closer.

"Okay," Hunter said as he straightened, "we use the human chain, but don't count on Jerry."

"What?" She widened her eyes.

"Orson claims Jerry tripped him, making him fall."

"How awful." She laid her hand on Orson's arm. "Are you sure?"

The older man nodded. "I know what it feels like to be tripped, and I was tripped." He moaned and grimaced. "And, I think he pushed Walter into the river."

Katie gasped. The concept that someone would harm another made her skin crawl. Still . . . first Steve, Walter, and now Orson. What could Jerry's agenda be?

Hunter laid his hand on her shoulder. "We can't prove that. We don't know."

"But . . . but . . ." She shook her head. "But Steve accused Jerry of pushing him into the river."

"All we have are accusations, nothing to back them up."

Her hands balled into fists. "But that's enough in my book! Jerry is dangerous. We have to do something."

Hunter crossed his arms over his chest as rain showered his face. "And what do you suggest we do?"

"I-I-I don't know." She lost herself in thought. Her mind wrapped around possibilities, but quickly dismissed each one. They were stranded, for pity's sake. What could they do against someone out to harm them?

Fight back.

She lifted her eyes to the men stomping the

ground above them. Katie cleared her throat. "Paul! Paul!"

The man moved to see her. "Yeah?"

"Can you toss down my bedroll?"

"Huh?"

She cupped her hands around her mouth. "Throw down my bedroll."

"Oh. Okay." Paul moved from her line of sight, then returned quickly. "Here ya go—catch!"

The light sleeping bag bounced down the hill, gaining force and speed as it went far left of where Katie stood braced beside Hunter and Orson.

She moved about ten feet to intercept. Planting her legs far apart, she crouched.

The bedroll shifted. Katie stepped to the right, keeping herself as a bulls-eye for the target. It bounced, then hit her square in the chest. Its driving force knocked her backward. Clutching the bag to her body, Katie flipped and rolled. Her body careened downhill. Rocks jabbed into her back and side, her legs and arms. She twisted. Saplings snapped. She lodged her feet against the ground, slowing.

"Katie! Katie!" Hunter cried.

Shadow's frantic barking was distinct.

She lifted her arm and waved, not yet able to turn around. "I'm okay," she yelled. Under her breath she added, "I think."

"Are you sure?"

The concern in his voice filled her chest with elation. Katie flexed her leg muscles. No shooting pains ripped through her, no bones cracked. She twisted her upper body and looked back up the hill. "I'm fine." Narrowing her eyes, she calculated the distance between her and Hunter. Not too bad—maybe a couple hundred feet. It'd just felt like a lot more when she'd been slipping and sliding.

"Can you make it back?"

She rolled onto her belly, keeping a strong hold on the sleeping bag. Taking inventory of the trees, saplings, and rocks along the way, she let out a sigh. "Yeah. Give me a minute."

As she kicked behind her for a foothold, a ruckus above her erupted. She lifted her head and squinted.

Shadow ran/slid down the hill, straight for her.

"No, boy. Stay!"

Either the dog didn't hear, or for the first time since his training, he disobeyed her commands. Within minutes, the Blue Heeler passed Hunter and Orson, still heading for her.

Katie held her breath. If something happened to Shadow . . .

He lunged for her, pressing his wet and trembling body against her shoulder.

Laughter of relief bubbled from her chest. She wrapped her free arm over the dog's shoulders and buried her face in his thick, drenched fur, soaking in the comfort he provided.

"You okay?" Hunter called down to her.

"We're fine. Coming up now." She grabbed onto Shadow's collar, careful not to pull. "Come on, boy, help me up," she whispered as she rose to her knees.

Shadow stood firm, his muscles quivering.

She gained her footing and balance, then let go of Shadow. "Good boy. Let's help Hunter with Orson now." She slipped her bedroll over her shoulder and picked her next point of leverage.

Hunter kept his hand on Orson's shoulder for comfort, but watched Katie and her dog make their way slowly to him. His heart had plummeted to his feet when the sleeping bag sent her reeling. Even now, his pulse raced as he sent up a silent prayer.

Katie and Shadow finally crouched by his side. Hunter gripped an end of the sleeping bag and unfurled it across Orson. "We should put him in the bag." His eyes locked with Katie's shimmering ones. "At least he wouldn't fall off our make-do shift."

She broke their connection and stood, leaning against the tree Orson had broken his leg on. She cupped her strong hands around her mouth. "Guys, we need a human chain. Space out at regular intervals toward us. Use a tree or something to brace yourself. We're going to need help to hoist up Orson."

Hunter finished unrolling the bag as Katie yelled out instructions. Tucked neatly inside were two complete changes of clothes. Heat encircled his neck as he stared at her lacy undergarments. His mouth felt stuffed with cotton as he touched the satiny material, now dark as rain saturated them. He closed his eyes.

Katie gave a gasp. He blinked his eyes open as she snatched the panties from him and shoved them into the pocket of a pair of jeans. Her face bloomed a bright red as she rolled the shirt into the jeans and shoved them into the bottom of the sleeping bag. He lowered his gaze, not wanting to embarrass her further.

"We can use this."

Her statement brought his head up. She held the dog's harness in her hand.

"Uh, Katie, how's that going to help?"

She pulled on the part that would lay against the dog's back. A snapping sound echoed. She pulled out a lead.

"How long is that?" Excitement at her find pumped through him.

"Eight feet. Not long, but better than nothing." Her smile sent his heartbeat careening throughout his body. Her voice came out velvety smooth. "How do you want to use it?"

Hunter unzipped the bag all the way down the

side, but left the bottom securely closed. "Let's get Orson inside, zip him up, then put the harness on Shadow."

Her hands stilled.

He glanced at her. Apprehension cloaked her expression. "What?"

"I don't know if that's a good idea." Her eyes rested on her dog. "Shadow's not strong enough to hold Orson."

"I didn't mean for him to pull Orson. Just to use as a backup in case one of us slips." A strangling phenomenon wrapped around his throat as he stared at her chewing her bottom lip.

Hunter diverted his gaze to Orson.

"Okay. But let's try not to put too much on Shadow."

He nodded and rolled/pushed Orson into the open bag.

Orson groaned. His body trembled. Hunter laid a hand on Orson's shoulder—his temperature had dropped.

"We need to hurry." Hunter let his eyes lock with Katie's.

She nodded, and together they secured the old man.

Once set, Hunter hauled in a deep breath. "You ready?"

Katie set her jaw. They stood as one.

It felt good to stand with her—to work side by side on something of worth. Determination pressed into the small lines as she shoved one of those mint things into her mouth. When this adventure drew to a close, when the truth was brought to light, would she still be willing to stand beside him?

Ten

The rain fought against their progress. Doing her best to keep hold of her corner of the sleeping bag, Katie's fingers constricted. The wet fabric made it slippery. More than once already she'd loosened her grip, and Orson fell to the ground with moans and cries. Shadow, who never ceased to amaze her, took up the slack when she or Hunter had trouble. The dog's strength kept Orson from tobogganing back down the hill.

Katie's arms ached, her legs cramped, but she trudged forward, pulling Orson. They reached the first man on the human chain as the burning in her thighs threatened to lock up her muscles. Carter's gnarled hand reached to grasp Hunter's.

Hunter crouched at Carter's feet, allowing the older man to hold the bag while Hunter scooted to the center of their makeshift stretcher. He tugged the bag until Orson's head laid in his lap. Hunter's eyes bored into Katie. "Sit down for a second and catch your breath. Carter and I have him. Let your muscles relax for a minute."

Too tired to argue, Katie slumped to the ground. Shadow licked her face.

Orson moaned and his eyes rolled.

"Is he going to be okay?" Carter's face scrunched.

"He'll be okay." Hunter wiped the rain from his forehead. "His shin is shattered, which is more painful than a regular broken leg."

Katie pushed off the ground and took hold of the corner of the bag. "We need to get moving. It'll be dark soon, and we need to be in a secure area by then." She had a duty to get the men to safety.

Careful of Orson's head, Hunter slipped from beneath the bag. "Carter, once we start moving, grab the bottom of the sleeping bag and help us keep as much of Orson's weight as possible off the ground. Each bounce has to be agony for him."

Carter mumbled something about not being strong enough, but moved to Orson's feet. Hunter nodded at Katie. The two of them hefted the top of the bag and began the next leg of their climb.

Keeping her attention focused on the ground, Katie gritted her teeth and lugged upward. Who would've thought Orson could be so heavy? Dead weight. A sliver of fear shot through her spine at her own phrase. Orson had come uncomfortably close to being just that—dead weight.

She dug her toe into a mound of earth, pulling

and jostling Orson, who gasped. She glanced at his face, the top of the sleeping bag partially covering his features. He'd murmured, but wasn't conscious. Probably passed out from the pain. Katie sighed and pushed her muscles further.

What would happen next? The whole trip was jinxed. First Steve, then the raft, then Walter dying. Katie sucked in her breath and blinked back hot tears, now Orson. She'd be responsible for this group, and so far, she'd failed miserabl in her job.

They reached the next link in their chain: Jerry. Katie eyed him cautiously as Hunter dropped to the ground again. Hunter inched Orson's head to his lap while Katie hunkered down beside him. Carter sat at Orson's feet, staring at the unconscious man's face.

Shadow kept close to Katie, almost in her lap. She looped her arm around the dog's shoulders, pulling him next to her. The canine's closeness warmed Katie.

This time as they caught their breath, Hunter didn't let go of the bag. Chewing on her bottom lip, Katie's gaze darted to Jerry, who squatted beside Hunter and studied Orson. Could he be worried that the guy he'd pushed didn't die this time? Or, instead, did he admire the results of his despicable actions? Trying to discern what lurked beneath his surface, Katie stared openly at Jerry.

Jerry glanced up and met her stare. His cold

and ruthless look made her shiver. Katie recognized a flash of evil in his eyes. He blinked, and the flash disappeared.

She swallowed and pushed to her feet once more. "Let's go," she murmured to Hunter, her voice hiccupping.

Hunter shot her a confused look, then followed her gaze. Jerry masked his face in innocence. She gave herself a mental shake. Had she imagined it? Her mind could be playing tricks on her.

"When we make it past you, help Carter with the bottom," Hunter ordered Jerry.

It looked as if Jerry might argue the point—his face turned red, all the way to the tips of his ears. Then, in the space of a heartbeat, he broke into a congenial smile. "Sure, man. Whatever you say."

The tone of his voice sounded light, yet Katie doubted his sincerity. He may appear to be helpful, but the sneaky little voice in her head warned her to be wary. Very wary.

Hunter hefted his side of the bag and looked to her. She hoisted her corner higher, and they made their way up the hill. The rain bands increased as they reached their next point, their destination. Paul stood anxiously, helping drag Orson up the last few steps.

Katie slumped to the ground, almost sliding, and hugged a tree. Paul knelt beside her, taking hold of her edge of the sleeping bag. "Are you okay? You look beat."

She brushed wet strands of hair from her eyes. "I'm fine," she snapped.

He looked at her as if she'd slapped him. Her heart clenched with guilt over her snippy response. She needed to stop jumping to quick conclusions that all of them were guilty. "I'm sorry. Just a little tired." She tossed him a weak smile.

"It's okay. I understand." He laid his hand on her shivering shoulder.

Katie couldn't allow her ideas about the situation to override the facts—each person on this trip fell under her responsibility. Directly or indirectly, it didn't matter. She already dreaded calling the authorities when she got home to report Walter's drowning. Acidic bile churned in her stomach. She wanted to retch as she visualized Gabe's face when he heard the news.

Hunter coughed, then cleared his throat. "Okay, Katie, we're back to where we started." He glanced toward the top of the mountain. "Now what?"

Letting out a long breath, Katie's mind raced. Going straight up would take them until the wee hours of night—not a desirable option. Orson's slipping in and out of consciousness couldn't be a good sign, either. They needed to get somewhere to set the tents, provide them with some cover, and settle in for the night.

The cave.

She stiffened and glanced around quickly. Almost certain someone had whispered in her ear,

Katie shook off the sensation. A renewed burst of energy sparked her on, and she pulled to her feet. "There's a cave not too far from here. Not really big, but large enough for us to have some shelter."

"Sounds like the best deal I've heard all evening." Hunter lumbered to his feet. "Lead the way, madam."

Hunter tried to pull more of Orson's weight toward him, giving Katie a lighter load. Paul offered to take her place, but Katie refused. The dedication and responsibility she accepted as a guide warmed his spirit. Considering the rapid drop in temperature as dusk settled over the mountain, he welcomed the sensation.

Katie came across as an odd woman, anyone could see as much. Sure, she tried to act as tough as nails, but her softness and concern snuck out when she let her guard down. She lived in the middle of nowhere, with two brothers on-site, and had gone into a profession not at all encouraging to women. Yet, she forged through and stood head-and-shoulders above the rest. At least in Hunter's eyes. How many more layers hid beneath her surface, not yet revealed?

At a plateau-type surface, Katie tilted her head to the left. "The cave's this way." Her dog rushed forward.

That she could even make out directions impressed Hunter. Amidst all the driving rain and battering winds, he had no clue where they were. He'd have to trust Katie. Trust—now there was the key word. How long had it been since he'd trusted anybody but God?

He tugged along, hoping the cave wouldn't be much farther. No daily workout at the gym could prepare his calf and thigh muscles for the blazing pain shooting up his legs with each step. Orson had regained consciousness of sorts, and whimpered. His cries echoed against Hunter's heart, filling him with desperation and devastation.

Katie picked up speed. "There. Just ahead." Her breathing came in pants. The dog returned to her side, pawing the ground.

Hunter squinted against the pelting rain. There. A dark hole in the side of the mountain.

She called *that* a cave?

His mental image conjured up a much larger, more concealing place. The reality hit him between the eyes as they drew nearer—the cave measured about twelve by twelve, with only a small overhang of protection. He gave a sigh and increased his efforts. Anything had to be better than tromping through the slushy ground of a steep incline in this weather.

Katie led them the final steps to the flatter embankment. The rocky overhang looming out from the mountain stuck out about five feet. It's once grassy knoll now dripped water, like a rainfall over a ledge. The cave, so she called it, dug into the hillside by about ten feet. At least they'd have approximately fifteen feet of protection over their heads.

He kicked the ground with his toe as he pulled Orson to the flattest area and set down the edge of the sleeping bag as gently as he could. The others soon stood at his side. Biting back his natural tendency to shout orders, he looked to Katie. "What do you want us to do now?"

She bended at the waist, her hands planted on her bent knees as she worked to catch her breath. "We need to get the tents set up inside first."

Paul, the recent eager-beaver, jumped to Katie's side. Did Hunter detect a bit of hero-worship in Paul's eyes as he gazed at Katie, or merely physical attraction? Once more, the ugly talons of jealousy ripped across Hunter's chest.

"Tell me what to do, and I'll do it." Paul looked more eager to do Katie's bidding than her dog.

"Thanks, you're sweet to offer." Katie's smile widened.

Hunter had never wanted to slam a fist into someone's face so badly. Turning so he wouldn't make a sarcastic comment, and also to swallow back the jealous fury rising in his chest, Hunter reached for the tent and tossed it to Paul. "Come on, I'll help you get started."

"Wait. I'll do it." Jerry moved past Orson's body, stepping in front of Hunter. "Paul and I can set up the tent while you help her get the old men settled." He grabbed the tent, stomping toward the mouth of the cave. His footsteps sending water flying in his wake.

Paul looked at Katie, shrugged, then turned to follow Jerry.

Shadow barked twice—alert. The hairs on the back of Katie's neck stood erect. She snapped her fingers. The dog, whining, immediately sat beside her.

Hunter turned to Carter, who leaned against a tree, fighting for air.

"You okay?"

Carter nodded.

A scream echoed from the cave.

Katie spun, her heart soaring to her throat. Not again! She pushed off the soggy ground, her feet slipping in her haste.

Hunter snapped at Carter, "Stay with Orson."

As one, Katie and Hunter headed to the opening of the cave.

Pop! Pop!

Katie froze as the gunshots reverberated down the mountain, slicing through the crash of the weather. She cut her gaze to Hunter and met his determined stare. Both slipped in their scramble to get inside the cave.

Paul ran into them, literally, fleeing from the mouth of the cave. Whiteness covered his face. His jaw quivered.

Hunter grabbed Paul by the shoulders. "What is it?"

"S-S-Snakes." Paul trembled.

Giddy laughter bubbled in Katie's chest. "It's snake season."

"What about the gunshots?" Hunter's piercing glare bore into Paul.

Shaking his head, as if coming out of a trance, Paul finally met Hunter's stare. "It's J-J-Jerry's. He shot at the snakes."

Without waiting to hear more, Hunter turned and bolted into the cave.

Katie laid her hand on Paul's shoulder. "It'll be okay. You go sit with Orson and Carter. I'm going to see about the snakes." She peered at him. Not seeing any understanding dawning in his expression, she squeezed his shoulder and raised her voice. "Paul? Go sit with the others."

He lifted his gaze to her face, seemed to focus on her words, and nodded.

She waited until Paul trudged in the direction of the older men, then turned toward the cave, nearly tripping over Shadow, the loud, angry voices of Hunter and Jerry carried over the rain and wind. She pressed forward, her dog at her side.

"That's still no excuse to have a gun on a rafting trip!" One of Hunter's hands curled around the nose of a handgun while the other gestured at Jerry.

Jerry stood with his hands on his hips, radiating arrogance and anger. "I told you, I brought my gun for reasons just like this: protection."

"You shouldn't have a firearm, period."

"And who, exactly, are you to tell me what I can and can't bring on a trip in the wild?"

Moving quickly, Katie positioned herself between the two men. She stood on tiptoes to intervene. Her back to Hunter, she concentrated her attention on Jerry.

Shadow bristled beside her, a growl building in his throat. She rested a hand on the dog's head, drawing from the canine's strength. "Guns of any sort are prohibited on this land. It's clearly posted in all the Gauley Guides by Gallagher material not to bring any." She straightened and curled her hands into fists on her hips. "What were you thinking?"

A scowl crossed his face, then he quickly replaced it with a look of annoyance. "Look, what's the big deal? I always carry my gun for personal protection." He shrugged, his defensive attitude still shouting. "Besides, it's a good thing I did too. I got those snakes. Now we can set up the tents and get out of this weather."

Katie sighed. She opened her mouth to agree to drop the matter—for now, when Hunter spoke from behind her.

"Do you have a permit for this gun?"

Jerry's eyes narrowed to tiny slits. Even in the

driving rain, Katie could see the fury shooting from his glare. "Not that it's any of your business, but yes, I do have a permit." He shifted his weight and wiped the water from his face. "So, give me back my gun and let's get the tents set up."

"I don't think so. I think I'll hold onto this for you until we get back to the lodge." Hunter slipped the muzzle of the gun under his arm.

"Why do you think you should have it and not me?" Jerry pushed Katie from between him and Hunter. "It's my gun. Give it back."

Shadow lowered his head, his growl intensifying.

Hunter let out a snort. "I don't think so."

Jerry took the last remaining step between them. "I didn't ask. Give it to me, or I'll take it back."

"You and who else?"

Heart pumping in her throat, Katie pushed Jerry back. "Enough! Both of you. This who-has-the-highest-testosterone-level game is wearing thin on my nerves." She turned and held her palm out in front of Hunter. "I'll take it and keep it until we get back." Shadow kept his back to Hunter, taking an aggressive stance toward Jerry.

She could almost feel the tension emitting from the two men trading power stares. Swallowing, Katie wiggled her fingers as she stared at Hunter. "The gun . . . give it to me."

Hunter laid the gun in her hand. The cold steel

against her skin sent shivers throughout her body. "Thank you," she mouthed to Hunter.

Turning, she gave a curt nod to Jerry. "You get in there and get the tents set up. Orson needs medical care." Without waiting for a reply, Katie moved from between them and headed toward the other men, Shadow on her heels. She tucked the handgun into the first-aid kit, then directed her focus on Orson. She withdrew a peppermint and slipped it inside her mouth as she knelt beside the injured man.

Why couldn't the imbeciles see they didn't have time for silly men's games?

Eleven

Could they just get a break?

From the crazy weather to Jerry's antics, Hunter couldn't get a grasp on the situation. Katie stepping in hadn't been added into his equation either. Who would've guessed she'd step between two angry men and demand to take custody of the gun? He shook his head—he had to admire her spunk. If only he could tell her who he really worked for and what mission he'd undertaken.

Neither he nor Jerry had moved an inch since Katie left. Almost like two dogs squaring off, neither one wanted to give up their ground and lose face to the other. Hunter knew he should be the bigger man and go get the tents set up. Orson needed attention and Carter and the others needed a dry place, but Hunter's determination wouldn't let him move. Somewhere in the line between his mind and his feet, his gut seemed to have waylaid the message.

"Oh, good gravy." Katie's voice oozed irritation and disgust as she walked back into the cave's mouth. "You two are like schoolyard bullies. I don't have time to deal with male egos and pride on overload." She pushed Hunter's arm, then Jerry's. "I want those snake carcasses out and those tents pitched before I make it in here with Orson and the others." Flipping around, she took two steps toward the other men, then looked back at them over her shoulder. "And that's an order. Both of you—move it."

Properly chastised, Hunter kept his gaze down as he stalked into the cave. It smelled of mildew, dirt, and forgotten memories in the still air. He grabbed the tails of the two snakes and pulled them free of the cave, letting their dead forms slither into the torrents of rain sliding down the hill. He returned, and Jerry had the big tent unrolled and stacked the metal stakes to the side. They hit against one another, sending a tinking noise bouncing off the hollow walls.

Still not speaking to Jerry, Hunter took the short end of the tent and pulled it as far back into the cave as possible. The tent flap would face the cave's opening. The larger tent nearly spanned the diameter of the confined space, but there'd be enough room to cram in Katie's tent.

He reached for a stake and used a rock to hammer it into the dirt floor, while wondering what Katie's reaction would be when she learned the truth. He vowed he'd be the one to tell her. Yet with the discovery of Jerry's gun, and in light of Steve and Orson's accusations, maybe he should tell her the truth now.

"Good." Her voice tore into his thoughts. She stood in the cave's mouth, her hands on her hips. No question about it, she pulled at his attraction when she got irritated or angry. "By the time you get done, Paul, Carter and I should have Orson up here." She didn't wait for a reply, just turned and left.

A sense of loneliness, one he wasn't accustomed to experiencing, swelled in his chest. His breathing became labored. The echoes of Jerry's hammering ricocheted against Hunter's head at a deafening decibel. A rush of heat rose within him, causing him to sweat. What was wrong with him? He swallowed and focused harder on hammering in the last stake for the tent.

"I'll start on hers." Jerry loomed over him, holding the roll of Katie's tent.

Hunter nodded, but his attention dimmed. His mouth went dry while his stomach churned. What was happening to him?

Lifting the stone to pound against the stake, Hunter's hands trembled. He brought the rock down with a hard thrust, only to miss his entire mark. His vision blurred as a wave of nausea swept over him. The ground shifted under him, and he swayed. He could make out Jerry setting up Katie's tent—the pounding against metal and the resulting pinging.

He fell to his side, his tongue growing larger by the minute. Air wouldn't come. He gasped for breath. Numbness crept up his body. His eyes watered.

"Oh, heaven help us, Hunter!"

Katie's panicked cry broke through the cobwebs of Hunter's mind. He wanted to respond, but the words strangled in his throat.

Her cold hands pressed against his cheek. The back of his head rested in the softness of her lap. He blinked, then tried to open his eyes. They wouldn't budge. Colors erupted before his eyes. Before blackness prevailed, Hunter did the only thing he could. He prayed.

Katie held Hunter's head in her lap, a dark void nagging her heart. As he slipped out of consciousness, her mind raced. What could've happened to him? Her gaze shot to Jerry, who stood over them. Had he done something to hurt Hunter? The memory of Jerry's anger over his gun swirled against her brain. That he'd hidden a weapon provided yet another piece of the puzzle. But what was his agenda? What was his end game?

Paul brought her a wet rag. Katie bathed Hunter's forehead. No longer bronzed tan, his face turned an awkward and frightening pallor. Little elasticity in his skin. Not good. Not good at all. Continuing to dab, she felt the heat of his flesh—he burned with internal fever. What could cause such a reaction?

Shadow whimpered beside her. The dog laid his head on his front paws, his big brown eyes watching each move Katie made.

Carter came out of the tent where they'd laid Orson and ambled toward her. His bones creaked and made snapping noises as he knelt beside her. He spoke, his voice cracking as much as his joints. "Looks like he's bad sick. Did he eat a poisonous plant or something?"

She concentrated on only one word he'd uttered. Poisonous.

"Paul, grab me Hunter's bedroll, please," she said.

When he handed it to her, she gently slipped out from under Hunter's head and used his bedroll as a pillow. She pulled to her feet and approached Jerry at the opening of the cave.

Even in the darkness, Katie could see the rain continued to pelt the ground. The wind whipped past the overhang, sending miniature typhoons dancing along the hillside. The sound grew louder, as if Mother Nature cast some premonition in their direction. Katie glanced down, expecting to see Shadow on her heels. He wasn't by her side. She glanced over shoulder to find Shadow hadn't left Hunter.

She moved to stand beside Jerry. "The dead snakes—who disposed of them?" She fisted her hands at her sides, hoping the shaking would stop.

"He-man Hunter did. I worked on getting the tents set up." He raised a single eyebrow. "Which, I had to do all myself since wonder boy passed out hammering in his first stake."

She clenched her fists tighter, letting her nails dig into her palms, resisting the urge to slap him across the face. "Where did you shoot the snakes?"

"Here in the cave."

Katie clenched her jaw to stop from screaming and pulling out her hair. "What part of the snakes did you shoot?"

"Oh." Jerry pursed his lips. "Well . . ." He rubbed his chin and looked to the roof of the cave.

She let out an exaggerated breath. Shifting her weight from leg to the other, she crossed her arms over her chest. "Try to remember."

"I aimed for their heads."

"Are you a good shot?" Her patience drew as thin as her belief they'd get back to the lodge by daybreak.

"Well, now," he smiled wide, his arrogance shining brighter than his perfectly straight teeth,

"I have been told I'm something of a marksman. So, yeah, I'm a good shot."

Katie shook her head and marched back over to Hunter. Shadow lifted his head to peer up at her. This time, instead of cradling Hunter's head in her lap, Katie lifted his arms and inspected his hands. As she suspected, one had a deep cut, now raw and angry. She looked over at Paul. "Please bring me the first-aid kit."

Paul rose. "Uh, what's it look like?"

She bit back the snappy retort on the tip of her tongue. It wasn't Paul's fault—none of this. Now, Jerry could be a whole different story. Katie shook her head, mentally pushing down the questions and accusations in her heart. "It's a white bag with a big red cross on the front. It should be in the bags with the food and coolers." That's where she'd left it when she'd stuck the confiscated gun in there.

As Paul rushed to do her bidding, Shadow leaned over and licked Hunter's face. Katie gave a soft smile. The dog, while friendly to most everyone, would never offer such attention to someone he deemed unworthy. Hunter must have impressed her Blue Heeler, and that was no easy feat.

Paul returned with the kit and set it beside her before kneeling down beside Carter.

Katie pulled out the syringe, pre-filled with anti-venom for the copperheads, the most common snake in the area. She ripped open the plastic packaging with her teeth. Taking a deep breath, she grabbed Hunter's arm and jabbed the needle into his skin. She swallowed back her pounding fear. He had to be okay. She had to have gotten the anti-venom into his system on time.

She chewed her bottom lip as all the first-aid courses she'd taken rushed across her mind, like racing over a class-five rapid. She grabbed the antibiotic cream, along with an antibacterial wipe. The tips of her fingers grazed over the cold metal of the gun lying in the bottom of the bag. She'd have to remember to take the kit into her tent for the night.

Using gentle care, Katie wiped the puffy and oozing cut in Hunter's palm, then coated it lavishly with the cream and found a large Band-Aid. She applied one loosely over his wound, then sat back on her heels to study him.

His face was too pale. No muscles in his jaw moved.

She reached to his neck, feeling for his pulse. It thumped against her fingers. Slow, but steady. Her heart hiccupped somewhat. He'd received the anti-venom, she'd addressed the contamination site . . . what else? What had she missed? There had to be something more she could do.

Glancing at Paul, she flashed a weak smile. "He'll be okay. I think we got to him in time."

"What happened?" Paul's voice sounded barely a whisper.

"One or both of the snakes must have released its venom right before Jerry shot it. The venom stays on the snake's body, even when it's dead. When Hunter grabbed the snakes, the poison slipped into his bloodstream through the cut in his hand." She ran her fingers absentmindedly through Hunter's hair. Its texture coarse, thick.

"But he'll be all right?" Paul asked.

She stared at Hunter's slack face. "I think so." Touching his arm again, she noticed the fever still rampaged. "Paul, grab me another bedroll. We need to cover him."

Paul rose and left. Carter sat on the ground beside Hunter. Shadow hadn't moved at all. Katie glanced over her shoulder. Jerry remained by the mouth of the cave, his body silhouetted by dancing flickers on the walls by the dimming light.

Paul returned with the sleeping bag and helped Katie spread it over Hunter's limp body. "This one is Walter's . . . was."

Katie's hand stilled over Hunter. The mention of the dead man's name sent pinpricks of remorse up her back. She shook her head, concentrating her efforts on seeing to Hunter.

Mission accomplished, Katie sighed and stood. "We need to go ahead and set up for the night." She offered her hand to Carter. "Inside the food bags are three stationary flashlights. Get them set up."

"Paul, we need to get Orson in his dry bag. I'll

use Hunter's bedroll. Get it and toss it into my tent, will you?"

Both men moved away. Katie gave a final gaze at Hunter's still body, then headed to the main tent, intent on transferring Orson to his dry bedroll and finding the supplies for supper. She slipped to the front of the cave and stood behind Jerry. "Want to help me get supper ready?"

He spun around, a wild look in his eyes. "Nothing on this trip is going as planned. What are we going to do? The rain's still coming down like cats and dogs. What if we're stuck here for days? Do we have enough food to survive?"

She smiled, willing herself to appear calm and cool. "We'll be fine. If we're careful, we've got enough food to last us a few days. My brothers will be searching for us long before then." She started to turn, but stopped. Staring at Jerry, she decided to test him once more. "Besides, we're two men lighter than we'd anticipated—that'll be extra food as well."

The prideful look crossed his face in a blink, but she'd been looking for it. She didn't miss it. Cold fear sent bullets of ice into her veins. Not bothering to hear anything Jerry had to say, Katie set about moving Orson and getting dinner for the group.

Hunter detected the murmur of voices. Warmth surrounded him. He swallowed, only to discover his mouth held no saliva. Something wet and coarse stroked against his cheek. Calling on every muscle to obey, he blinked open his eyes to see brown ones staring back at him from a furry face.

He groaned when the dog licked him again.

"Hey, you, welcome back." Katie's voice echoed across his brain as she moved into view. He turned his head slowly to look at her. His temples throbbed. Licking his dry, cracked lips, he gave a little cough. "W-What happened?"

She knelt beside him, tucking the cover over his chest. He reveled in her care and attention. Her smile cheered his soul. "You got snake venom in the open cut in your hand." The faint, yet distinct odor of peppermints clung to her breath.

Vaguely remembering a slight stinging sensation, he tried to lift his right hand.

She pushed his arm down gently. "No worries. I have it all cleaned out and bandaged now." She smoothed his hair from his forehead. Her touch sent his heart pounding. "I gave you the copperhead anti-venom we always stock in our kits. You should be back in top form in a couple of days. Until then, you need to take it easy."

"I'm thirsty."

She moved out of his line of sight, her shadow flickering over his face. He glanced at the surrounding darkness. They'd moved him inside the big tent alongside Orson, the place quickly turning into a sick bay.

Katie returned and lifted a cup to his lips, holding his head while he sipped.

The cold water reinvigorated him. He worked to sit up. Katie helped him by wrapping her arm around his back. Once he sat, she offered him another sip. He gulped heartily until she pulled the cup back. "Whoa. Take it easy. Nice and slow, or you'll have it coming back up."

Now that his mouth didn't feel like the dessert during summer, Hunter licked his lips again.

"Are you hungry? We finished having some sandwiches and chips. I could make you one." She bounced up, seemingly eager to wait on him.

He shook his head and took a quick inventory of how he felt. "I'm not hungry. My stomach feels a little out of whack. The water did the trick."

She lowered herself to his side again. "Anything else hurt, besides your stomach and your hand?"

Shaking his head again, he shrugged. "How'd the poison move so fast?"

"I'm no doctor, but it's my guess your adrenaline pumped it through your bloodstream quicker than normal." Her gaze darted over her shoulder, then settled back on him. "You were steaming mad, remember?" She smiled and cocked her head.

"Yeah, I was. I'm sorry you had to see that."

"No worries. I'm glad we figured it out in time."

"We?" He hiked up his brows.

"I questioned Jerry and guessed what had happened, but it was Carter who made me think of the venom."

"Ah." He nodded, but stopped when fissures of pain knocked against his temples. "Well, I thank God you were here."

The smile dropped from her face and her eyes dimmed. "You can thank whomever you like— that's your right."

A piece of his heart broke off. "You don't believe God had anything to do with saving me?"

She gave a snort of laughter. "I don't believe God has much to do with anything." Her eyes misted over. "Not anymore."

"Katie . . ." He whipped his hand out from under the sleeping bag and laid it on hers. "What happened to your faith?"

Her exquisite eyes widened. "How do you know I ever had any?"

"Everyone has a measure of faith. God placed it in your soul when He created you." He smiled, even though it felt crooked. "Besides, you didn't question His existence, you commented on His lack of working. That normally indicates a loss of something you once had. A loss of faith."

Glancing down, Katie shrugged. "I learned several years ago not to trust God. He's proven time and again He doesn't care."

Hunter's heart tightened. "He loves you, Katie. Very much."

The coldness in her look made him shiver, even though he grew hot under the thick sleeping bag. "He hasn't loved me in a very long time." Snatching her hand free, Katie pushed to her feet. "And I don't think He's likely to start again anytime in the near future."

Twelve

Katie stalked the short space to her tent, snapped her fingers and pointed for Shadow to enter, then ducked inside. She zipped the tent door, desperate to finally slip into her jeans. Emergency after crisis had prevented her from getting out of the wetsuit. She lifted jeans and found them damp, but at least they weren't wringing wet.

Her gaze settled on Hunter's bedroll that took up the main space of the small two-man tent. She should walk it over to him. His personal belongings were rolled up in that bag. Sucking hard on the peppermint candy, Katie wondered if she'd be as embarrassed to see his underwear as she had been when he'd seen hers. Shadow stared up at her, as if understanding her dilemma. Katie sighed. Probably.

Entering the other tent, Katie looked around before she set Hunter's bedroll down beside him and lifted the first-aid kit. She cleared her throat, garnering everyone's attention. "We need to build a fire. For warmth, of course, but also to keep animals away." Her gaze settled on Hunter. "Like snakes."

They carried out her wishes without argument. Jerry and Paul gathered what small branches they could, especially the ones that'd some protection from the rain by lying under trees and other forest litter. Carter retrieved all the discarded paper wrappings from their previous meals along with the empty candy wrappers Katie dug out from her fanny pack. Hunter searched through the supply bag and located a book of waterproof matches.

Katie secured the first-aid kit with the gun in her tent, then went about doing what she needed. At the edge of the cave, but a safe enough distance from the tents, Katie built a fire. As the flames licked the wet wood, the cave filled with hissing and popping. A steady sizzling sounded once the blaze grew.

All except Orson huddled near the fire. They'd left the main tent unzipped, allowing the emitting heat to penetrate toward the injured man. Warmth seeped into the air.

Katie stared into the bright orange and blue flickering fire, her mind wandering. What could Hunter be up to? He came across as a strong man's man, yet talked about God in such an intimate way. The contradiction confused her. Shadow nosed under her arm. Katie pulled him next to her, relishing the close physical contact.

Jerry rose, heading out from the cave into the sheets of wind and rain.

"Where're you going?" Hunter mumbled.

Twisting around, Jerry flashed a sardonic smile. "I'm answering the call of nature." His brows hitched up. "Want to come?"

Even though he looked as if he'd drop where he sat, Hunter struggled to his feet. "Actually, I do, now that you mention it." He swayed, his center of gravity off, and gripped Paul's shoulder.

Jerry made a point of letting out a huff and cocking out his hip. "Well, come on, then."

A burst of anger sparked in Hunter's face before he covered it. Katie sat at the ready, in case she had to step between the men again. But Hunter, even though still unsteady, followed Jerry out into the driving rain in silence.

"Do you think they'll argue again?" Paul's voice edged across the dancing flames.

Shrugging, Katie said, "Who knows?" But worry stomped across her chest.

"You know, I never would have imagined those two would be at such odds." Carter inched toward the fire. "They seem to have similar personalities."

"Maybe they're too much alike." Paul kept his eyes on the fire. "Which isn't necessarily a good thing." He spoke softly, almost as if to himself.

"Why do you say that?" Katie resisted the urge to send Shadow outside to look after Hunter. A grown man surely could go to the bathroom by himself, even if he did just recover from the snake's venom, as well as the draining side effects of the anti-venom. Then again, Jerry was at the top of her suspect list. She shifted, uncomfortable with her thoughts.

Paul shrugged. "I don't know. Sometimes . . . well, sometimes . . . let's just say Jerry isn't always the nicest person."

His own business partner admitted Jerry could be a jerk? Katie chewed the mint and scratched behind Shadow's ears. An icy finger traced her spine. She shook off the chills and drew to her feet. "I need to answer the call of nature myself." Snapping for Shadow, she turned and headed out of the cave.

Away from the comfort and security of the fire, Katie's flesh popped with goosebumps. She rubbed her hands over her arms and kept her ears perked for angry voices. Only the raging sound of the elements sounded. Jerry and Hunter must have called a truce. She turned in the opposite direction the men had gone, and headed toward a small thicket of woods.

By the time she returned, the men sat by the fire, looking no worse for wear. She moved to sit, then changed her mind. "I think I'm going to call it a night. It's been a long day."

Paul immediately pushed to his feet. "Can I help you do anything?"

Katie smiled at the eager man, and noticed a scowl crossed Hunter's face, which made her want to grin wider. "Actually, Paul, you can get me Walter's bedroll, since mine is still wet." Paul turned to go into the main tent.

She turned to Hunter. "Sorry, but you'll have to use your bedroll as a sleeping bag instead of a pillow."

He arched an eyebrow.

She smiled. "Don't worry, I didn't open your bedroll and handle your Fruit-of-the-Looms."

He threw his head back and laughed. "Now I know for a fact you didn't. I only wear Hanes."

Oh, no, he wouldn't embarrass her again. "Boxers or briefs?"

He didn't have to reply as Paul returned with the folded sleeping bag. "Would you like me to put it in your tent?"

"No, thanks. I've got it." Accepting the bag, Katie said to the men in general, "I'd suggest you gentlemen get to bed soon. We don't know what the weather promises for tomorrow."

Ducking, she tossed the bedroll into her tent and snapped for Shadow. She threw a final glance at the group, stepped inside, then zipped the tent flap shut. She laid out the sleeping bag, bunching the top under her head as a makeshift pillow. Not exactly the comforts of home, but at least she had dry clothes and warmth. Shadow plopped down beside her, offering even more heat.

Katie blinked as she spied the first-aid kit.

The gun. What kind of person carries a gun on a rafting trip? She wiggled, trying to get comfortable on the hard dirt under the tent's floor. She could be wrong about Jerry. Maybe he did bring the gun for protection. Still, she couldn't discount both Steve's and Orson's accusations. Katie let out a long sigh and flipped to her back.

And Hunter. What about all that *God* nonsense? The contradictions of the man infuriated her. He carried himself with poise and confidence. Because of who he was, or because of who he leaned on? Having seen him in action during a crisis, she no more believed him an accountant than she'd buy a sinking boat. That same train of thought reminded her of the cut raft. Katie wanted to give Jerry the benefit of the doubt, but someone had cut the raft.

Her mind tripped back to Hunter. And his religion. How had he tapped into her questions so well? He didn't know—couldn't understand. God had turned His back on her years ago. Left her and her brothers motherless. The grief had only been compounded when they'd lost their father eight years later.

Pinching her eyes shut, Katie willed herself to relax and go to sleep. Too bad her mind wasn't paying attention.

Hunter shifted inside his sleeping bag. He'd had a tough moment earlier, unfurling his bedroll and stashing his things out of sight from prying eyes. He wasn't strong enough yet to back up his explanation. Besides, he refused to fail. Success hovered within his grasp.

Orson mumbled in his sleep. Hunter had checked the man's leg before turning in, and hadn't noticed any signs of cutting or infection. Good, Orson needed to be kept calm and as pain-free as possible. No telling what secrets he'd blurt out if his fever spiked. Hunter couldn't afford a slip of any kind.

Paul snored softly near the back of the tent. His pitch didn't even come close to the fervor of Carter's nasal orchestra. Hunter strained to stare at the dying embers of the fire, dimming into the darkness. He'd heard Jerry's breathing level out, but wouldn't put it past the dude to fake his sleep. Who knew what he'd pull next? Jerry was the culprit—all of Hunter's training screamed it. Now, he needed to prove it.

Rustling from inside the other tent pulled Hunter's gaze in that direction. Katie. The woman had her hooks in him, and she didn't even know it. He recalled their conversation earlier and swallowed. What had been so traumatic for her that she'd turned her back on God? Now, for a much better reason, he'd have to keep his control under wraps. If she wasn't a Christian, no hope glimmered for a possible relationship.

Whoa! Had he really said relationship? Him?

He needed to just put those thoughts aside and concentrate on the task at hand.

He rolled onto his side and slipped his hand under his improvised pillow. The secure feeling of cold steel against his skin allowed him to relax and drift into the arms of slumber.

Shadow's barking roused Katie from a deep sleep. Heart pounding in cadence with her faithful companion's warning, Katie fumbled to free her feet from the sleeping bag. She stumbled in a cloud of disorientation and unzipped the tent. The dog darted between her legs and stood at the mouth of the cave, trembling and whimpering.

Dawn had broken, but the sky, dusted an ashy-orange tint, remained void of sunlight. Katie inched to the edge of the cave. Rain, carried by the wind, pelted her face. Her stomach flipped, then crashed to her feet. The river raged dangerously close, less than two hundred feet below the cave.

"What's the dog barking about?" Hunter yawned as he slipped out of his tent and moved to stand beside Katie.

"He's letting me know something's wrong."

He let out a heavy breath. "What now?"

She pointed to the raging water below. "River's still rising."

He moved to the edge and looked down. The sheets of rain moved with a vengeance across the hillside, drenching his dark locks. Hunter stepped back under the overhang and shook his head. Droplets of moisture flew in every direction. "What do you suggest?"

Wiping splatters from her arm, Katie tilted her head to the sky. "We hike farther up." She peered at the torrential downpour, shielding her eyes with her hand. "We can make it a couple more hundred feet. That should keep us out of harm's way until this downpour stops, at least."

Hunter joined her, looking in the direction she gazed, then back at her. "Are you sure?"

She nodded. "Emily's still throwing rain bands at us. Unless it stops coming down like cats and dogs, the river will continue to rise. We have to move to higher ground." They had no choice.

He wiped his face and ducked back under the overhang. "Okay. What's our game plan?"

"You wake up the rest of the group and have them get back into their wetsuits. We'll need to repel all the water we can." She chewed her bottom lip as she glanced around the cave. "We'll need to break everything down and try to get as much as we can inside a rolled up tent or supply bag. At least that'll keep our food and bedrolls dry."

"Okay. I'm on it."

Katie stared into his eyes . . . mistake. Attraction slammed hard against her chest. Even now, when facing yet another calamity. Or maybe she experienced the yearning for a connection because of the urgency. His strength drew her to him, as well as the way he'd cared for Orson so gently and the way he'd comforted her when Walter drowned. The urge to let him carry her burdens over-whelmed her, and she gasped aloud.

"Are you okay?" He took a step closer.

She held a hand out in front of her, stopping his progress. She couldn't allow him to touch her. No, if he touched her, she'd turn into a whimpering idiot and she needed to keep her control to stay in charge of her responsibility, the group. "I'm fine. We need to get busy."

He nodded.

Katie rushed into her tent to don her wetsuit. She pulled her hair back in a braid, took down her tent and wrapped her bedroll and clothes tightly inside. Then she checked the progress of the others.

Orson sat on the dirt floor, little tufts of white hair standing out on either side of his head. Katie flexed her hands to refrain from smoothing his hair down. Jerry, already wearing his wetsuit, shoved two bedrolls into the supply bags.

Katie looked over his shoulder. "Be sure and tie those securely."

Jerry scowled at her. "You don't say?"

She chose to ignore his sarcasm—people dealt with stress differently. Hunter stepped out of the tent, his face still ashen. He, too, wore his wetsuit and hiking boots. Panic circled in the pit of Katie's stomach. Images of her brothers' faces stomped across her mind. Gabe? Christian? Were they okay? Had they realized the danger and called off Christian's trip? Fear lodged in her throat. Were they out looking for her, in this weather? They could be in danger.

"We'll be ready to move in a few minutes." Hunter's smooth words snagged her from her rambling and dangerous thoughts. He moved closer to her and lowered his voice. "How are we going to get Orson up the hill?"

Inching out free of the overhang, Katie pointed upward. "See that big oak up there? The one with the low branches?"

"Uh-huh."

She stepped out of the rain. "If we can get a rope anchored there, we could pull him up." Shaking her head, Katie freed her bangs of excess water. "We could also use the rope to make sure nobody else slips."

"And we could pull up the supplies without having to carry them."

Smiling, she nodded. "Exactly." At least somebody was on the same page.

He spun, glancing around the cave. "Do you happen to have a rope?"

"Actually, I do." Why did he do such crazy things to her insides? The strain must be getting to her—her emotions flip-flopped and bordered on hysteria.

She shook off the random thoughts and pulled a

nylon rope out of the supply bag and tossed it to Hunter. "See how long this is." She grabbed the first-aid kit. "I'm going to re-wrap Orson's splint and give him a couple more ibuprofen."

Katie addressed the old man's injury as best she could, put the first-aid kit back in the supply bag, then went to stand beside Hunter.

"Looks like it'll be long enough to reach the tree. How do you want to do this?"

"We'll need someone at the top to help pull."

"I'll go."

She gave him a soft smile. "You're still weak and will be for another day or so. No offense, but I need someone stronger right now."

A blank expression covered Hunter's face, hiding his true emotions. She touched his arm. How would she react if he actually opened up to her? "Only because I know how the anti-venom can knock you out. Don't take it personally." The heat shooting up from her fingertips at the connection between them made her jerk her hand away. The man touched something deep within her heart, and the emotion worried her. He was only here for a weekend, and losing her heart would cost her after he left.

Besides, who found forever in days?

The muscles in his jaw flexed. "Who do you suggest?"

Turning her gaze to flit over the group who finished packing, she pressed her lips together.

"Well, Jerry's the strongest of the group, but . . ."

"You don't trust him." His words were a statement, not a question.

"Not really. I mean, all we have are accusations at this point, but still." Katie let out a slow breath. "Paul's the only other one we could try."

Hunter studied the man. "I guess. I don't see him being able to hoist Orson up that far alone."

"I figured I'd send him up to tie the line, then let Carter and Jerry climb once the line's secure." She puckered her lips and sucked in air, making little noises with her mouth. Shadow, soaking wet, rushed to her side. He shook, drenching both Katie and Hunter with his spray. Katie laughed. At least her pet's antics were constant. "Shadow, boy, stop that."

Hunter laughed as well. "Well, at least we got our shower this morning."

The intimate implications of his words, even unintentional, sent power surges through her. Her eyes honed in on his face. She willed herself to look away when he stared back at her, but her body refused to obey her brain's commands.

His expression softened, his mouth slacked. The air stuck inside her lungs. All moisture left her mouth. Desperate for a peppermint, she licked her lips, then swallowed. Nothing worked. The inside of her mouth felt like the Mojave Desert. She reached into her fanny pack, pulled out a candy, and popped it in her mouth.

"So, what're we doing so early this morning?" Jerry's cocky attitude rubbed against her zinging nerves as he joined them.

Katie straightened. "We're going to secure a rope above and use it to move upward."

"Who's gonna do that?" Jerry smirked.

Biting back the snappy retort waiting to explode, Katie said, "I thought Paul would."

Paul's eyes widened as large as the face of a paddle as he joined the group. "M-M-Me?"

"Yes, you. You're strong enough." Moving to stand beside him, Katie laid a hand on his shoulder. "All you have to do is tie the rope around the tree."

"What tree?" Insecurity covered his face like a wet sleeping bag, but his eyes lit in the barely-dawn light.

Stepping from under the overhang, she pointed out the tree.

He grimaced. "That's kinda far up there. Not many trees to grab onto during the climb."

"You can do it, Paul." Smiling as wide as she could, Katie squeezed his bicep. "I know you can."

"I'll do it, for pity's sake." Jerry glanced toward the massive oak. "No problem at all."

Her heart stumbled as she groped for the words. "Uh, Jerry, I need you down here for now."

"Why does he get to go and I have to stay?" Even the whites of Jerry's eyes darkened.

"I'm stronger than he is. Besides, I'm not a wimp."

Paul stiffened under her touch. She glared at Jerry. "I need you to help with Carter on the climb after the rope's secured."

Jerry's face twisted into an ugly scowl. "Why do I have to baby-sit the old man?"

"Nobody needs to baby-sit me. I can climb as well as any other man here." Carter stomped to the edge of the cave and gazed up the steep incline. His Adam's apple bobbed.

Katie clapped her hands. "Listen. This is the way it's going to be—Paul, you'll climb first and secure the rope." She wagged her finger between Jerry and Carter. "You two will go next. I'll need all three of you guys in place before we try to get Orson up."

"What about venom-boy here?" Jerry nodded toward Hunter, acidic sarcasm dripping from his words.

Hunter opened his mouth. Katie shot him a look that she hoped he understood meant to keep quiet and let her handle this, then grimaced at Jerry. "I need Hunter down here to help me boost Orson, as well as tie the supply packs for y'all to pull up."

Jerry's expression was one of pure loathing. "How sweet."

"Look . . ." Hunter took a step toward the mouthy man.

Katie stepped between the two men, her heart

thumping like a Mexican jumping bean. "We don't have time for this. We have to get moving."

Hunter stalked into the cave, then squatted beside Orson and spoke in low tones. Shadow parked himself at Katie's feet.

Planting himself directly in front of her, Jerry rested a hand on his hip. "I still don't see why I shouldn't go first."

Her wariness of him dissipated, consumed by the swirling anger in the pit of her stomach. "You know what, Jerry, I don't have time for this spitting contest you want to have with everyone. For just a moment, would you let your pea-brain pretend to be larger than your testosterone level?"

She popped her shaking hands on her hips, digging her fingers into her waist. "Wrap your mind around this: we need to all work together to get out of here alive. Got it? There's not enough room on this mountain for all of us and your over-stroked ego."

A dark hue of crimson shot up his neck to his face. Bright red circles blazed on his cheeks. He clenched and unclenched his fists as a wide range of fury streaked across his face. Shadow shot to his feet and growled, low and guttural. She snapped her fingers and pointed to the ground, her gaze fixed on Jerry's face.

"Hey, let's just get it done, okay?" Paul said.

"Good idea," Katie spat out from behind clenched teeth. She snatched the yellow rope from atop the rolled bags and stalked to the right of the cave.

Paul hovered at her elbow. "Just tell me how to do it."

She took in quick breaths. Jerry made her so mad.

Hunter patted Orson's shoulder, then moved in her direction. Jerry remained rigid, not taking a step from his position. His face reflected his anger was still in control.

Concentrating on the task at hand, Katie explained to Paul the path to take. Hunter stayed close, positioning himself between her and Jerry.

Once Paul had a grasp on his task, he looped the rope bundle over his shoulder. He cast a final look to Katie, like a condemned man plodding to the execution chamber, and began his trek up the mountainside.

Katie snuck another peppermint as she followed his progress with her stare. Shadow pawed the ground until she commanded him to sit. Even then, the Blue Heeler didn't seem content to merely watch Paul's ascent.

Paul made his painstaking climb with the speed of a sleep-depraved tortoise. He slipped several times, causing Katie to bite her lip and draw blood. Yet, Paul managed to steady himself before sliding and crashing down on their heads. At long last, he reached the tree. He secured the rope, then tossed down the end with a yell. The prideful glee in his voice reverberated over the wind and rain.

Hunter caught the end of the rope and wrapped it around a large sapling, holding the end securely behind his back, letting his body weight play anchor. He nodded to Carter. "You and Jerry go ahead and start climbing. I'll keep the tension tight."

Carter moved toward the rope and muttered, "Goood night!"

"Just keep a tight grip on the rope. Use it like a handrail." She flashed what she hoped came across as a confident smile.

Paul cupped his hands to his mouth. "It's easy. Come on."

Thirteen

Hunter held his breath as Jerry stalked past Katie, his head down and jaw set. Jerry gripped the nylon and gave it a tug, almost jerking it free from Hunter's grasp. Jerry gave a twisted smirk and pulled himself along the incline.

"Go ahead. I've got it," Hunter said to Carter.

Shrugging, the old man picked his way up the hill.

Katie moved beside Hunter, lending her own strength to the resistance of the rope in order to keep tension on the line.

He ignored his protective urging, focusing on

Jerry and Carter's climb. Even as he wanted to knock Jerry's block off for his mouth and attitude, Hunter appreciated Katie's sharp tongue. But if Jerry was responsible for the cut in the raft, she was now on his bad side. Not a good move for her.

She grunted as she tugged, wrapping the nylon tighter around the tree. Her calf muscles flexed, drawing his attention. Katie Gallagher was one strong woman.

Carter's exuberant shout broke through the rain and wind. Jerry and Carter stood beside Paul. Katie turned to Hunter. "Okay, let's get Orson tied and see if they can drag him."

Within minutes, they'd put the jacket-style life preserver on Orson and wove the end of the rope through its belt loops. He gritted his teeth. "It'll be okay."

Hunter laid his hand on Orson's chest. "It's gonna be a rough ride, buddy. It'll probably hurt —a lot."

Katie ran a hand over Orson's thinning hair, tears shimmering in her eyes. "Just try to stay on your back." Her lips trembled as she smiled. "If you find yourself rolling or shifting, use your good leg as a guide."

Orson nodded. Hunter fought squirming under the older man's scrutiny. The blame burned from Orson's eyes. Looking to the men above to avoid any more condemnation, Hunter hollered, "Okay, guys, pull."

Cries and groans marked Orson's progress. Each time he cried out, Katie cringed. Her compassion filled Hunter's heart with a rush of attraction. He kept his body rigid to refrain from swooping her into his arms and telling her none of this was her fault.

Paul yelled that they'd secured Orson. Hunter let out a sigh of relief. The rope fell back at their feet, and Hunter lifted his gaze to meet Katie's.

"Let's tie this off and get you moving." Her voice remained calm and even.

"Why don't we send the supplies, then you and I can climb together?"

"No, I want you there to watch Jerry."

So, she really didn't trust the little weasel. But apparently, she trusted him. Hunter smiled. "Okay, but then you send the supplies and hurry." He yanked the rope twice to ensure it would hold, gave her a smile, and took his first step.

The climb took him longer than he'd anticipated. Katie had been right—his body still suffered from the anti-venom. He hated feeling less than 100%, especially when the stakes were so high. He reached the plateau where the others waited, then turned to yell for Katie. The words died in his mouth.

A loud crashing caused his body to tremble. Then he realized it wasn't a reaction—the mountain actually trembled.

He grabbed Orson and pulled him against the

support tree. Jerry and Carter pushed Paul closer to the trunk as well.

Echoes of the crashing moved like an earthquake around them.

As if standing in front of Summersville Lake Dam when the discharge tubes opened and ten thousand cubic feet of water spewed out, a wave of mud jetted down over them.

Cold and wet, the dirt sluiced, covering them like chocolate over almonds. Calling on every ounce of strength left, Hunter held fast to the tree, sandwiching Orson between himself and the bark. Even as the forceful sludge pounded against them, the distinct sound of a dog barking pierced the deafening roar of the mudslide.

His heart flipped. Using the inside of his shoulder, Hunter wiped the muck from his face and peered down the hill. The mudslide rushed down, picking up momentum and power on its descent.

Dear God, help us!

Katie looked up at the group. The dog barked, then shot sharply to the left.

Hunter's body trembled as the unforgiving mud slammed into her. Horror filled his chest as he spotted her legs shoot free, then disappear into the crashing mush. An arm cleared the surface, vanishing a second later. Supply bags tossed in the air, then landed in the rapid movement of the mire.

Terror stole Hunter's breath from his lungs until he lost sight of Katie in the burbling thickness.

The earth slipped under Hunter's feet. He anchored his position against the tree, trying to take on as much of Orson's weight as he could, and held firm. Mud sledged against them, racing down the hill like a winter Olympic luger race.

Keeping his eyes trained on the place where Katie had been mere seconds before, Hunter's gut knotted into a mass of tangled nerves. She hadn't resurfaced in several minutes. Images of her being sucked into the murky mass made him shudder. *Father God, protect her!*

The thick sludge met the rising river, feeding its hunger. It swirled into the raging water, wind pushing it like the beater of a mixer.

Around him, Hunter recognized the desperate cries from Paul—the litany of curses from Jerry— the grunts and groans from Carter. He felt Orson's shuddering back against his chest. Quivers of fear—or pain?—racked the injured man's body. Hunter squeezed closer, using his body as a shield over Orson.

Almost as suddenly as the slide had begun, it lost force and intensity. The flooded river consumed the mud, taming its hungry temper.

Hunter loosened his grip on the tree. Orson slumped against him.

"I-I-Is it o-over?" Paul's words broke the tense silence.

Wiping his face with his palm, Hunter cleared his vision. "I think so." He'd do just about anything for a cell phone right now.

The men shoved away from the tree—the foundation to which they'd clung for dear life. Slinging mud about as they tried to acclimate themselves to the ravages nature had thrown at them, they stomped and shook. Hunter eased Orson down and propped him against the sheltering oak. He secured the man, then his hand grazed the knot of the nylon rope. Hope soared through him.

"You guys stay here. I'm going down for Katie." He tugged on the rope, slipping it higher on the tree trunk, clearing it from the level of mire.

"Man, are you nuts?"

Hunter glared at Jerry. "We can't leave her down there. What if she's hurt?"

"Hurt?" Jerry flicked his hands, sending little globules of muck flying. "She's a goner, man. There's no way she could've survived that." He shook his head. "No way."

"Well I'm going to find out for certain." Hunter lifted his feet to reposition himself closer to the rope. A pop sounded as he released the air pocket. He lifted his face to the sky, letting the onslaught of the rain wash away the mud stuck to his face. *Please, God, let her be okay.*

"Waste of time, man. Total waste of time."

Without a conscious thought, Hunter gripped the

neckband of Jerry's wetsuit. His fingers sank into the pliable material. "I don't care if it's a waste of time or not, I won't leave until I find her. You stay here with the guys and try to get over by that rock formation. Got that?" He let Jerry go with a shove.

Jerry stumbled two steps backward, then found his footing. His stare could freeze the sun. "Fine. Whatever." He turned to Paul. "Help me get Orson moved."

Satisfied the group would be secure, Hunter held onto the rope and took his first tenacious step down the hill. Stomping in the thick mess made his progress unproductive. He could move faster by sliding his feet along the ground, letting the slippery mud glide him along. The closer he drew to where the cave was, the faster he slid.

He tightened his hold on the rope, careful to watch the level of the river, which with the addition of the muck, appeared to have risen faster. His hands stung, especially his injured one, as the rope burned against the exposed tender flesh.

Fat raindrops battered his head, sending chunks of mud swabbing down his shoulders. Hunter twisted his head back and forth rapidly, removing as much of the sludge as possible.

Carefully, he crept the remaining feet to reach the tree where the rope remained tied. He grabbed the tree and let his gaze drift over the area. No sign of Katie.

Please, Lord, let her be alive.

"Katie! Katie!"

He stood as stiff as the mud drying on the back of his neck, listening for a reply. Only the roar of the wind whipping across the river echoed in the air. "Katie! Katie!"

"Ugh."

His heart surged at the sound—could that be her? Hunter strained to hear over the pounding in his head. Fear choked his mind. "Katie!"

"Here."

He could barely make out her voice coming from his right, toward the cave.

Thank You, Lord. Thank You.

Shifting to firm his balance, Hunter moved in that direction. "I'm coming Katie. I'm coming."

She didn't answer.

Taking two more sliding steps, the adrenaline coursed through his veins, urging him on. "Katie!"

A dog barked, loud and repetitiously.

"Shadow!"

The Blue Heeler's barks came louder.

Hunter slugged as fast as his sense of balance would allow him. At last, he reached the lip of the cave. And saw her. The knot in his stomach tightened.

Looking like he felt, Katie lay crumpled against the back wall of the cave. The dark mud coated her hair like a dye. Her face, streaked by the assault of rain, stood out stark in the dim cave. Standing guard beside her, still barking, stood Shadow.

Hunter approached cautiously, holding his hand out to the dog. "Hey boy, remember me? I'm the good guy."

Shadow licked his hand, then whined.

Dropping to his knees, Hunter gently touched Katie's shoulder. "Katie?"

She rolled to give him a weak smile. "Hey, you." Dried mud cracked on her cheeks.

"Are you hurt?" Using the back of his hand, he brushed the offending mire from her face.

"Just my side. I think I only had the wind knocked out of me, but my ankle hurts." She licked her lips and cringed. "There was so much mud."

"I know." He wiped away the majority of the remaining dirt from her face with his knuckles, pushing back the errant strands of hair clinging to her cheek.

Her eyes widened. "Is everybody else okay?"

"Everyone's fine. Just fine." He swallowed. "Can you stand?"

"I think so."

Hunter slipped his arm around her waist. He helped her rise and use the wall of the cave for leverage. He bent over, loosened her hiking boots, and inspected her ankle. His hands trembled as he re-tied her boot, keeping it loose around her ankle, then straightened. "I think you only twisted it."

"Yeah." Her words came out choked as her

incomparable eyes met his. She raked her top teeth over her bottom lip, tugging his attention to her mouth.

It felt like a giant vacuum hose sucked all the air from his lungs. His gaze locked onto her full lips. The cave suddenly became warm—still—close.

Oh, Lord. Give me strength.

The subtle movement of her mouth stopped. Her breathing came in ragged breaths. The hint of peppermint filled the space between them. He lifted his stare to her eyes. Their silvery depths glimmered, moisture pooling in them as she gazed at his mouth, then looked at him and blinked. A rosy pink spread over her face, peeking out from the mud.

His heart tripped. She swayed, or maybe his perception of movement had become distorted. He reached out and grabbed her, pulling her to him in a fluid movement.

Katie's mouth opened a fraction of an inch. Her quick, short breaths made little gasping sounds. He ran a finger down the side of her face. She shivered. It became his undoing.

Drawing her closer, until he held her in the circle of his arms, Hunter slowly lowered his head. His gaze dipped from her eyes to her mouth again. He pressed his lips on hers.

He pulled slightly back, ending the peck of a kiss. He rested his forehead against hers, his stare entangled with hers. Fingertips caressed her face, unmindful of the remaining mud marring her unblemished features. The light in her eyes illuminated the entire cave. She was beautiful from the inside out. Now if he could understand why she'd turned her back on God . . .

Shadow barked, startling them. Hunter stepped back as the dog danced in circles at their feet. Hunter stared at the rapidly rising river.

Katie smiled at the dog, even as her insides turned to oatmeal. She lifted her fingers to her mouth, pressing against her lips. How could a kiss, as chaste as could be, send her heart aflutter?

Hunter turned back to her, his eyes as dangerously dark as moments before. "We need to start heading back up. The river's still rising." His voice came out like a sick bullfrog's croak. He gripped her elbow, steadying her. "Will you be able to make it?"

"I think so." She tested her ankle's stability by putting some weight on her left leg. Shards of white-hot pain shot up her calf and into her thigh. Bouncing, she bent her knee, relieving all pressure on her injured ankle. "Well, maybe not."

"I can help you." Hunter slid his shoulder under her arm.

Hopping on her good foot and leaning heavily on him, Katie made her way free of the cave.

The murky waters lapped over the tips of her

boots. A rush of adrenaline pushed her heart into her stomach. She turned her head to look up at Hunter. "We have to hurry. The river's already here."

Hunter remained silent, yet continued to lead her toward the path they'd constructed earlier. They reached the tree, and he waited until she held the rope firmly before turning back toward the raging river.

"What are you doing? We need to get climbing." The sudden realization of urgency hit her smack in the face.

"I'm looking for any of our supply bags. Everything was lost in the mudslide." His head twisted against the gusty wind.

The rain bands blasted them with icy droplets. Katie shivered. Shadow pranced on the muddy incline's floor.

"I see one!" Hunter jumped forward into the slushy mess creeping up. His head disappeared under the swirling darkness, then popped up a few feet away.

She watched as he continued his trek until he reached a small sapling with a low-lying fork. One of their bags was wedged against the bark. He hoisted it over his shoulder, securing it with the ties.

In her peripheral vision, she spied another pack a mere twenty feet to his left. "Hunter!"

He glanced over his shoulder to meet her stare.

"There's another one." Her finger shook when she pointed.

Following her direction, Hunter nodded. He performed a couple more dips and sloshes before retrieving the second pack. He secured it over his other shoulder, then turned back to face her. "See any more?"

Her eyes quickly scanned the area. "No. Come on, we've got to get moving."

Hunter trudged like an elephant in quicksand to join her. He supported her injured side, allowing her to hold the rope. "All right, let's do this as quickly as possible, okay?"

Nodding, Katie set her jaw, determined to push away the pain and do what she must.

Catcalls and whistles erupted from above.

Lifting her head, Katie smiled as Paul and Carter whooped over her progress. A sudden jolt of pain in her ankle forced her attention back to the climb. Clenching her teeth, she gripped the rope harder and pulled herself up to the next level.

Each step marked slight progress, yet Katie occupied her mind with Hunter's kiss. Replaying it over and over and over. A secret smile tugged at the corners of her mouth. If she concentrated, she could recall the gentleness and concern in his eyes. The memory caused her heart to race.

Shadow barked, pulling her from her reprieve. She squinted as she lifted her gaze.

"What's he barking for?"

Letting her gaze flit across the hillside, Katie saw nothing amiss. She leaned over to the dog, who pawed the ground beside her. "What is it, boy? What?"

Shadow burst into a sprint toward the top of the hill. He reached the other men, then spun around and tore back down the incline to her feet.

"What's wrong?" Hunter's grip tightened on her waist.

"I don't know. He's trying to tell me something." She laid a hand on the dog's head. "What is it, Shadow boy?"

The little dog whimpered, then barked. His paws clawed at the ground. Wiggling, he sped up the hill again.

Katie straightened. "I don't know what's wrong with him. Let's get to the top and I'll try to figure it out."

They continued their trek with a heightened sense of importance. Fifteen minutes later, they reached the group.

Carter accepted the mud-caked packs from Hunter while Paul knelt beside Katie when she slumped to the ground. "Are you okay?" A worried tone carried in Paul's voice.

She smiled, even though fingers of hot pain trailed up her leg. "I'm fine." She glanced around and her heart dipped. "Where's Orson?"

"We found us some shelter." Paul's chest puffed

out. "We've already got Orson all situated and comfortable."

"We didn't find anything, lamebrain. I did." Jerry, as arrogant and condescending as ever, glared at her. Obviously he hadn't forgotten her tirade against him.

"Show me," Hunter said as he touched Paul's shoulder. Paul stood, turned, then led him toward a small thicket of trees to the left. Carter ambled behind the men.

Katie wiped her mud-caked hands on the bottom of her wetsuit and surveyed her ankle. She'd have to get out of the boots soon—the swelling already caused splinters of discomfort. Glancing up, she met Jerry's appraising stare. She hitched an eyebrow. "What's your deal, anyway?"

Jerry shrugged, but threw her a disgusted look. She bit her tongue to keep from retorting as Hunter and Paul returned.

"It's a nice little set-up. Looks like a rough lean-to of sorts." Hunter held out his hand to help her to her feet.

She laid her hand in his, letting the heat from their contact warm her. "Yeah. It's one the rangers put up here for lost hikers."

"You knew?" Jerry's eyes scathed over her.

Smiling, she cocked her head to the side and slipped on her most saccharine-sweet voice. "Why do you think I climbed in this direction?"

Fourteen

Hunter swallowed back the roar of laughter clogging his throat. The look on Jerry's face was priceless—simply priceless. As he helped Katie hobble toward the lean-to, his attraction to her grew.

God, please help me out here. She doesn't trust in You. Show me the way to lead her back to You.

Hunter shoved into the little shanty, then helped Katie onto the dirt floor beside Orson before directing his attention to Carter. The old man stood right outside the doorway, letting the rain clean away the mud from the pack. Hunter joined Carter, hoisting the other pack under the bombarding downpour and rubbing away the muck. Katie's dog paced between the door and his mistress. Jerry stood outside.

Their shelter looked to be about twenty-by-twenty, with a tar roof atop a wooden frame. Cobwebs flecked the corners. One long table sat to the left of the door, with a fire pit in the upper left corner of the room. Beside the pit sat a firewood rack loaded with smaller logs and kindling. It had a feeling of comfortable decay—wood and nails, rigid and unimaginative, but shelter none-the-less. A thick layer of dust stirred into the air as the group ambled inside.

Paul shuffled to Katie's side. The green-eyed beast within Hunter surged. He gritted his teeth and swiped the pack so hard it slipped from his grasp. Bending to pick it up, he spied Jerry casing out the area. Hunter watched Jerry pick his way around to the back of the lean-to. Distrust replaced jealousy as Hunter slung the pack into the lean-to and sprinted to sneak up on the investor.

Keeping his body pressed as close to the make-shift building as possible, Hunter listened for Jerry's footsteps in the sluggish dead leaves among the thicket. Shadow bounded beside him. Hunter snapped his fingers once and pointed, as he'd seen Katie do many times. The dog dropped to his haunches with his ears erect.

Hunter drew up short when he heard Jerry's mumbled curse, followed by stomping and splashing. Hunter deftly returned to the doorway, mere seconds before Jerry appeared from the other side.

Feigning surprise, Hunter glared. "Where've you been?" The dog rushed past him into the lean-to.

"Just looking around." Jerry shrugged, but avoided eye contact.

The body language training he'd undergone screamed in Hunter. He's guilty—he's the murderer! "Find anything useful?"

"Nah." Jerry pawed at his wetsuit, knocking off thick clumps of mud.

Hunter ducked and crossed the threshold. Carter

stood at the small wooden table, still swiping at the packs with the back of his arm. Katie, with Shadow laying at her feet, sat sandwiched between Orson and Paul, the younger man's head bent close to hers. Hunter exhaled sharply through his nostrils, then made purposeful strides toward Carter.

"Let's see what we have here." Hunter took the larger of the two packs and fumbled with the strings. Wet and infiltrated with muddy granules, the knots were secured tight as a miser gripping his last dime. Hunter's numbing fingers couldn't pry them apart.

Jerry thumped inside the shanty and peered about. His steps were unsteady, like a toddler's first attempt at walking, as he headed to the opposite side of the room. He slumped against the wall, self-secluded from everyone else. His eyes trained on Paul's, although the man didn't appear to notice—Paul's attention focused solely on Katie.

Paul's whispered tones reached Hunter's ears. As he moved his head to glance over his shoulder, Katie let out a throaty chuckle. Hunter tensed his muscles, flicking his biceps.

"Here." Carter's gravelly voice jerked him back to the packs.

Hunter gripped the string between his hands and pulled. The knot popped loose, tearing the twine in two. Carter snatched the corner and unfurled the roll. Once flat, Hunter recognized the main tent. Nestled securely inside were three sleeping bags, one of which belonged to him. He let out a quiet sigh of relief—just knowing his sidearm hid within grabbing distance made his nerves calm. For five years, he'd never been far from the Beretta, and felt like it was more of an extension of his hand than a weapon.

He tossed the sleeping bags to the corner of the lean-to and then lifted the second pack. He and Carter laid it completely flat, and found one food bag and two more sleeping bags. Hunter sighed as he glanced toward Katie. They hadn't recovered any of her things. He strode to hover over her, his eyes narrowed at Paul. "Okay, you two," he said to Orson and Katie, "that mud isn't doing anything for either of you. Let's get you outside in the rain and wash off the yuck."

Katie smiled at him and held out her hand, her brightness piercing the dark cloud of jealousy over his heart. "Sounds like a plan to me—help me up."

He couldn't resist smiling back at her as he took her hand and gently tugged. She overshot her target, smacking flat into his chest. He wrapped his arms around her, steadying her. The feel of her in his arms again made his knees threaten to buckle.

"Why don't I help support Katie and you help with Orson?" Paul's voice shattered the moment Hunter savored.

Taking deep breaths, Hunter turned to face Paul, throwing poison arrows with his eyes.

Paul blinked. "I mean, you're stronger than I am and can hold up Orson better."

Hunter let out a snort, but let his hands drop from around Katie's waist and pulled Orson to his feet.

Katie hopped against Paul, glancing over her shoulder, past Hunter and Orson. "Hey, Carter, why don't you see what you can rustle up for lunch out of the supplies we have?"

Reclaiming her place as leader of the group, she cut her eyes over to Jerry, who leaned against the wall staring at them with disinterest. "Jerry, why don't you get up and help Carter?" The dog exited the shanty first, rushing off toward the area behind and above the shack.

Even injured and uncertain, Katie continued to take charge. The smile tickled Hunter's mouth. He had to admire her attitude and outlook. Hunter took on more of Orson's weight as the man groaned, but pinched his lips together tightly. As they made their way to stand under the down-pour, Hunter lifted his face to heaven.

Hunter stood under God's shower, then led the others back into the lean-to. Carter and Jerry stood at the table, opening cans of stew with handheld gadgets. Hunter's stomach rumbled. The shanty had no cooking appliance, but a fireplace pit sat nestled in the corner. Shadow rested at

Katie's feet, his brown eyes watching each man's move-ment.

Orson shivered. Hunter steadied the man against the wall before letting his eyes roam the room. No space allowed for privacy within the confines. He swallowed as he stared at the injured members of the party, Katie and Orson. Both trembled as the air kicked up outside, roaring and battering against the rough shelter. They needed to get into dry clothes, as quickly as possible.

Hunter stared back at the packs on the floor. He smiled as he lifted the large tent. Dragging it across the room, Hunter moved it by the door and peered outside. Directly adjacent to the shanty lay a flat, clear area. A perfect place for a tent that would allow the building to provide shelter from the kicking winds.

Katie kept her eyes trained on Hunter. He'd been pacing like a caged tiger, his expression so intense she could almost see the pulleys in his mind turning. He now stood in the doorway, a crumpled tent at his feet, his eyes affixed beside the lean-to, and she knew what he planned. Of course . . . how brilliant. Set up the tent for privacy issues in changing clothes and such, but also a place for her to sleep separately from the men tonight. A warming sensation spread across her body as his stare connected with hers. So thoughtful of her needs. She smiled.

"Paul, come help me pitch this tent." Hunter lifted the tent and stakes.

Instantly, Paul moved to his side, but Jerry glared at Hunter. "We have a shelter—why do we need the tent?"

Hunter passed Paul the stakes and wadded the tent into a tight ball against his chest. "For privacy in dressing, and a place for Katie to bunk tonight."

"What's wrong with her sleeping in here?" Jerry's lips pulled into a misaligned curl.

"It's inappropriate for her to bunk in the same room with four men." Hunter turned on his heel and strode from the shanty. Shadow followed in Hunter's wake.

Jerry shot his scowl over to Katie.

She arched an eyebrow.

"Don't feel comfortable lying among us, do you, Ms. Gallagher?"

She swallowed the acid retort, and forced herself to smile. "I think we'll rest better if Shadow and I hole up in the tent." Reaching into her fanny pack, she pulled out a peppermint, noticing she only had a handful left. She pushed the mint into her mouth and closed her eyes, letting the soothing flavor relax her.

Orson grunted.

Jerry shot his eyes over to the aging tax attorney. "What're you moaning about, old man?"

Katie bit back her retort. Jerry's attitude

worsened . . . how much longer until he totally snapped and went off the deep end?

Orson's voice echoed, filling the room. "If you were any kind of gentleman, you'd let the lady sleep in this shack and we all would take the tent."

"Us four give up our comfort because she thinks she's too good to bunk in the room with us?" Jerry snorted. "You must be kidding. Let loverboy out there stay with her." His cold eyes snapped to her face. "I'm sure she wouldn't care too much about resting better then."

Her heart racing, Katie narrowed her eyes and lowered her voice. "I wouldn't dare ask you to be inconvenienced."

Jerry's fist popped down on the table, causing the wooden legs to creak in angry protest. "I'm already inconvenienced enough as it is, aren't I, Ms. Gallagher?" His body stance implied a man with a vested interest in chaos and dissention. "And we're the paying clients here."

He was right. Katie's body trembled and she balled her hands into fists. Her chipped nails dug into her palms.

"We're all put out, Jerry, but you appear to be the only one harping on it at the moment," Orson said.

Katie used Orson's shoulder as leverage to draw to her feet.

Shadow burst into the room, moving to stand in

front of Katie, but snarling at Jerry. The hairs on the back of his head bristled. A menacing growl sounded from down in Shadow's throat.

She didn't command the dog to back down. Instead, she met Jerry's frigid stare with one of her own—the one her brothers swore would freeze hell over.

A shuffling caused her to turn. Hunter's broad shoulders filled the doorway. He glanced over Katie's stance before he faced Jerry. "What's going on in here?"

Her heart lunged. With his eyes squinted and his muscles jumping under his wetsuit, Hunter portrayed every inch a warrior. A protector. Katie wrestled with her independent streak, carrying on a mental battle whether to stand down and let Hunter deal with Jerry, or to remain in charge as the guide and have a showdown with the mouthy investor.

The decision was made for her.

Shadow lifted his head, then tilted it to the side. He barked once, filling Katie with trepidation. In one motion, the dog turned and fled out the shanty. His bark carried from behind the lean-to.

Hopping on one foot, Katie made it to the doorway.

Hunter gripped her elbow. He moved so close she could feel his breath against her ear. "What's wrong?"

"Someone's here. That's Shadow's greeting

bark." She hobbled from the building, letting Hunter assist her. A sense of completeness surrounded her as Hunter stayed close to her side. Completeness and security.

Hunter turned his head back to the doorway. "You guys stay here."

Katie pressed on, following the sounds of Shadow's barking. Hunter squeezed her elbow until she stopped. Glancing at him, she used her hand to shield her eyes from the offensive rain. "What?"

"Maybe you should wait here. I'll go see what the dog's found."

"Shadow hasn't found anything—someone's here. I trust him . . . he's never wrong."

Hunter shook his head slowly. "Still, maybe I should check it out first. Just to be on the safe side."

His words struck home, allowing her imagination to play havoc with her mind. She stiffened. "No. It's my job as guide to look out for the group. I have to go."

"Okay, but if it's unsafe, promise me you'll let me handle it."

She wanted to ask how he'd be able to handle an unsafe environment any better than she, but refrained. Nodding, she moved toward the echoes of Shadow's barks.

As they rounded the back of the lean-to and gained ground up the incline, the dog's barking became louder, more intense, more insistent.

Katie's stomach churned. Shadow had found someone. She picked up her hobbling-hop, leaning heavily on Hunter's support.

They moved to forge ahead, when Shadow bounded back into the clearing.

A crashing through the brush carried on the gusts of wind.

Katie froze while Hunter stepped in front of her, moving into a defensive crouch. His legs spread about two feet apart, planted in the mushy ground.

Two figures stood silhouetted against the incoming rain bands. A wide-shouldered man dressed in a black rain slicker, fumbled into the clearing.

Katie peered around Hunter as the mysterious man rushed toward them. He wore a huge backpack, making him appear even larger. The black hood covered his head and shielded his face, making him look formidable, reminding her of the cartoonish impression of the Deliverer of Death. Her pulse thudded loudly in her head, drowning out the cacophony from the wind and rain.

Shadow rushed to the man, his nub of a tail wagging. Katie stared at her dog as he greeted the stranger. Only whoever approached wasn't a stranger to Shadow.

Pushing around Hunter, Katie hopped toward the man. Hunter grabbed her elbow, gently tugging her back.

"What happened to your leg?" The familiar

voice made her want to jump regardless of the pain as the man pushed back his hood. Christian's bright eyes stared into hers.

"Christian! Oh, I'm so glad to see you." Katie let herself be swallowed in her brother's engulfing hug. She clung to him longer than normal, trem-bling.

He pulled back and peered into her face. "What's wrong? What's happened?"

Fighting back the tears, Katie shook her head and grabbed his hands. "I'll fill you in later." She made a playful punch on his arm. "But you. How'd you know where to find us?"

"I'd already called off my trip when Rory told me about the boat and where you'd put in. I figured you'd head to the lean-to." He shrugged and smiled the boyish grin she loved. "I thought I'd be the good brother and bring you supplies and such."

"He was so worried about you." Ariel, a smaller pack affixed to her back, stepped beside Christian.

In Katie's excitement, she'd forgotten about the second person. Now, the young woman stood with her hand comfortably in the crook of Christian's arm. Why on earth would Christian bring her? Why not one of the park rangers or a sheriff?

Hunter's hand on her shoulder startled Katie. She swayed for a moment before Hunter's strong arm wrapped around her waist. He winked at her, but spoke to Christian and Ariel. "Why don't we get inside, out of the rain, to catch up? I'm soaked to the bone here."

Although she appreciated his staunch support, something stunk to high heaven—something she couldn't quite put her finger on, but it lay there, irritating her under the surface, much like a festering splinter. She needed to figure it out. Soon.

Christian smiled and laid a hand over Ariel's, who pushed her perfectly manicured hand into the crook of his elbow. Katie allowed Hunter to help her turn and hobble back toward the lean-to. Shadow pranced along in front of the group, stopping every so often to look back, as if checking on Katie.

They crossed the threshold and entered the room. Jerry's eyes narrowed on Christian and Ariel. Katie leaned against the table, letting her forearms take the bulk of her body weight. She smiled at Carter, who shoved kindling from the rack into the small fire pit. He nodded at her. "We need some matches. I haven't found any around here."

Slipping the pack off his back, Christian chuckled. "I have a lighter in here. As well as plenty of food and dry sweatshirts."

Katie breathed a sigh as her knees buckled. Just having Christian beside her lessened the burden of responsibility that had settled over her shoulders, but she needed to tell her brother of her failure. "A member of our party, Walter Thompson, fell into the river." She blinked at the tears pooling in her eyes. "He got sucked into a hydraulic and swept into a death cave." She swallowed.

"Oh, Katie." Christian wrapped an arm around her and hugged her tight. "We'll call the police as soon as we get back." He kissed the top of her head before releasing her.

She hauled in a deep breath, struggling to control her emotions. "I'm assuming Emily came ashore?" She brushed her bangs from her eyes.

"Actually, she's been sitting off the coast, throwing in rain bands and wind." Christian unloaded the pack, setting canned goods and supplies on the table. "She only made landfall midmorning. Rain should settle down today and slack up by morning." He tossed the empty backpack in the corner. "We should be able to start hiking out by noon tomorrow. The four-wheelers are waiting in the parking lot at the top of the hill. We should all be able to make it because we pulled the wagons."

"Good."

Carter lit the kindling. Pops and cracklings filled the room. The smell of smoke wafted about, hanging in the stale air like an oppressive cloud. Shadow leaned against Christian's leg . . . her brother bent down and scratched the dog's muzzle.

Paul raided the cabinets and lifted an old cast-iron pot they'd dumped cans of stew in. He settled the handle in the hook above the pit.

Katie faced Christian. "So, Steve made it okay?"

"Yep. He and Rory arrived before the rains settled in." Christian took the pack from Ariel and pulled out a pair of jeans and sweater, along with a bag of candies. He smiled as he plopped them on the table in front of Katie. "I took the liberty of grabbing a spare set of your clothes from the lodge, as well as a bag of those blasted peppermints you can't seem to live without."

She grabbed the offering and straightened. "Oh, thank you, Christian. I'm so ready to get out of this wetsuit. All my stuff got lost in the mudslide."

"Mudslide?" Christian tilted his head and squinted.

"Long story." She hopped back from the table, gathered her balance, then nodded at her brother. "Get the guys to fill you in on our adventures. I'm going to slip out to the tent and get changed." Shadow moved to stand by her side. She stroked the dog's head, then gave the command for him to stay. Shadow sat back at Christian's feet.

Moving closer, Ariel asked, "Can I help you?"

"Sure, I'd appreciate that."

The two women crossed the threshold, then headed to the tent.

A fine bead of sweat dotted her upper lip by the time Katie had slipped inside and zipped the tent closed. The trip took more out of her than she'd anticipated. She slumped to the floor, panting with exhaustion.

Ariel handed Katie the dry clothes. "I was disappointed when we had to cancel my group, but I'm glad I was able to help."

"I'm a little surprised to see you. I'd have thought you would've left when the weather turned so bad." Katie pulled the sweater over her head—it clung to her wet bra.

"I would have except I couldn't get my flight canceled."

"I understand that."

"When Christian said he was coming out to bring supplies and see if he could get your group back, I volunteered to drive the other four-wheeler since that Rory fellow didn't want to leave the lodge."

Not with anyone there he wouldn't. "Well, I'm really glad to see you." Katie lowered her voice. "And really glad to have another woman out here."

Ariel smiled and stood by the tent's flap. "Unless you need me to help you with anything else, I'll give you some privacy."

"Thanks."

After the tent's flap was zipped once again, Katie worked to pull off the wetsuit. The heavy fabric pushed against her ankle. She cringed and let out a loud moan.

"You okay?" Hunter's soft voice from outside the tent made her heart quicken.

Did he have to stand so close to the tent? She licked her lips as the memory of his kiss skidded across her mind. "Um, I'm okay," she called out.

"Just checking. You're taking quite some time."

"Hard to get out of a wetsuit with a bum ankle."

Hunter chuckled. "I can imagine."

"I'm almost done." She quickly jabbed her good leg into jeans. The worn, dry denim nestled softly against her skin. Almost sighing in satisfaction and comfort, Katie took a breath, then worked to get her hurt leg into the jeans. She gritted her teeth against the discomfort her movements caused.

"No hurry."

Despite the awkward position of lying flat on her back and inching up her pants, Katie smiled. It dawned on her that he'd stand out there and wait on her—wait to help her back into the lean-to. His gesture of consideration warmed her frozen toes.

Hunter Malone embodied all the traits of a man she could really fall for—strong, considerate, dependable, and able. All the qualities she'd vowed long ago to hold out for when she'd believed in love. Believed in a happily ever after.

She slipped the jeans over her hips and buttoned the snap, then clipped her fanny pack around her waist, which she quickly restocked with the peppermints Christian had brought. Katie reflected on her and Hunter's kiss, surmising that surely he felt something too. He didn't seem the type to trifle with someone's emotions. Then again, she could never be certain about people. Her own past proved that beyond a doubt.

Struggling to stand, Katie knew Hunter hid something, but what? She'd keep digging at Hunter's layers until she uncovered what lay beneath the surface. Then, and only then, would she consider her emotions.

Fifteen

Hunter waited outside the tent, listening to Katie's light moans as she apparently struggled to get dressed. Had it not been for impropriety's sake, he'd have rushed in to help her minutes ago.

Katie unzipped the tent and practically fell into his arms, jolting him. He pulled her close, steadying her, but also savoring the feel of her in his arms. The knitted sweater nestled over her curves, the soft yarn rubbing against his forearms as he kept her in the circle of his embrace. Her vivid eyes collided with his.

In the space of a heartbeat, he lowered his mouth to hers. The sweet warmth of her sent tingles down his back. He deepened the kiss, drawing her tighter against his chest. Her heart pounded against his, pulling him in. Her hand fisted at the nape of his neck, her fingers playing in his hair with a gentle yet probing tug. His strength dissipated like morning mist.

Realization tapped his shoulder, as if the Holy Spirit appeared in the flesh. He lifted his head and took a half-step back, but kept an arm circling her waist. Her eyes fluttered open and stared into his. Hunter swallowed, then gave a shaky smile. "I'm getting you all wet again."

Her eyebrows shot up. "Oh."

He couldn't resist—he ran a finger down the side of her face. Her flawless skin felt so soft, his fingers itched to touch her.

"What's happening here, Hunter?" Her voice hiccupped.

His hand froze, finger settling on her chin, as her question penetrated past his attraction. "What do you mean?" His voice sounded husky to his ears.

"With us, you and me. What's going on?" Her eyes reflected so many emotions, ones he couldn't even begin to read, much less comprehend.

"I, uh . . . Katie, I have these feelings for you." He ran a hand through his wet hair. "But, we need to get you out of the rain before you get soaked again."

Her face crumbled in obvious disappointment. Every fiber of his soul wanted to hold her again, to snuggle close and stay there forever. He wished he could reassure her, to insist his feelings were real, but he couldn't. Not yet. Not while he still had a job to do. So instead, he helped her into the lean-to, all the while sending up prayers.

They entered the lean-to and the enticing aroma of stew filled his senses. His stomach growled. He left Katie at the table and moved to the fire-pit. Carter stirred the bubbling thick broth. Hunter's mouth watered. "Smells marvelous, Carter."

The older man smiled. "It's almost ready."

Paul helped Orson to his feet. Moving to assist, Hunter grabbed Orson's other side. "What do you say we get you into some dry clothes?"

Orson grunted through chattering teeth.

Hunter and Paul slipped Orson outside and into the tent. Once the three men changed into dry clothes, they lumbered back into the shanty. Carter spooned generous portions of the stew into bowls as Hunter sat Orson on the floor beside Katie. He grabbed two of the full bowls and passed them to the two injured members of their party. He went to grab a third bowl, and his hand met with another's.

Lifting his gaze, he stared at Ariel's face. Reading her silent request, he gave a slight tilt of his head before reaching for another bowl. She winked at him, then turned to join Christian across the room. He moved to sit beside Katie, but met her icy stare, and his steps faltered. A sinking feeling shot into his gut.

She'd seen his exchange with Ariel.

Swallowing back the strong urge to grab Katie and tell her the truth, Hunter lowered himself to the floor beside Paul. He had to trust God to see him through and prayed she'd understand when it became safe enough to explain.

He closed his eyes and said grace, then lifted his spoon to eat. The sensation of being watched caused him to look up. Across the room, Ariel smiled, almost shyly. He reflexively returned her smile. An almost physical burning sensation ripped into his side. Turning his head, Hunter set his jaw as Katie's pained expression shredded his heart.

Katie chewed her stew until it had ground into liquid. Each chomp delivered more force than the one before. Now her jaw ached. Not that she cared. Ariel, who she'd really started to like, blatantly flirted with Hunter—winking and smiling —while seeming to be attached to Christian's hip. And Hunter had flirted right back, after kissing Katie and telling her he had feelings for her.

Frustration mixed with jealousy clogged her throat. She choked when she tried to swallow. She set down her bowl while she coughed and sputtered.

Paul popped her back. "Are you okay?"

She coughed so hard her eyes watered. Everyone stared at her. She waved off Paul's hand while gulping in air. Katie lifted her eyes, and Hunter's probing gaze burned into her. She wrinkled her nose, then pushed the bowl with the rest of her stew toward Shadow. The dog lapped the hot food.

Leaning against the wall, Katie glared at Ariel until the woman glanced at her. Katie hoped her facial expressions portrayed the anger and disappointment churning inside her. She forced every ounce of her emotions into the glare.

Ariel fidgeted, then dropped her gaze to her stew bowl.

A gloating sensation rose inside Katie. Elation that she'd made Ariel so uncomfortable the woman needed to look away. Then, without warning, the feeling sank to the depth from which it came. Disgusted with her petty jealousy, Katie shoved from the floor and grabbed the empty bowl from Shadow. She limped and hopped toward the table.

Hunter rose and met her before she'd made much progress. He took the bowl from her and set it on the wooden counter.

Katie stiffened. Could she have misread the situation? Could Hunter have only been being polite? Was she blowing everything out of proportion? Maybe. She relaxed and offered him a demure smile. His return grin, wide and reaching his eyes, made her heart ping. He couldn't have kissed her moments before and then flirted with another woman. No, Hunter wasn't like that.

He moved beside her, snaking his arm around her waist and pulling her against his side. His touch burst through the dam holding back her attraction. He held her tighter, closer to him, and she relished the warmth of his body heat.

Her emotions spiraled, spinning like a hydraulic in the Gauley.

His gaze drilled into her, igniting the rekindled attraction sparking in the pit of her stomach.

Another hand lighted on her shoulder. She jumped and turned.

Christian's eyes darkened as they peered at her. "Katie-cat, what's up?"

Not a sound came out. No words, not even a soft creak. She pressed her lips together. Tears welled in her eyes. Katie blinked them back, letting the sting propel her anger. She hated to cry, especially in front of other people. It crawled all over to know Hunter witnessed her loss of control.

Katie jerked away from Hunter's side, hopping as she laid a hand on the table. She brushed away the few tears that found their way down her cheeks. "I'm fine. Just tired and overwhelmed." Katie hauled in a deep breath, held it for a few seconds, then exhaled slowly. Her heartbeat slowed to its normal rhythm.

"Are you sure?" Christian turned her to look at him.

"Yeah." She sniffled, refusing to give into the emotional tidal wave threatening to consume her. "I just need to rest." Katie straightened her shoulders. She was, after all, the older sibling here. "I'll be right as rain after a sleep."

"Why don't you go ahead and get settled in the tent?" Christian dropped his hand and smiled.

"I'll have Ariel bring in some sleeping bags for you both."

Katie froze, frigid blasts of uneasiness settling against her spine. Ariel. She'd thrown dagger-stares at the woman over something so silly, and she felt bad. She'd have to apologize.

She limped away, shrugging off both Hunter's and Christian's offers of help. She needed to do this alone—be alone. Maybe a couple of hours away from the strain of responsibility and leadership, as well as free from Hunter's in-depth stares, would right her world back on its axis.

Hunter decided to take the bowls out to wash them, but Christian's slight brush against his arm stopped him. He shot the young man a quizzical look. "You have something to say to me?"

"Yeah, I do." Christian nodded toward the door.

Holding the dirty bowls, Hunter moved outside. "What's on your mind?" He held the dishes out, letting the rain rinse them clean.

"My sister."

Hunter met Christian's stare. He held it, forcing his breathing to remain normal. "Well, that's really none of your business."

"I think it is." Christian folded his arms over his chest, acting oblivious to the rain sheeting over his face. "Katie's not the type of woman you can toy with. She doesn't play well with others."

Arching a brow, Hunter slipped the bowls inside

the doorway. He straightened, then turned back to Katie's brother. "I'm not toying with Katie." His voice lowered and became unintentionally rough.

"I think you are. You're playing games, and I won't have you playing them with Katie's feelings."

"Again, it's none of your business."

Christian's eyes narrowed. "She's my sister, so I'm making it my business. She's been hurt badly before—I don't think she could take such heart-ache again."

Silence filled the space between the two men as they faced off.

Hunter let out a long sigh. "I'm trying to do the right thing, Christian. I really am."

"You haven't told her who you are, or why you're really here, have you?"

Clenching his jaw, Hunter shook his head.

"So, you aren't being honest with her." Christian ran a hand over his hair. "Katie's real big on honesty. And trust. When she finds out you're really . . ."

Hunter held up his hand. "I'll tell her when the time is right."

Christian gave a curt nod. "Have it your way, but I'm telling you, she's going to get hurt. And when Katie gets hurt, hold on to your hat because she gets beyond ticked off."

"I'll take your advice under consideration." Hunter walked back into the lean-to.

Christian grabbed his arm and pulled him back.

Hunter stared at Christian's hand, then glared at him.

Christian dropped his hand to his side. "Don't hurt her more than you have to. I love her and don't want her heart broken."

Torment and guilt gnawed at Hunter's chest. He met Christian's stare once more, then nodded. He wished there were another way to get his job done, but there wasn't. Not that he could see. And his job had to come first. No matter what, it had to get done. But God forgive him for the pain he knew he would undeniably cause Katie.

Ariel unzipped the tent slowly. Katie lay still on the sleeping bag. Where was Ariel going?

The other woman had been sweet and helpful in setting up the sleeping bags. Katie had apologized to Ariel for her ugly looks and attitude, explaining that she'd been exhausted. All had been well when they'd lain down for their nap. That had been less than an hour ago.

So where was Ariel going now?

Katie crawled to the opening, pressing her ear against the mesh netting. Muffled voices drifted over the rain. Who would be whispering with Ariel in the rain? Christian?

At least the wind had died down some. Katie shifted and squatted with her weight on one leg. She strained to hear the conversation.

Hunter's unmistakable baritone reached her ears. "Are you really okay? I mean, if you've got doubts, I can call it all off and get you out of here."

Ariel laughed, sounding throaty and flirtatious. "I'm fine. It's you I'm worried about."

Katie's stomach knotted.

"Me? Why on earth would you worry about me?" Hunter sounded closer—his words were clipped and clear to Katie's hearing.

Once more, Ariel let loose that seductive laugh of hers. "Don't play stupid with me, partner. I've seen the way you're acting toward her. You're not fooling me."

"What about the way you're playing with Christian, huh?"

They were both playing games! Katie's hands trembled. She balled them into fists and pressed one against her mouth.

"Maybe I'm not playing with him, sweetheart." Ariel's voice held a lilt of teasing. Katie wanted to punch her square in the mouth.

"Hmm. If you say so." A long pause thudded. Hunter spoke again. This time, his voice lower. Katie strained to hear. "You be careful, babe."

"You too," Ariel said. "Watch out for Katie . . . I think she's wary of me."

Katie almost missed Hunter's next sentence. Almost, but not quite. "I'll handle Katie Gallagher. You just be ready to move on a moment's notice."

"Just make sure you handle her, and she doesn't handle you, partner."

Slushy footsteps made their way to the tent.

Katie awkwardly scrambled back to her sleeping bag. She plopped down and pinched her eyes closed. Her muscles tensed when the zipper sounded. Katie wanted to watch, but didn't dare move a muscle.

Katie squinted an eye. Ariel slipped back into her sleeping bag, let out a long sigh, then flipped to her back. She groaned loudly, following with a big, fake yawn.

Heart pounding, Katie fluttered her eyes open, as if just awakening. She blinked a couple of times before allowing her gaze to settle on Ariel.

Lifting her arms over her head, Ariel gave an exaggerated stretch. She dropped her hands and smiled across the dimly lit tent. "Did you have a nice nap? I sure did."

Katie ground her teeth. She hated to lie— detested falsity in any size, shape or form—had endured enough of it to last a lifetime. Apparently, the same ideals didn't matter to Ariel.

Working to keep the anger from her tone, she opted to simply avoid answering Ariel's question. Wasn't Gabe's favorite mantra that the best defense was a good offense? "Did you sleep okay out here in the tent? Were you warm enough?"

"Oh, fine." Ariel stood and offered her hand to Katie. "Let's go see what all the guys are up to."

Although it galled Katie to the core, she took Ariel's hand and stood. As soon as she got her balance, she dropped the physical contact with the woman who had an ulterior motive. Katie's ankle wasn't as sore as before and it looked as if the swelling had gone down. She put her weight on it, testing it, and fiery pain jabbed into her thigh. Definitely improved, but still injured. Limping, she moved toward the front of the tent, leaving Ariel to her own devices.

Once inside the lean-to, the enticing smell of something delicious wafted to her nostrils. Katie's stomach rumbled. Having not finished her stew earlier, she was famished now. She made her way to Paul, who leaned over the fire-pit, stirring something in the cast-iron pot.

"Something smells wonderful, Paul." She leaned over the pot, inhaling the aromatic steam.

The man straightened. Afternoon light flooded through the window and doorway, casting a shine on his bald spot. He smiled as he set the spoon on the table. "We're having venison jerky stew."

She had to return the man's smile. "Well, it smells *mahhh-velous*."

Paul laughed at her horrid impression, then turned back to the bubbling stew.

Hunter stomped inside, his arms heavy with small branches and limbs. He carried the wood to the hearth beside the fire-pit and dumped it there. Hunter spread the pieces out as close to the fire as was safe.

Paul joined Katie at the table. He leaned close, nearly whispering in her ear. "How's your ankle?"

She flashed a weak grin. "It's better, I think." Her smile dropped as Hunter's dark eyes settled on her. Her heart lurched at the attraction nestled into the chocolate-looking orbs. Then she recalled his secret conversation with Ariel. She spoke to Paul, but kept her eyes glued to Hunter's. "I think resting did it some good."

"We probably ought to wrap it with a bandage or something." Paul's statement jerked her attention back to him. His face lit with adoration.

Instead of flattering her, it annoyed Katie. She frowned. "I might wrap it before I go to bed tonight."

Paul's face fell. Katie felt like a heel, but wanted him to understand she wasn't interested. She didn't want to lead him on. Not like some other women did. He hurried past her, out of the shanty.

"Where's Ariel? Still resting?"

Katie turned at the sound of Hunter's voice. They were alone in the shanty. She shrugged. "I don't know where she went. She got up when I did." She leaned her hip against the table. "Do you know where Christian is?"

Hunter nodded toward the door. "He went out to get some more wood. We need to have plenty for the night and it'll need to dry out as much as possible."

Katie wrinkled her nose. "Then I assume that's where Ariel went." Her gaze drifted over the room. "What about Jerry, Carter and Orson?"

"Jerry and Carter are helping Orson answer the call of nature."

Her eyes locked with Hunter's. Could he see she thought it a horrible decision? "How long have they been gone?"

Hunter's eyes widened, then he glanced at his watch. His Adam's apple bobbed. "About thirty minutes."

Katie's pulse raced. Thirty minutes. How long did it take two men to help an injured person use the bathroom? She pushed off from the table and hobbled toward the door. And ran smack into her brother.

Christian dropped his armload of wood.

A log hit Katie's thigh—another jarred against her hurt ankle. Pain tore through her leg. She let out a yelp, followed by a sharp cry. All balance gone, Katie crumbled to the ground.

Shadow, who'd followed Christian, licked her face.

Tears burned her eyes. She didn't bother trying to blink them back as the pain in her ankle intensified.

Christian dropped to his knees. "Oh, Katie-cat, I'm so sorry."

Ariel stood behind Christian, her face writhed in sympathy.

Katie bit her bottom lip, choking back the burning pain.

"I didn't see you coming out." Her brother pushed her bangs from her face. "Are you okay?"

Katie groaned. The words wouldn't form in her throat. Shadow danced beside her, whimpering.

"Let me get you up."

Katie turned to glare at Hunter, but he bent over and swept her into his strong arms. He cradled her against his chest while crossing to the table. The odor of wet wood and laundry detergent clung to his flannel shirt. The buttons pressed into the side of her face. He sat her on top of the rough wood with care and consideration. His eyes dropped to her injured ankle and he untied the laces of her hiking boots. "Let me look at it."

She flinched. Shadow growled, but remained sitting. He stared at her, his puppy dog gaze stuck to her face.

"Does this hurt?" Hunter's warm fingers gently probed her ankle, not allowing her to follow a train of thought to the station.

How could she tell him she didn't want him to touch her—couldn't take the intimacy? Not while uncertain of his involvement with Ariel. She dug her nails into her palms, jerking her foot free of his grasp. "It's fine."

Hunter shrank back as if she'd smacked him. The vise on her heart tightened.

A scream echoed across the late afternoon air, tromping over the wail of the wind and rain.

The hairs on the back of her neck stood at attention. Goosebumps popped up over her arms.

Another scream, this one louder and blood-curdling, ripped through the forced silence in the shanty.

Everyone moved at once.

Hunter and Christian raced from the room. Ariel followed behind them. Katie hopped down from the table, then hobbled to the door, Shadow at her side.

A keening wail bypassed a cry, right into a full-fledged scream. The sound tore over the sheets of rain, long and piercing. Then it suddenly stopped, as if cut off.

Sixteen

Hunter ran with the speed of a cheetah, his mind racing as fast as his feet over soggy ground. He sprinted around the back of the shack. He ducked low-lying tree limbs. Hunter's right hand tightened. His weapon! He needed his Beretta.

He stopped running, stood still, his ears trained to pick up any sound.

Christian and Ariel came to a halt beside him. Ariel bent at the waist, propping her hands on her knees and breathing in puffs.

Hunter heard muffled sounds from the thicket of trees. Shooting into motion, he raced in that direction. His legs brushed against soaked bushes as he ran, wetting the side of his jeans. The clamoring from behind let him know Ariel and Christian were right on his heels.

Reaching a clearing, Hunter stopped. He caught his breath, listening for any sounds of movement. Nothing, save for Christian's and Ariel's feet pounding and their heavy breathing.

"What is that?" Christian's face glimmered red and sweat beaded on his upper lip.

Hunter held up a hand for silence.

Ariel spun, her eyes surveying the area. She pointed toward a thicket of trees just as a rustling sound drifted over the wind.

Pushing himself into motion, Hunter ran full speed ahead. His gut wrenched. He'd been around the block enough times to understand what could have stifled the scream he'd heard. Forcing his legs to pump faster, Hunter plunged into the shadows of the trees. At least the leafy canopy provided some shelter from the torrential downpour.

He stopped when trees blocked his path. Spinning around, Hunter blinked to focus. *Lord, show me.*

Ariel touched his shoulder. He turned. She inclined her head to the right. Hunter inched closer to where she indicated.

Muffled sounds reached Hunter's ears. Snapping and popping noises, like limbs being moved. He hauled in a deep breath and burst through the dense line of trees.

Jerry held Orson's shoulder. Carter lay on the ground, blood oozing from his temple.

"What happened?" Hunter dropped to his knees beside Carter's lifeless body. He laid two fingers against the man's neck—just as he'd feared, no pulse. Hunter pressed harder. Still nothing. He tilted Carter's head back and bent to administer CPR.

Ariel dropped to her knees and helped. Three minutes passed. Five. Eight. Twelve. Finally, she stilled Hunter's hand. "It's no use. He's gone."

Why, God? Why couldn't I save him? He looked at Jerry. "Somebody want to tell me what happened?"

His eyes cold as the stinging wind, Jerry peered at him. "I don't know. I was helping Orson in those bushes," he nodded toward the area Hunter had only moments before burst through, "and I heard Carter whimpering and mumbling. I sat Orson down, then ran here as quick as I could."

"We heard screams," Ariel said.

Jerry stared at her, then lowered Orson to the ground. "Yeah. I couldn't find him until I heard the screams." He straightened and shook his head. "By then, he was already there, like that."

Hunter stood, looming over the dead body of Carter James. He fisted his hands on his hips.

"There were three screams. I found you in that time, and I was back at the lean-to. Why couldn't you get to him?"

"I guess I'm not as attuned as you are, radar-boy." Jerry's snarl made him look like a rabid dog ready to take a bite out of someone. "When I found him dead, I went back for Orson." He narrowed his eyes and glared at Hunter. "Didn't want two bodies out here."

Jerry lied, and was probably a murderer. Hunter swallowed back the anger. He stared at Ariel. She gave the briefest nod, then moved to Orson's side.

Orson, looking as if in shock, mumbled to himself. When Hunter tried to talk to the man, his gaze shot to Jerry's, then to the ground.

Hunter clenched his jaw. Apparently, the fiend had gotten to Orson.

"What do we do now?" Christian's face turned pale.

Hunter pitied, yet envied the man. Moments like this made Hunter long for the days when death shocked him, back before he'd become cynical and jaded. He let out a long sigh. "You help Ariel get Orson back to the shack." Settling his gaze on Jerry's grimacing face, he jutted out his chin. "Jerry will help me get Carter's body back."

"I'm not toting a corpse anywhere." Spreading his legs apart, Jerry took a defensive stand with his arms crossed over his chest. His eyes as cold and lifeless as Carter's.

Not wanting to have it out in the pouring rain, Hunter ignored the man's stance. "We can't just leave him here."

"Then you carry him since you seem to be so hot and heavy to get him to the shack." Jerry followed Ariel and Christian as they helped Orson down the path. "I could care less."

Hunter's hold on his temper snapped. "That much is obvious."

Jerry whipped around to face him once more, his expression distorted into a mask of rage. "What's your beef, Malone? Huh? You've been a real pain in the neck this whole trip. Who died and left you in charge?"

"Carter did."

Shrugging, Jerry fisted his hands at his sides. "Get over yourself, man. Carter just died."

"Just died?" Hunter's heart raced as it did before every important job. "Just died?" He took two steps toward Jerry. "Someone bashed the man's head in. That's murder, man. Plain and simple."

"Yeah? So?" Jerry's nonchalant attitude came out full stride.

Hunter's veins clogged with ice. "So the murderer is still out here somewhere."

"Is that supposed to scare me?"

"If you had any brains it would." Hunter took another step toward Jerry. "Unless you're the one who killed Carter."

Jerry's jaw quivered. In an instant, it locked back into place, holding firm and steady. His eyes darkened as he squinted. "Who do you think you are—accusing me?"

Hunter lifted a casual shoulder. "If the shoe fits . . ."

"Get over it." Jerry shook his head with intentional slowness. A tactic Hunter recognized as a power-play. Every top-A-executive learned the move before being allowed into the boardroom. Jerry spun on his heel and muttered, "I'm getting out of the weather. Suit yourself."

He stomped off, following Ariel and Christian. Hunter looked at Carter's body. The rain had washed the blood from the man's temple. Blue and black hues darkened around the left side of the head. Footprints surrounded the corpse. Talk about muddying up a crime scene. Hunter sighed, then bent down and hoisted Carter over his shoulder.

Paul joined Katie as she reached the edge of the tree line. Ariel and Christian broke into sight, supporting Orson between them, with Jerry sulking behind. Shadow barked, then ran ahead to the trio. Katie let out the breath she'd been holding as she spied her brother. Her heart lodged in her throat when she didn't see Hunter and Carter on their heels.

"Go help them," she said as she pushed on Paul's arm.

Paul moved to the trio, then took Ariel's place.

Katie shuffled back to the shanty, Shadow at her feet. Katie didn't know if Orson had been hurt again, but she knew he would be soaked. Carter could be injured as well, which would explain his and Hunter's delay.

Once inside the shanty, she added more wood to the fire, sending the flames shooting up. Smoke shifted as she stirred the embers, permeating the room with the inviting pull of warmth. She lifted the lid on the pot, releasing the steam and the enticing aroma of solid food. Her mouth watered.

"Let's go ahead and get him changed—he needs to be as dry and comfortable as possible." Christian's voice lumbered in the lean-to. "Ariel, can you grab a pair of pants and a sweatshirt and toss them to us in the tent?" Keeping an arm around Orson, he headed outside.

Jerry stomped into the room, his eyes holding a wild look.

Katie leaned against the table for balance. "What happened?"

"Carter got himself killed." He slumped against the wall, sliding down until he sat. His eyes went flat, emotionless as a corpse.

She gasped. "Carter's d-d-dead?" Raising her hand, she gripped her chin.

"Dead as a doorknob."

"B-But how?"

Jerry's eyes took on the appearance of someone under the influence of drugs, with his glazed-over stare. "I don't know. Why are you asking me?" He shoved to his feet as Ariel strode back into the room.

Ariel's eyes locked on Jerry. She popped her hands to her hips and glared. "So, what else can you tell us? What really happened out there?"

Jerry met Ariel's glare with one of his own. "I told you, I heard the old man, then I heard the screams. I tried to find him, but couldn't. When I finally did, he just laid there dead, like you saw."

"My question is why'd you go so far out to relieve yourself." Hunter stood in the doorway, water dripping from his hair and slipping down his chiseled face.

Katie laced her trembling hands in front of her. She willed her muscles to freeze, not to give into her foolish heart's demand to run to Hunter and embrace him.

Jerry lifted his upper lip into a sneer. "We didn't realize we'd gone so far. Carter needed some privacy." He narrowed his eyes. "At least, that's what he said."

"Uh-huh." Hunter shook his head—water flew from his dark curls, splattering the floor around him. "So it was Carter's idea to go that far? With Orson, an injured man? Sorry, I'm not buying it."

"What are you saying?" Jerry took three steps toward Hunter.

Katie sucked in air. Helpless to intervene, her heart thumped.

Hunter met Jerry in the middle of the lean-to. Standing toe-to-toe, Hunter pushed his face so close to Jerry's, they were only a breath apart. "I'm saying I don't think Carter wanted to go out that far. I think you did, for some other reason."

"What are you accusing me of?" Jerry punched a finger into Hunter's chest.

Hunter shoved Jerry. "Just what I'm saying, what I said before—I think you led him out there with the intent to hurt him."

Ariel moved swiftly between the men squaring off. She kept her back to Hunter, but pushed Jerry farther away. "Stop it. We need to figure out what happened." She stared a moment longer at Jerry, then faced Hunter. "Where'd you put the body?"

"I wrapped him up in a wet sleeping bag. He's at the back of the shanty. We'll move him out in the morning when we go."

The unspoken messages shooting from Hunter to Ariel made Katie's stomach turn.

Something definitely sparked between them. Even if she hadn't eavesdropped on their conversation, Katie would know by the way the two stared at one another.

Betrayal rose within her, waving like a red flag in front of a bull. She'd been played, and apparently, by a master. Her heart cracked as the waves of nausea crashed into her soul. How could she have let her heart trust again? Hadn't she learned her lesson?

Christian and Paul carried Orson into the room. Katie let out a long breath. She might've been played the fool, but now she knew better. Just having Christian there bolstered her resolve not to have her heart trampled on. Squaring her shoulders, she crossed the room with a limp and knelt before Orson. "How's your leg?"

His weathered face grimaced into a weak smile. "It hurts like the dickens."

"I'll rewrap your splint for you." She moved to retrieve the first-aid bag, but Paul laid it in her hand.

Gracing him with a smile of thanks, Katie turned back to Orson. Behind her, shuffling resonated throughout the room, followed by the clanking of the cast-iron pot. Another whiff of savory-smelling stew filled the air. Katie hastened in her care and attention. She needed food, but she needed answers more.

Katie finished wrapping Orson's shin, then stood. She wavered for a moment on her good foot. A strong arm, warming her though her sweater, wrapped around her shoulders and tugged her toward a wall of muscle. The masculine smell of Hunter nearly made her knees buckle.

Looking into Hunter's probing eyes, she licked her lips. She laid a hand on his chest, taking a brief moment to appreciate the ripples before pushing back. "I can do this."

She could do everything on her own, just like she'd done since her mother had abandoned her family.

Even though the loneliness threatened to rip her apart.

Hunter let Ariel diffuse the situation with Jerry. He knew better than to lose his temper—been trained not to let his emotions get the better of him. Yet, the stakes were higher than when he'd taken the job. He hadn't planned on his personal feelings being pulled into play. He hadn't counted on Katie Gallagher.

Glimpsing in her direction, he took in the details of shock and outrage marching across her face. A darkness filled her eyes as she stared at Jerry, narrowed when she looked at Ariel, and glistened with fury when she met his scrutiny. Somewhere between their stolen kisses and now, he'd done something to infuriate her. Something upsetting enough to make her stare with disdain as soon as their eyes met. His gut twisted.

Ariel handed him a bowl of stew. From habit, he took a bite. It scalded his tongue. Reflexively, he swallowed. The burning seared his throat down to his belly. He moved around the table and grabbed a water bottle from the table, then took huge gulps.

Beside him, Katie took a step back, stumbled, and would've fallen if he hadn't grabbed her.

He pulled her against him. The smell of rain clung to her hair as well as a trace of peppermint assaulted his nostrils. The warmth from her body next to his soothed the primal beast within who screamed for a kiss. Here—now—in front of everyone. Peering over her head, his eyes met Ariel's. Ariel arched a finely tweezed brow and gave a slight incline of her head.

Whirling around, Hunter lifted Katie from the ground and carried her outside. He set her down inside the tent's flap. Shadow rushed between them. He wedged the dog away with his calf.

Katie lifted her palms to his chest, pushing him away. Pain lurked in the depth of her eyes.

"We need to talk, Katie."

"I don't want to talk to you." She turned her face away from him.

"You need to listen."

"Let me go."

He held his hands out, flexing them into fists, but kept her pinned in place with his stare. "I think you've gotten the wrong idea somehow."

She shifted her weight. "The wrong idea? Gee, Hunter, how do you think I got that?"

Sarcasm dripped from her tongue, emblazing against his conscience. He swallowed while the logical part of his mind scrambled to find the right words to say. "I'm assuming you think something's going on between me and Ariel . . ."

"Really?" She crossed her arms, momentarily

throwing off her balance. She recovered quickly. Her face wrinkled into a disapproving glare. "Now why would I think that?"

"You have to listen to me." He laid a hand on her shoulder and fought to keep his voice even. He had to make her understand.

She shrugged off his touch. "No, I really don't. Matter-of-fact, I refuse to listen to anything more you have to say." Taking a wobbly step from the tent, Katie shoved past him.

His heart lay cold in his chest. On impulse, he grabbed her elbow, spun her around, then trapped her in his embrace.

Her eyes widened as he lowered his mouth to hers, capturing her lips.

Katie twisted her head, ending the barely-there kiss.

Tread carefully, my son.

The words bounced around in Hunter's brain. Wanting more—needing more of Katie, Hunter also understood his priorities. Battling his conscience, he took a step back. His gaze danced over her face and stopped when they met her stare.

Her face flushed, but her eyes remained dark. He recognized the revived emotion lurking in her beautiful silver eyes. He swallowed. "Katie . . ." His voice cracked as he whispered her name.

The mood shifted . . . her wall slammed back into place, barricading her emotions. She shook her head and pushed away with more force than necessary. "No. Don't confuse me." Tears coated her irises.

"There's something I need to tell you . . . something I need to explain." He took a step to close the distance between them, his hand jutting out to touch her. Which, now that he stopped to think, might not be a good idea. He lacked in the self-control department around her. She did something strange to his senses, made him want more, need more.

She hobbled backward, holding her hands out in front of her. "No, I don't want to hear it. You've proven you can jack around with my attraction. Are you proud?" Not giving him a chance to respond, she continued in her litany. "I can't do this. I won't. I don't know what your involvement with Ariel is, but frankly, it doesn't matter. It's none of my business what you two do. But don't think I'm going to keep it from Christian. He deserves to know Ariel's playing him for a fool, just like you played me."

He reached for her, but grabbed air.

Katie slapped his hand away. Hard. The stinging of his flesh broke him from his heady trance. His voice strangled. "Katie, wait . . ."

She pushed him aside, limping toward the shanty. "Just leave me alone, Hunter. Don't even talk to me. Ever."

Seventeen

"You need to listen. About me and Ariel . . ."

She jabbed a finger into his chest. "Stop. I told you I don't want to hear it. Do you have a hearing problem? You two may be into that swinging scene or something, but leave me out of your sick little games. Do you understand? Save it. I'm not interested." Katie narrowed her eyes. "If you so much as get into my space again, I'll sic Shadow on you."

At the mention of his name, the dog shot to her side. The fur on his neck bristled.

"But, Katie . . ."

Without bothering to reply, she turned and shuffled closer to the lean-to. Her heart slipped and lay smashed at her feet. Tears threatening to consume her, she changed direction, heading toward the small clearing left of the shanty.

Katie lowered herself to the ground, ignoring the moisture seeping through the denim and soaking her skin. She pushed away the discomfort of the cold air. Drawing her legs up to her chest, she then laid her forehead against her knees. Cold, wet, and alone—she cried.

Hunter had betrayed Katie's trust. Crushed her heart and left her emotions in shambles. Hadn't she tried to keep her distance, to stay away from people who could gain the power to hurt her?

A hand on her shoulder made her jump.

Christian lowered himself beside her. "Are you okay, Katie-cat?"

She rested her head against his chest, letting his warmth comfort her. The reassuring *thwarmp* of his heart echoed in her ears. Katie sniffed. "Yeah. I'm okay."

"You sure?" He twisted and used his knuckles to lift her chin. "I don't think I've seen you cry since Gabe and I hid your clothes when you went skinny-dipping."

Katie let out a cough-laugh. "I still can't believe you did that to me. I was only in the seventh grade and there were boys jumping into the river." She wiped her eyes with shaking hands and smacked him playfully. "You guys sure were the gruesome twosome."

Chuckling, Christian tightened his hold on her. "Nah, just having fun."

"Yeah, right—at my expense." She jabbed him in the side with her elbow, but not too hard.

"Want to talk about it?"

The compassion in his voice nearly made fresh tears spring from her eyes. She sucked in short, ragged breaths. "I'm not ready. Not yet."

"Okay." He hugged her tight. "Just know I'm here when you're ready."

She peered into his eyes. "Thanks, Christian."

She planted a soft peck on his cheek, then snuggled against him.

"Katie-cat, I love you."

She searched her memory. Had he ever uttered those words to her before? She glanced at him.

His dark-as-the-river eyes, so much like their mother's, shone on her. He smiled. "I mean it. I love you, sis."

This time, she wouldn't deny the cleansing tears. She blinked and let them fall freely down her cheeks. "I love you, too, Christian."

Tucking her head under his chin, her brother held her, rocking her. Katie felt safe and secure in his arms. She needed to tell him about Ariel and Hunter . . . needed to warn him, but she wanted this rare and tender moment to linger.

"Hey . . ." His voice boomed in her ear.

She startled, peeking at him again. "What?"

"Check it out—it's stopped raining." He smiled, then hoisted himself to his feet, pulling her up with him. "Looks like we'll be right on schedule to head out tomorrow."

"Yeah, it does." Good news, right? So, why did her heart feel so heavy?

"Let's go tell the others and start getting things packed up. We need to get moving at first light."

Katie leaned on him for support, then stopped. "What?"

"Thanks, Christian. I needed you."

His returning grin and warming hug sent a feeling of peace deep into her.

Hunter followed Katie into the lean-to, his heart thrumming as it sunk to his gut. He'd blown it—bigtime! In his bumbling, plow-through manner, he'd isolated her. Now, she wouldn't even listen to an explanation. His stomach turned.

Someone had lit two little oil lamps that sat on the table, the light casting odd shapes on the rough walls.

Katie whispered to Christian before turning around and speaking to both Paul and Orson. From his place across the room, Hunter couldn't hear what she said, but her seductive voice drifted on the breeze, stirring his desperation. Katie kept her eyes focused on who she spoke to, never letting her gaze sweep his way.

He clenched his jaw to avoid snapping—at Paul, who gaped at her with clear adoration—at Orson, who received her gentle hands on his wounds, and—at her, for not even giving him a fighting chance. Without even saying as much as good-night in his direction, she pushed by and hobbled to the tent.

Now Ariel spoke to Christian in hushed tones, their heads bent close together. Hunter eased himself to the doorway of the lean-to. Once Ariel kissed Christian on the cheek, she snagged a bottle of water and one of the small lamps, then headed toward the tent. Hunter grabbed her arm and pulled her around to the side of the shanty, opposite the tent.

"What?" she whispered.

He lowered his head so his mouth hovered right beside her ear. "I don't trust Jerry. Keep your piece handy tonight."

"I know. What about you?"

Shaking his head, Hunter watched the last rays of the sun disappear behind the trees in the distance. "I can't risk having mine at the ready. I've got it in my sleeping bag, but that's not where I normally like to keep it."

She laughed, but kept her voice down. "Not many people use a Beretta as a teddy bear."

He ran a hand over his hair, pulling the longer bangs from his eyes. "Just be alert."

"Okay." Ariel laid a hand on his arm and took a step. His grip on her elbow tightened and she peered up at him, a questioning look in her eyes.

"About Katie . . ."

She plopped her hands on her hips and tilted her head. "Yeah?"

"She, uh, thinks there's something physical going on between you and me."

Ariel snorted, only to have him shush her. "Between us? Is that why I've been getting the drop-dead-please glares?"

"It appears she overheard one of our conversations."

Instantly, Ariel's stance stiffened. "Which one? Does she know?"

He shook his head. "No, I don't think she understands. Right now, she has the wrong idea about us. She thinks we're a set of players, and that you're leading her brother on for some odd reason, and that I'm doing the same with her."

"So, the job is still intact?"

"Yeah, seems that way."

"But?"

Hunter lowered his brow. "But what?"

"The tone of your voice implied a but coming up."

He smiled. Ariel knew him too well. For five years they'd worked side by side, growing attuned with one another. He let out a long breath. "I almost told her."

Ariel's jaw dropped. "But . . . you can't do that. You don't have authorization to make that kind of decision."

Tilting his head back, he stared at the dark, starless sky. The wind had died with the dis-appearance of the rain, but a soft breeze kissed his face.

"Hunter!" The harsh whisper held a note of accusation.

His eyes locked with Ariel's. "I know, I know. But, it's just . . ."

"You're falling for her, aren't you?"

Staring at the ground, Hunter pressed his lips together. He lifted his head and slowly nodded. Sometimes he considered having a partner who knew him so well a bad thing. This could be one of those times.

She let out a loud sigh. "You know better, Hunter. We've been through this time and again."

Hunter's defenses kicked in and he snorted. "Don't tell me you're only playing the part with her brother." He hitched up his eyebrow.

Even in the dark, he could see the color spreading across her face before she glanced down. "It's a job. We'll be out of here in the morning. You'd do well to remember that, Hunter. We're gone tomorrow."

"I know, but I can't help it, Ariel. I didn't plan it." He fisted his hand in the back of his hair and pulled. He welcomed the stinging pain to his scalp. He needed to feel something right now, anything besides his heart splintering apart.

She sighed again and patted his chest. "You'll get over it. Let's do our job and get out of here, okay?"

He nodded, pushing the knowledge of his departure as far from his mind as he could.

"We'll concentrate on getting the job done, right, partner?" Her voice carried the sound of needed assurance. "We can't slip up, Hunter. We've already had casualties, and the boss isn't going to be too happy about that."

He smiled and placed a kiss on her temple. "Yeah, I know."

"Night, Hunter." She gave his arm a final squeeze, then moved toward the tent.

"Be safe, Ariel."

Katie stepped back from the tent's flap, using the darkness for cover as she moved to her sleeping bag. Why had she watched them, silhouetted by the swaying lamp, making them look like a Hallmark romance card?

How had she become such a sucker for punishment? Even though she couldn't hear their conversation, she couldn't mistake their intimate touching: hands on shoulders, arms, chests. And he kissed her. The slight kiss he'd planted on Ariel's temple spoke volumes to Katie's heart—told her he cared deeply for Ariel.

That knowledge alone drowned out the hope in Katie's soul.

She unwrapped her ankle, inspected her injury by touch, then lifted the bandage to wrap it again. Katie winced as she pulled the Coban material tight.

Ariel slipped inside the tent. She set the lamp on the floor and sat on her sleeping bag, across from Katie, watching her.

Even in the dimness, and without looking up, Katie felt Ariel's eyes on her. She sighed as she secured the bandage. "What?"

"How's your ankle?"

"Better." Katie stretched out on her sleeping bag, wiggling the toes of her foot to ensure the bandage wouldn't cut off her circulation.

"Good. At least it stopped raining."

Irritation coiled around Katie's mind like a worn-out spring. She released an exasperated sigh. "What's on your mind, Ariel? This small-talk is boring me."

"Getting right to the point, aren't you?"

"No sense in just chewing the fat. We both know there's no love lost between us. Personally, I'd rather go to sleep." She reached behind her head and released her braid, running her fingers through the wet and stringy strands. "But it seems you have a bee in your bonnet about something, so spit it out."

Ariel fixed her stare on Katie and lowered her voice. "Hunter tells me you suspect there's something going on between him and m—"

"I really don't care, Ariel. Except that you're leading my brother on, and I can't allow that to continue." She exhaled slowly, pushing back her own feelings of jealousy. How Christian, or Hunter for that matter, could be attracted to such a high-maintenance woman like Ariel went beyond her level of comprehension.

"But that's just it, there's nothing between me and Hunter. I mean, well . . ."

"Right." Katie crossed her arms over her chest.

"Look, it doesn't matter to me, you two can play whatever sick game you enjoy, but you leave me and Christian out of it." She curled her hands into fists, tightening her arm muscles so much her arms shook. Her shoulders tensed. "Understand?" Her rage swarmed the more she thought things through.

"What's between me and Christian is—"

"Over." Katie spoke louder than she'd intended. The woman made her so mad, Katie wanted to slap her pretty face. Punch her perfect nose. Pound her tiny figure into the ground. The mental image made Katie smile, despite her anger and envy. Right on the heels of righteous anger for her brother's sake, followed her misery over allowing herself to care for a womanizer.

She let out a huff. "Tomorrow, when we get back to the lodge, I'm going to tell Christian everything about your little schemes. You'll regret that you and Mr. Malone decided to tangle with the Gallaghers."

"Really?" Through the heavy air in the tent, the smile behind the words came shining through. "I think you're in for a big surprise."

She didn't like the sound of Ariel's baiting tone. "Don't push me, Ariel. I'm not in the mood for your cockiness. I'm tired and not inclined to stomp you into the ground like you so deserve." She flexed her fingers. "But, I will if you insist."

Ariel chuckled, the sarcasm penetrating the

tension between the women. "I don't think so."

Katie sat straight and shifted to face the opposing side of the tent. "Oh, I do. Even on the worst day of my life, and you on your best day, I could still take you. So, don't tempt me."

Ariel didn't have time to respond as Shadow jumped up from his place on the foot of Katie's sleeping bag. He growled from deep in his chest and throat.

The hairs on Katie's arms stood at attention, then goosebumps prickled her skin.

Shadow pushed to the tent's flap. He lowered his head, growled again, before letting out a distinctively warning bark.

Katie shifted toward the tent door. Ariel shuffled around on her sleeping bag and put out the lamp. Katie slapped her shoulder and whispered, "Shh!"

Rustling in the bushes shattered the frogs' songs from the trees. The noise of sluggish movement on wet ground sounded close to the tent.

In the darkness, Ariel moved to Katie's side. The two stood still and listened. Whoever—whatever lurked out there, sounded like it moved closer.

Shadow barked twice, his alert bark.

Every nerve ending stood at attention as Katie moved her hands to snap for the dog to get to her side. Too late . . . Shadow snarled once more before shooting out of the tent, barking his head off.

Eighteen

The clamor of rushing blood pounded against Katie's ears. Hearing Shadow's warning barks, followed by his deep growls, wrenched her free from her fear-induced paralysis. The adrenaline pumped through her veins at class-five speeds as she pushed back the tent flap and rushed into the blanket of night, ignoring the pain in her ankle.

Ariel placed her hand on Katie's shoulder. Katie glanced at the other woman, determined to shove her aside, and recognized the flash of steel in Ariel's hand.

A gun!

Why did Ariel, of all people, have a gun?

Like a frame-by-frame projector, Katie's mind clicked through her memory bank. No way Ariel could've known about the gun she'd taken from Paul, much less known where she'd hidden it. And the gun still lay tucked inside her bedroll, which laid somewhere in the Gauley River, lost in the mudslide. So this gun had to be Ariel's. The notion clipped in Katie's mind, numbing her with questions.

Ariel lifted the handgun, keeping it close to her body. She nudged Katie's shoulder with hers. "Hunter's sleeping right inside the shanty door. Go get him. Tell him to come armed," she whispered.

Katie willed her legs to move, but her feet refused to budge, as if they were rooted deep into the ground.

Shadow barked, this time with a high-pitched tone. A thundering growl responded. No way could that be a dog.

Ignoring Ariel's tugs, Katie pushed herself forward, rushing toward the sound of Shadow. She rounded the side of the tent. What she saw sent icicles of dread into the pit of her gut.

A fully mature black bear stood on his hind legs. His teeth glaring as he swatted at Shadow, who darted in, out, and around the bear's legs.

"Shadow!" Katie's voice came out merely as a hoarse whisper. The dog didn't turn his head to acknowledge her presence. Snapping her fingers twice, Katie called him again. Shadow continued to torment the bear.

Ariel appeared at Katie's elbow. She spread her legs and lifted her gun. Its muzzle pointed at the bear.

Katie laid a hand over Ariel's extended arms. "No!"

Ariel glanced at Katie, but didn't lower her weapon.

"The shot will only enrage the bear—it can't bring it down." Katie squatted. "Shadow, come!" She pulled a stern tone into her command.

Shadow turned to look at her. In that moment,

the bear's massive paw arced to his side, then descended, gaining momentum.

Her heart jumping, Katie screamed. "Shadow!"

The bear's claw made contact with the canine's side. The Blue Heeler yelped a fraction of a second before he bounced across the way, striking the ground with a sickening thud.

Resisting the almost overpowering urge to run to her beloved dog, Katie rose and gripped Ariel's arm tightly. "We need to back away, slowly."

Still keeping the gun aimed at the bear, Ariel took a step backward.

The bear dropped to all fours and pawed the ground. Mud sloshed up, scattering mucky droplets about five feet in surrounding directions. Opening its mouth wide, the bear let out a long, chest-quivering roar.

Katie took a step backward, ignoring the pain from the weight she put on her injured ankle. She jerked Ariel back with her.

The bear growled and slapped the ground once more before taking a lunging stance.

Recognizing the bear's position, Katie pulled Ariel harder. Her balance tilted. She let go and fell flat on her behind.

Ariel hunkered beside her, placed a hand under her elbow, and tugged her arm.

The bear roared, then charged.

Katie opened her mouth and pulled a scream

from the bottom of her lungs. Her shout split the night's silence.

Hunter bolted upright. Without taking the time to process the shriek that yanked him from a restless sleep, he reached into the bottom of his sleeping bag and retrieved his Beretta. Shoving himself free of the thick bag, Hunter rose, then raced out the door.

Weapon in hand, he sped past the open tent, intent on finding Katie. Her scream, and he knew deep inside his gut it'd been Katie who shrieked, tore his insides apart.

Please, God, keep her safe.

He rounded the tent. His heart stopped beating for a moment, then raced. A big bear rushed. Katie sprawled on the ground, Ariel crouching beside her.

Hunter planted his feet in the saturated earth, lifted his gun, took aim, and fired.

In his peripheral vision, he saw Ariel stand, take a targeting position, and open fire alongside him.

Bullets dug into the bear's flesh. It yowled and stopped. Rearing up on its hind legs, the big bear opened its mouth and roared. A row of sharp, white teeth glistened in the moon's soft light.

Hunter continued to fire his weapon until he'd discharged all bullets. Two more shots thumped into the bear from Ariel's gun.

The massive bear swayed, leaning heavily to

the right, only to swing toward the left. Time stood still as the animal bellowed and clawed at the air, then turned and lumbered off, leaving behind a trail of blood in the mud.

Hunter shoved his Beretta into the waistband of his jeans, then scooped Katie into his arms. "Let's get out of here," he told Ariel before stomping back into the lean-to.

Katie's fists pummeled his chest. "No! Put me down. Shadow's out there. He's hurt." Her words came out in a rush, tumbling atop each other. The wounded, vulnerable tone in her voice gave him pause.

He set her down inside the threshold, then turned to Ariel. "Where's the dog?"

Ariel's trembling hand pointed toward a clump of trees. "The bear tossed him over there somewhere." Her voice hiccupped. He hesitated. He'd never seen anything rattle Ariel. Not in the past five years. Hunter tweaked her nose. "You okay?"

She nodded.

"Reload in case that bear comes back." He gave his partner a wink.

"Move out of my way!" Katie shoved against him. "I have to get my dog."

"I'll get him." Hunter turned in the direction Ariel indicated. He stopped and glanced over his shoulder. His eyes latched onto Katie's. "You stay inside."

"He's my dog," she replied while crossing the doorway.

He gripped her shoulder tightly. "You're hurt. I'll get him. Stop being so stubborn and stay put." She opened her mouth, and he met her with a kiss.

He crushed her lips, and his hands framed her face. He felt her soften under his embrace, and backed away.

She blinked several times.

Turning, Hunter stalked into the darkness to find the dog. He shook his head. Even when obviously scared spitless, the woman had to argue with him. The only effective way he'd found to stop her bickering was to kiss her thoroughly. Hunter smiled. Then again, her kisses left him senseless as well.

Whimpering drew Hunter toward the largest tree in the small thicket. Treading softly, he crept along. "Shadow? Boy?" He scanned the ground around the area. Nothing caught his eye.

He turned and took two paces into the trees. A weak whine erupted to his right. He crouched lower as he moved toward the sound. "Shadow? Where are you, boy?"

A slight movement snared his attention. A hump shivered, barely noticeable in the thick black of darkness. He dropped to his knees beside the dog.

"Hey, boy. You okay?" Hunter fought to keep his voice calm as he laid his hand on the trembling fur. Rubbing his fingers together, he gauged the moistness. Shadow had to be hurt badly from the amount of blood congealing on his fur.

Hunter slipped a hand under the dog's limp body.

Shadow growled, then followed immediately with a whimper.

"I know, boy. I'm not gonna hurt you. I'm taking you to Katie."

As if the dog understood his words, he remained still and quiet while Hunter lifted him. Standing, Hunter kept the Blue Heeler clutched close to his chest. He tried to walk steady and slow, jarring the animal as little as possible.

Once he got within five feet of the lean-to, Katie rushed out to meet him. Tears streaked her face and continued to fall as she held out her arms to take the canine. She buried her face next to the dog's muzzle and crooned.

Hunter transferred the now whining dog into his mistress' waiting arms, then wrapped his arm around Katie and guided her into the shanty. The rest of the men huddled around the table, with the lamp relit, whispering to one another.

Katie moved toward the first sleeping bag. Hunter assisted her as she lowered the dog to his bedroll. Her hands ran over the dog's body. "The first-aid kit is in the tent. Grab it, will you?"

Pushing to his feet, Hunter stood and studied her for a moment. Unashamed tears caked her face as she caressed and coddled her pet. Something inside of him snapped. I'm falling in love with her! He stiffened as his mind searched his heart and blared the ensuing results.

"Please get it for me." Katie's silver eyes shone with moisture.

His heart swelled. Nodding, he turned to go to the tent.

Katie cleaned Shadow's wounds as best she could with the dwindling first-aid supplies. Shadow whined and stared at her with his soulful brown eyes before finally drifting off to sleep. She rose and stood at the doorway of the lean-to, looking out into the night. Moonlight flooded the area, casting shadows that looked like stalking cats ready to pounce across the side of the shanty. Her heart ached while she rewound the events in her mind.

An arm wrapped around her waist. She looked into Christian's concerned face. "Shadow going to be okay?" His voice softened with concern.

She let out a long, breathy sigh. "I think so. The bear's claws left some pretty deep gashes in his side, but I think they'll be fine as long as they don't get infected." Katie ran a hand through her hair, separating the strands with her fingers. "His back leg is fractured, maybe broken. I splinted it, but he needs a vet to set it properly."

Christian kissed her temple. "I'm sorry. I know how much you love Shadow. He'll be okay."

Katie leaned against the doorframe. Her mind continued to churn. "Christian, Ariel and Hunter have guns," she whispered.

His audible sigh loomed heavy on her heart. "Let's step into the tent, okay?" He glanced over his shoulder, as if checking to ensure no one watched them. "I'll tell you everything."

"I'm really tired of all this cloak-and-dagger stuff. If you know what's going on, tell me here."

"It's not that easy, sis." He pulled her next to him, hip to hip, and took a step toward the tent. "Come on, Katie-cat."

Dread propelling her each step of the way, Katie allowed Christian to help her into the tent, away from the others. She sighed, lowered herself to her sleeping bag, situated her injured foot as comfortably as she could, and stared up at her brother. "Shoot."

Instead of sitting on Ariel's bedroll, Christian lit the little lamp on the floor, then took a seat next to her. "There's really nothing going on between me and Ariel. Well, not yet."

Katie guffawed. "Yeah, sure, right." She lightly flicked his hands, which dangled in his lap. "But, Christian, you need to know this. There's something going on between Ariel and Hunter." She gripped his hand and squeezed it. "I've seen them together. I've overheard their conversations."

"It isn't like that, Katie." He muttered as he stared at the ground.

"Yes there is. I've seen him kiss her."

Christian's head shot up. "He kissed her?"

"Well, he kissed her forehead, but still."

Chuckling, Christian nudged her arm, then leaned against her. "That's because they're partners."

"Partners?" Katie wrinkled her nose as her mind tried to wrap around what that implied.

"Yeah, partners. With initials—as in F.B.I."

She sucked in a quick breath and held it until her lungs screamed for release. Letting it out in a fast swoosh, Katie's heartbeat sped again. "But . . . I thought . . ."

"Listen, I shouldn't even be telling you this, but the FBI has evidence that money is being laundered through Lassiter James Accounting. Hunter went in undercover six months ago to try and pinpoint who is involved. They narrowed down their list of suspects to the people in the boat."

Katie pursed her lips, letting the information soak in. "But, Ariel . . ."

"She's Hunter's partner, but the firm is a good ole boys' club. They couldn't slip her in. So, she's been working in the background, following up the leads Hunter discovers."

"But you . . . she . . ."

Christian smiled. "When she showed up at the lodge, I didn't have a clue who she was. The FBI had gotten together a small group of agents to join

Ariel to back up Hunter. The only problem was, she came in the night before, which had her beating the weather, but the other agents' flights were canceled. When Gabe and I canceled my group, she had to come clean and tell us everything." He shook his head. "Gabe's beyond furious at the danger Hunter put you in without telling you."

Hitching an eyebrow, she tilted her head.

"I know, I know. Gabe and I couldn't let you fend for yourself, but the river wouldn't allow us to follow you. We knew you'd head this way when you realized the river had risen. Ariel almost had to put Gabe under arrest to stop him from coming. So, she came with me."

A thought niggled hard against Katie's mind. She ran her hand through her hair again. "What do you know about the gunshot the night the group arrived? The one you claimed you didn't hear."

Christian shuddered. "Ariel had tried to sneak around to meet up with Hunter, but got turned around in the woods. She met a snake, thus the gunshot."

"Oh."

"So, you see, there's nothing between Hunter and Ariel. At least, not like you're thinking. They're just partners." Reaching over, he tugged her hair. "They're the good guys, Katie-cat."

A sudden flare of anger flashed through her. "Hunter put me, as well as those men, in danger for what?"

"It wasn't like that, Katie. According to Ariel, they're working on a money-laundering scam. Nothing dangerous was supposed to happen. Hunter was taking advantage of a situation to see if he could determine who might be involved."

Using his shoulder, Katie hoisted herself up. She let the feeling of betrayal circle her heart, fanning her fury. "But it did. And now, two men are dead. Dead, Christian. Do you get that?" She pointed her finger in his face. "It could have been me. All for what? To uncover some two-bit criminal?"

"Keep your voice down." Christian scrambled to his feet and stood beside her. "They're pretty certain the big-shot running the show is Jerry. Up until this trip, they didn't know if he or Paul called the shots."

"I don't want to keep my voice down. I've been lied to, again and again, and now Shadow's hurt because I wasn't told, and I got stuck out here in the middle of nowhere with a deranged money launderer." She pushed Christian's shoulder. "You, of all people, know how I feel about deceptions. You should have told me as soon as you got here."

"Katie-cat—"

"Don't try to patronize me. I'm done with it. Hunter . . . Ariel . . . everyone can all go play super spies with guns and violence somewhere else. I had my fill of secrets years ago. Count me out."

She jerked the flap back and headed to the lean-to, chewing her bottom lip. The urge to bury her face in Shadow's fur nearly choked her. She needed time alone with her thoughts, with no one telling her more lies.

Lies . . . lies . . . lies—she'd tasted the bitter sting of rejection and refused to allow herself to burn with betrayal and deception again.

Why hadn't her brother told her the truth immediately? Hadn't Christian suffered, too, from their mother's lies of loving them? Did he forget so easily that she upped and walked out? Just left them. Couldn't he see how deceptions, of any form, ripped lives apart?

She made her way into the shanty, her emotions erupting like volcanic lava, burning her and leaving her raw.

Nineteen

Hunter looked up from the anxious faces surrounding the table as Katie stumbled in. She didn't so much as glance in their direction. She dropped to her knees beside Shadow lying on Hunter's sleeping bag. His heart clenched at the sight of her hunched over her injured pet. Giving himself a mental shake, he returned his gaze to the men around the table.

"So, we're in no more danger from that bear?" The color had yet to return to Paul's oval face.

"We injured it, but didn't kill him." Hunter spoke to Paul, but let his eyes drift over the other faces.

Orson rubbed his head, pain still etched in his weathered face, then smoothed the frazzled ends of his thinning hair. Deep in the crow's feet at the corner of his eyes, fear.

Hunter experienced a fleeting sensation of guilt. The old tax attorney had been the one to suspect the money-laundering scam occurring at Lassiter James and contacted the FBI. On his recommendation, his alone, the firm hired Hunter. He could tell Orson now regretted his decision. The old man had yet to spill the details of what had happened to Carter. Maybe if Hunter could get him alone for a few minutes . . .

Jerry, on the other hand, appeared as if nothing were amiss. His eyes had locked on Hunter's weapon, still snuggling against the small of his back. Hunter knew the game was up—Jerry suspected too much, and with him and Ariel having to draw their Berettas, his instincts and training told him it was only a matter of time before Jerry realized the gig was busted, if he didn't already. Hunter would have to keep a close eye on him, a very close eye indeed. Maybe Jerry would get sloppy and make a mistake. A mistake that would lead to his downfall. Just one slipup, one mention of how the money-laundering chain went, and Hunter would be able to act. Now, however, the stakes had been raised. Someone was desperate to keep their involvement a secret. Even if it meant murdering innocent people.

Under Hunter's analysis, Jerry jutted out his chin. "Since you gave me so much grief about my gun, how about you explaining yours and super-chic's, here?"

Ariel spoke up. "Christian and I brought them when we came. For protection." Years of training had served her well . . . she didn't even blink an eye as she told the bald-faced lie.

Hunter let out a sigh when Jerry merely harrumphed, but made no further comment. Christian lumbered to the table. He leaned his elbows against the wood, resting his chin in his hands, and scuffed the floor with his toe. Christian's gaze lifted to meet Hunter's, seemed to understand the unspoken questions lurking in Hunter's eyes, and gave a slight shake of his head.

So, Christian had told Katie and she hadn't understood. Hunter's nerves twisted like a wind chime in a category-five hurricane. He wanted to force her to listen, to understand, but he needed to do his job first. He cut his stare to Ariel, who responded with a casual shrug. The whole situation didn't bode well for him.

Christian cleared his throat. "We need to settle down for what's left of the night, guys. We have a long hike at first light. We'll need our rest."

Hunter ran his hands through his hair, which had finally dried.

"Will we be able to make it out of here?" Paul's eyes blinked in the dim room.

"It's a steep climb, but totally do-able," Christian answered.

Clapping his hands together, Hunter nodded. "So, let's get what rest we can."

Paul and Christian automatically went to Orson's side and helped him back to his bedroll. Jerry glared at Hunter for a moment longer, then pulled a smirk across his face before turning to strut to his sleeping bag.

Ariel hesitated. "What about Katie, Hunter?"

"She needs her rest. Her ankle's got to be hurting and she's had an emotional evening."

Christian returned to the table, tossing an arm over Ariel's shoulders. His voice hummed barely above a whisper. "I tried to explain it all to Katie, but she's hurt. She feels betrayed—that you lied to her, and I didn't tell her as soon as I could. You need to know, Katie has some issues with betrayal and abandonment. If you had been up-front about the situation, maybe two men would still be alive and Shadow wouldn't have been hurt." He dropped his arm and traced a groove in the table with his fingernail. "She's pretty mad."

Stiffening his spine, Hunter forced himself to stay in take-charge-agent mode. "She'll get used to it."

Looking up, Christian let out a dry chuckle.

"You don't know Katie very well then. She can hold on to her temper for a long time. A real long time." He glanced at his sister before looking back at Hunter. "Trust me, I know."

Ariel patted Christian's hand. "Well, the damage is done. Hunter's right, we need our rest to hike out of here in the morning. I'm turning in." She stood on tip-toe and planted a kiss on Christian's cheek. "It'll all come out in the wash."

She strode to the tent, the lamp casting warmth through the canvas material. Hunter sighed and looked at Katie's brother. "We need to get Katie to turn in, too."

Christian snorted. "Good luck with that. She ain't gonna leave Shadow." He stared at his sister, hovering over the sleeping animal. "That dog's been her one constant in life—ever since Dad died. He's her best friend."

"We have to try."

"Uh, no, we don't." He gave an impish grin. "You can. I've already had my Katie-chewing today and am not in the mood for another round. I'm going to bed."

Hunter couldn't help but smile as Christian trekked to his bedroll and plopped down. His gaze drifted back to Katie, leaning across his own sleeping bag. Desire and despair warred in his heart as she ran her hand over the dog's back, over and over again. He swallowed, then moved toward her.

He knelt beside Katie, his attention focused on the dog. "He'll be okay," he whispered as she petted the animal.

"I hope so." Her voice came out cracked, broken. The sound made his heart thud harder. She sniffled. "I don't know what I'd do without him."

Switching his gaze to her eyes, Hunter couldn't stop himself from tucking the hair back from her face, slipping it behind her ear. The first time he'd seen her hair down, not in a braid or ponytail, and it made his breath catch in his throat. Its long and luxurious length felt like smooth silk against his calloused hands. He swallowed against the desire to bury his fingers in its thickness. "He'll be fine. He's sleeping."

"I know." She wiped the tears from her face and looked up. She licked her lips. "Um, thanks for going to get him."

He smiled, barely lifting the corners of his mouth. "I wouldn't have left him out there." His eyes settled on her mouth. The way she chewed her bottom lip. He stared back at the dog, ordering the demons of his mind to back off. He let out a pent-up breath. "Christian said he told you the truth."

The worry eased from her expression, only to be replaced by another emotion. Which was it—pain or disgust, he couldn't tell. "He did." She dropped her gaze to Shadow.

"And?" He held his breath.

Cold eyes flashed back to his. "And it doesn't make a difference. You lied to me, right from the beginning." Although she kept her voice low, her tone left no room for misconstruing her displeasure. "I can't tolerate liars—I won't."

"But, Katie, I had to. This is my job. Surely you can understand that?" He worked to keep his voice down so the others across the room couldn't hear them.

"No, I can't. I can't comprehend why you felt it necessary to keep me in the dark. Ariel let Christian in on this little scheme. I was the one in the boat. Shouldn't I have been forewarned?" She ran a thumb over the side of her chin. "The damage is already done. Two lives gone, and me, Orson and Shadow all injured." Her stare pierced his consciousness. "Isn't that enough?"

Hunter ran a hand through his hair, feeling the coarseness in contrast to the softness of hers. "Looking back now, maybe I should have. But I get my orders from my supervisor, and I had my instructions not to tell you."

She snorted, then stroked the dog's head. "That's no excuse and you know it. You could have told me at any time." She spoke so quietly, he had to concentrate to hear her. Her eyes slipped to his face, her expression unreadable. "I don't like being lied to."

"But that's not all, is it?" He leaned forward,

intentionally invading her personal space. "What's really bugging you, Katie?"

"That you lied to me."

"There's more than that. I didn't exactly lie to you, just didn't tell you everything. But you're more upset than only that. Tell me what's really going on."

Her eyes widened before narrowing into tiny slits. "You played me, Hunter. Played with my emotions, led me on with your smoldering stares and breathless kisses. All the while knowing you were here to do a job and get out. To leave me . . . abandon me when you'd accomplished your mission." Tears pooled in her flickering eyes. "I don't like to be messed with like that. You may get a kick out of doing that on all your jobs, assignments, whatever, but I don't. It's not fair."

"It wasn't a game to me." His voice thickened, a heaviness masking his tone. Never letting his eyes move from hers, Hunter touched her face. "Never a game. Katie, I've—"

Katie pushed his hand away. "I don't believe you. I can't deal with this right now." Her attention focused back on her pet. "I have to take care of Shadow."

He let out a frustrated sigh. Would the woman ever stop putting walls around her feelings? She was soft and sensitive. She was so attuned to her pet and treated her brother with a gentle firmness.

Hunter wanted a place in her heart and to lead her back to God's love and mercy, but she threw an icy stare at him instead. "Well, we need to get some shut-eye for the hike out tomorrow."

"Will you help me move Shadow to the tent?"

"He's resting fine here. Why don't you let him stay?"

"But . . ." Her eyes widened and she shook her head. "Where will you sleep? He can't be kicked or anything."

"I'll grab one of the bedrolls Christian and Ariel brought." He touched her shoulder, wanting to hug her, needing to get across that his feelings for her were genuine, but understanding she needed time to sort out her emotions. "It'll be okay."

Katie finally nodded. "You're right. I guess he shouldn't be moved." She laid her palms on the ground and pushed up.

Hunter stood, helping her to stand. He suddenly wanted to tell her all his hopes and dreams, but knew she'd blow him off. His body tensed, each muscle tightening in the battle between his heart and his mind. He had to fight his personal battle of restraint.

Something indefinable lurked behind her eyes as she stared at him. A shudder coursed through her body, breaking the spell she'd cast over Hunter. Tossing a final glance at Shadow, she moved past him to the tent, not offering him another word.

He waited until he heard the zipper close before

crossing the room to get a musty sleeping bag. Paul snored softly from his bag next to Orson. The tax attorney's breathing echoed harshly against the dark silence of the lean-to. Christian looked up as Hunter passed. "She still mad?"

Hunter raised a brow and nodded. "Pretty much, yeah."

Christian's chuckle, while low as to not disturb the others, reverberated loudly in Hunter's skull. "I figured. She does like to hold on to her anger."

Squatting beside Christian's sleeping bag, Hunter tilted his head. "You said that earlier. Any tips on breaking through that wall of hers?"

"You'd do better to ask Gabe. He's always been the one who's able to slip under her guard, not me."

"Any advice at all?" Hunter hated the desperation prevalent in his voice.

"Don't push her. Let her work through her emotions in her mind first." Christian shifted around in the bedroll. "Katie's a complicated girl, has been ever since our mother died. Well, Mom disappeared. Dad waited seven years and had her declared legally dead. Katie was caught in the crossfire then. She has a lot of issues hidden beneath the surface. Let her figure it out. If you press her on it, you'll lose."

Wait . . . the sage advice Hunter did *not* want to hear. Waiting was the wind gusting down halls, slamming every door of opportunity. Had his opportunity passed?

He stood. "Thanks."

"No problem. Good luck, you'll need it."

Hunter crossed the room, then laid the sleeping bag next to his, where Shadow slept soundly. He stretched out on the thick fabric, arranging the room in his mind, now a force of habit. Paul and Orson slept against the north wall—Christian slept closest to the table, on the west side—Jerry's rhythmic breathing sounded against the east wall—and Hunter laid closest to the door on the south side. Come morning, they'd be up at first light. He needed his sleep. If only the taunting image of Katie would stop controlling his thoughts.

Katie scrambled into her sleeping bag, moving as silently as she could. Ceaseless, endless questions hammered against her mind. Hunter's eyes haunted her. She remained trapped by the memory of her emotions. She'd never forget a single detail of his face.

Ariel rolled to the side, facing her. Katie realized she hadn't been quiet enough. "He really cares about you." Ariel's low voice crawled up Katie's side.

"What?" The annoyance level she endured diminished quickly.

"Hunter. He really cares about you."

Katie flipped onto her back. "I really don't want to talk about it."

"I'm just telling you." Ariel rustled in her sleeping bag. "I'm his partner and know him better than anyone. He's really taken with you."

"Look, I'm trying hard not to be rude, but I don't want to discuss this. Especially not with you."

"Fine. Whatever you say. Suit yourself." Ariel snuffed out the lamp and turned her back to Katie.

Guilt pressed on Katie's chest. She inhaled deeply, arguing with herself over whether she should apologize or not. She pinched her eyes closed, wishing she had someone to talk with. Someone she could trust, like her father. Maybe if she believed in the whole religion thing, the God-thing, she'd have someone. But God wasn't listening. At least, not to her. No matter what Hunter preached. Although she couldn't deny he walked in peace. Could that be a reflection of his relationship with God? She, too, once had a personal relationship with the Lord.

She turned on her stomach, letting the bumpy ground dig into her flesh, the pain far surpassed by the ache in her heart. How could she explain her tangle of feelings? She hadn't ever felt like this toward a man before Hunter. As much as it ripped her apart to consider what she must do, she had to do it. Had to remove him from her mind, from her emotions. If she didn't push him aside now, her heart would be lost. The admission dredged from a place she'd thought missing in her psyche.

Expelling a long breath, Katie forced her muscles to relax. The memories drifted over everything that happened today, letting exhaustion overwhelm her. Her entire body became engulfed in tides of despair and weariness. Drained—spent and hollow. Katie closed her eyes and drifted into the wisps of sleep's welcoming arms.

Twenty

Katie's even breathing stalled. In the twilight between awareness and slumber, she battled the cottony gauze encasing her mind. Her eyes jerked open as she tried to gulp in air, and couldn't take in a deep swallow. A strong hand covered her mouth. The distinct odor of sweat filled her nostrils, nearly making her gag. She frantically twisted her head, but the hand held firm.

She tried to move to no avail, trapped inside her sleeping bag. A man straddled her, his knees pinning the bag tightly over her. A strange greenish hue shone inside the confining tent, casting odd shadows on the tarpaulin. A glow stick laid on the ground beside her. She struggled to focus on the man's face looming above hers.

Jerry's eyes held that familiar, uncertain glazed look.

She bucked and thrashed, terror taking hold of her. Katie arched her back and jerked. The rocks under the tent's floor dug into her shoulders. Cold sweat beaded on her upper lip and brow.

He pressed his face closer to hers. "Stop fighting me," he whispered harshly. His pupils were dilated, the whites of his eyes mapped with red jagged lines. He brandished a gun in his free hand, digging its cold muzzle into the side of her neck.

Katie stilled her movements as the gun pushed against her pulse. Backlit with the eerie greenish hue from the glow stick, Jerry's face appeared distorted. The vision before her conveyed a man hovering on the brink of insanity.

Heart pumping blood through her veins as fast as the undertow of the Gauley, Katie could smell the stink of her own fear. She swallowed, but remained frozen in place. The gun against her throat kept her muscles from tweaking.

"That's better. I'm going to remove my hand. If you scream, I'll kill you. Then I'll kill your brother." His narrowed eyes glared at her. "Got it?"

She kept her stare focused on his eyes and nodded, slowly and deliberately. Her mind drifted into a muddy haze as disbelief pervaded her senses.

This couldn't be happening to her!

"Good." He removed his hand and pulled the gun back to his side. She drank in big breaths of air, letting her lungs fill to capacity. He shifted off of her.

Raw panic rose within her. He allowed her to sit. Her gaze drifted across the tent.

Ariel.

She lay on her side facing Katie, arms stretched behind her. A thick belt nestled right above her knees, effectively tying her legs together. Dark knots wove around her ankles. Only the light from the green glow stick split the blanket void of darkness. Katie squinted against the shadows of the night. Were those shoelaces around Ariel's ankles? A long piece of duct tape covered her mouth. As Katie stared at her, Ariel's eyes blinked furiously.

Katie pressed her lips together. Ariel was trying to send her a message, but Katie couldn't understand. A knot of wild horror tightened in her stomach.

Jerry hovered over her, waving the gun. "Get your shoes on, we're leaving."

"L-L-Leaving? To where?" Her hands trembled as she automatically reached for her hiking boots.

"You're taking me out of here—tonight." His eyes shone with . . . what?

Her hands froze over the boot's laces. "I can't take you out of here, Jerry. I have a twisted ankle."

"Too bad." He curled back his lips, snarling. "You'll do what I tell you, or I'll shoot your brother and everybody else here."

"Why are you doing this?" Panic rioted within her. She had to keep him talking—get him to listen to reason. Didn't he realize he'd tied up an FBI agent?

Jerry waved the gun at her. "Put on your boots."

Katie finished donning her shoes and looked at him. She wrestled with keeping her heart cold and still.

Jerry grabbed her arm and jerked her to her feet.

Her breath solidified inside her lungs. Breathing became impossible. She coughed and sputtered.

Whack!

Katie's head popped back. Her face stung and grew hot.

She raised a hand to cover her cheek where he'd slapped her. Tears of pain and fury blinded her. She couldn't control her spasmodic quivering.

"Now get moving." Even though he whispered, a cold edge laced his voice. He jabbed the barrel of the gun into her spine.

She flinched. He pressed harder.

Her back cried out in protest. She took a wobbly step.

He leaned close to her, his breath in her ear. "If you so much as make a sound, I'll kill everyone here. Including your brother and that blasted dog of yours."

Christian's tenderness and declaration of love rang out against her heart. The knife in her chest twisted. Determination sat like a rock inside her gut.

She hobbled from the tent and moved soundlessly around the lean-to. Her eyes pealed for any sign of movement from inside the building. Nothing. Clenching her jaw to kill the sobs in her throat, Katie pressed on.

The moon shone through the clouds, muted illumination slicing through the darkness. The shiny metal of Jerry's gun flashed in the light. Katie bit her bottom lip to stifle the cry building.

Behind the shanty, Katie spied the wadded sleeping bag. Her heart lurched. Carter.

Had Jerry killed him? Dismay crowded her mind. She had no hope of getting out alive. She forced herself to continue walking, climbing. An idea whipped into her mind so suddenly, she nearly faltered. She may die, but at least she could lead Jerry far away from the others.

She could give them a chance.

It had stopped raining, but the saturated ground made their climb slippery and treacherous. Several times, Katie lost her footing and slid back against Jerry. In each instance, he'd thrust the gun into her back and shove her in front of him.

Having left the glow stick behind, Jerry demanded she use the waning moonlight as her only navigation. Clouds still blanketed the sky, hiding the twinkling stars behind their gloomy depths. A gentle breeze pushed cold air across the space, and she shivered.

Their progress, sluggish at best, was hampered even more by Katie's injury. Every step up sent bolts of intense agony up her leg. She remained silent and defeated—fear and despair tore at her. Her spirits sank lower with each step, knowing it took her farther away from what she held nearest and dearest. A bitter frigidness dwelt in the cave of her lonely soul.

The raspy snoring from Orson's open mouth roused Hunter. In the dark, his disorientation hovered over his consciousness. Shaking himself, he sat and glanced over at Shadow. The dog laid still, the only movement coming from the gentle rise and fall of his little furry chest. Hunter smiled and rubbed his chin. Had anything happened to the dog during the night, Katie would never for-give him.

He ran his hands over his face, then through his hair, wiping the cobwebs of sleep from his mind. As quietly as he could, Hunter slipped from his sleeping bag and crawled to the foot of it. He shoved his feet into his boots, didn't bother to tie them, then stood and crept from the lean-to.

Morning's first light beckoned mere moments away. He gasped against the burst of chill. He ran his hands over his arms as he continued to the edge of the trees. Having listened to the torrential rains they'd endured, the still silence unnerved Hunter. Birds that'd been silent for the entire trip, tweeted from their branches. A promise that all would be fine.

An uneasy sensation slithered up his spine. Hunter looked around, taking stock of his surroundings. A warning voice whispered in his head. He remained still, gaze filtering along the horizon for anything amiss. Nothing jumped out at him, nary a thing appeared out of place. Still, the sensation settled over his shoulders.

Hunter paced himself as he headed back to the shanty. His mind congested with doubt and disquiet. He glanced around at the doorframe. The tent's flap still zipped tightly shut—no movement from outside, save the graceful swaying of the trees in the pre-dawn breezes. His imagination must be working overtime.

Back inside the lean-to, Hunter noticed Jerry absent from his sleeping bag. Hunter grunted softly. The other man must have had to see to personal business. Most likely, his presence in the great outdoors had been what caused Hunter's shroud of uneasiness. Shrugging off the sentiment, Hunter began laying out breakfast for the group. If Jerry didn't return within a few moments, Hunter would go searching for the troublemaker. As soon as first light broke, Hunter wanted to be ready to get them moving.

Someone tapped his shoulder.

Hunter jumped and spun around, looking into Christian's smiling face.

"Good morning," Katie's brother whispered, not bothering to mask his snickering.

"Morning." Hunter grinned and returned to assembling breakfast supplies. They had plenty of food and water, thanks to Christian's and Ariel's packs.

Christian scratched his head. "Anybody else up?"

"Just Jerry."

"Lovely." Christian ran a hand over his hair, pushing his jagged bangs from his face. "I need to visit the little boys' room."

Hunter chuckled. "I hear ya."

Christian ambled toward the door.

"If you see Jerry, tell him to come on back and get his bedroll ready to go," Hunter whispered out to him.

"Will do," Christian said over his shoulder before crossing the threshold.

Shadow rousted to his three good legs and hobbled behind Christian. Sympathy for the faithful dog washed over Hunter. Poor thing, probably desperate to see his mistress. Hunter could relate . . . anxiety knotted his nerves at the thought of seeing Katie this morning.

Alone again, the odd feeling of something wrong, something terribly wrong, filled Hunter's sense of self. All the training, all the years in the field, and his instincts had never failed him before, not a single time. He spun slowly, surveying the room. His stare fell to Jerry's empty bedroll, not looking mussed. His mind raced with possible scenarios, and none of them good. His gut twisted.

Hunter rushed from the shanty and approached the tent. His hand hesitated over the zipper. What if Katie and Ariel were asleep? What if paranoia were merely playing havoc with his mind? He leaned his head against the canvas, listening for snores. He heard nothing, so Hunter pressed closer, practically straining against the material. "Ariel? Katie? You awake?" He spoke in a loud whisper, desperate for a reply.

Shadow appeared at his side, sniffing the tent. He whimpered and pawed at the heavy canvas.

A muffled moan sounded.

He unzipped the tent and stepped inside. His heart turned into a giant glacier.

Hunter rushed to Ariel's prone form, then yanked the duct tape from her mouth. "Are you okay?"

Shadow sniffed at Katie's sleeping bag. His canine body went rigid as he barked twice.

Ariel nodded. "Katie." Her voice sounded raw and scratchy. "Jerry took Katie. He's making her lead him out of here."

Dark fury fogged his thoughts. He ripped the binding from Ariel's wrists, cringing as she flinched against the harsh removal.

"Hunter . . ."

He locked his gaze on her face.

"He has my backup firearm."

Katie kept her eyes trained on the terrain in front of her. The moon tucked back into the clouds, forcing Katie and Jerry to journey by the purplish hue of the impending sunrise. Now, the first sunbeams filtered through the canopy of oaks, dancing across the dim patches of trees. Red and yellow leaves drifted on the gentle breezes, announcing fall's arrival. Impending doom cloaked her like a well-worn shawl, and Katie studied the beauty of the mountain she'd lived close to all her life, but never really appreciated. The bright colors of autumn calmed her soul, soothed her agitated state. Having a plan also helped assuage her fears.

An idea occurred to her after the first fifteen minutes of the climb—to lead Jerry in a roundabout way, thus allowing the others to make it to the top before them. It could be her only chance of survival. Implementing the plan wouldn't be as easy. Knowing she couldn't veer sharply to either side, and with the gun in her back, she had to keep making progress upward. Taking baby steps around trees and rocks, she'd managed to deter their course by at least twenty yards to the left of the path the others would take up the hill. She let out a ragged breath as she calculated she would need to move them several more yards to ensure the others' safety.

Jerry's constant grunts and shoves only fueled her determination. Somewhere along the way, she'd let go of most of her fear, allowing anger to take its place. Katie resolved to keep an iron will imposed on her self-control. He might well kill her, but at least she'd save her brother, Orson, Paul, Ariel, and . . . and . . . Hunter.

Hunter. His name hovered on the edges of her mind. The harder she tried to push the truth away, the more it persisted. In all likelihood, she wouldn't get the chance to tell him how she felt, even if she could admit it. Nor would she be able to lose herself in his embrace. Katie shivered, recalling in vivid detail the kisses and the way they'd made her feel.

The memory of her emotions trapped her, holding her as much a hostage as Jerry. Her cold words came back to haunt her, tormenting her relentlessly. He'd asked for her to listen, to understand, and she'd refused. The mocking voice in her head blasted insults at her. Her day of reckoning couldn't be postponed for long. Talons of guilt and regret clawed at her soul.

At a large boulder, Katie took another three feet to the left.

Jerry grabbed her sweater and jerked her backward. She fell against the soggy ground, the cold moisture soaking her jeans. She glared at him.

"What are you doing?" He waved the gun about. "You keep going sideways. What are you trying to do?"

Using the rock as leverage, she pulled herself up, glaring at him. "You want to get up to the parking lot, where the ATVs are, right?"

"That's up, not over." His expression told of his vexation. He pushed the gun in her side, jamming it against her ribs.

Katie flinched from the sharp jab and took a reverse step. She pressed the back of her legs against the boulder. "Christian told me last night they'd secured the four-wheelers on the far end of the lot."

His eyes scanned up the hillside, then jolted to her. "You'd better not be trying anything funny."

She held her hands in front of her body, palms outward. "I'm not." She lowered her voice, using the same tone she employed when speaking to wounded animals. "Jerry, why are you doing this? This isn't you. You're better than this."

Hesitation flashed in his eyes. She studied him carefully, mindful to watch his expressions. He squinted against the cresting sun. "What do you care?"

"I'm wondering what would push an obviously intelligent man like yourself to such a desperate measure." Katie held her breath. Would he realize the flattery was false? Would he fall into the trap of talking to her?

"I didn't have any other choice." He broke eye contact.

This wasn't an insane madman, merely a man who felt trapped by his circumstances, even if they were brought on by his own actions. "We always have a choice, Jerry. Always."

"I'm a dead man now anyway. Marked." He sniffed and straightened his stance. The snide look returned to his eyes. "You don't know anything."

"I know it's not too late to turn around." She took a tentative step toward him. "It's not too late to stop this."

She never saw him raise his hand, only felt the impact of his fist against her chin. The force of the blow knocked her to the ground. Her head crashed in blinding, white pain. Dots danced before her eyes, then darkness enveloped her in its icy embrace.

Twenty-one

Hunter's shout brought Christian running from the woods. Paul stumbled out of the lean-to, while Orson grumbled. Christian's face fell as he listened to Ariel's recollection of Katie's abduction. He stood with a tight jaw, fisting his hands, spreading them, then fisting them again.

Paul's face turned white as a spirit haunting the

mountains, as Shadow snarled at his feet. The dog bared his teeth and growled at the man.

Ariel touched Paul's shoulder. "Hunter and I are FBI agents. We've been working this case undercover and know your firm is involved in a money-laundering scam." Her voice dropped a notch. "We need your help. You know Jerry better than anyone. Tell us what you know."

Paul's bottom lip trembled. "Well, uh, I had no, uh, idea he'd go this far. He never said . . . this was never part of the plan."

Hunter shoved Paul against the outer wall of the shanty. He pushed his forearm against Paul's throat, and got in his face. "Tell me the truth."

"O-O-Okay. Ease up." Paul's voice cracked. A sheen of sweat glistened on his bald spot.

Hunter released enough pressure so Paul could swallow. Shadow moved in front of Hunter, teeth bared at Paul while he emitted low growls.

Paul gulped in air. "I confess, we were laundering drug money through Lassiter James Accounting."

Hunter dropped his arm and glared at Paul. "Go ahead, keep talking."

"We, uh, would get the cash from the drug deals, then make investments at Lassiter James. Two months later, we'd cash out one of the accounts and give the cleaned cash back to the drug dealers. Keeping out our own cut, of course."

Hunter's rage became a scalding fury. "Who

was in on it at the firm?" An icy chill hung on the tattered edges of his words.

"C-Carter."

"And who else?"

"No one that I know about." Paul's admission did nothing to soften Hunter's stony stance.

"So why kill them? Walter? Carter? Attempt on Orson? Why?" Hunter spit the words out with disgust. His anguish sat like a steel weight in his chest.

"We knew the FBI was on our tail. Jerry figured out the leak came from Lassiter James. He demanded Carter put together this trip and invite anyone who'd had access to our files over the past year." Paul shifted his weight, only to have Hunter pounce on him like a lion on a gazelle. "He intended to uncover the rat who leaked the information to the FBI."

Pinning him to the wall again, Hunter refused to accept the dull ache of foreboding. "Well, guess what—I'm your leak. Now, what else?"

"Nothing. I swear." A spark lit in Paul's eyes, only to be replaced immediately by a flash of primal terror.

Hunter released him and paced the trodden and wet ground in front of the doorway.

Ariel slipped handcuffs on Paul's wrists. "You have the right to remain silent. Anything you say can and will be used against you . . . ."

Hunter drowned out the Miranda Rights. The

shock of the lengths to which Jerry had gone left him immobile. He experienced a wretchedness of mind he'd never experienced before. And he never wanted to again. He clenched and unfurled his hands. "Ariel, I need the extra magazines you brought."

She reached into a bag right inside the tent, retrieved two clips of bullets and tossed them toward Hunter, then took her service gun and tucked it into her waistband.

He caught them with ease, then shoved them into his back pocket. He pulled out his Beretta, checked the magazine he'd loaded last night after the bear attack, then shoved it back into the waistband of his jeans.

"I'll go with you." Ariel moved to his side.

"No." His tone left no room for argument.

"I'm your partner. Of course I'm going with you." She widened her stance, refusal to back down shining in her eyes.

Hunter recognized the movement of tossing of her hair performed in defiance. He shook his head. "You need to secure the prisoner and protect the civilians."

She jutted out her chin.

"He's in custody. I have to go after Katie." Just saying her name sent stabs into his heart. He wanted to snap someone's neck over the injustice of it all, yet knew he had to master his emotions. Letting loose the fury curling in his gut wouldn't help her. He needed to be the professional his reputation claimed him to be. "Start moving the others out of here. You know protocol—an agent must escort the prisoner into custody. Call for backup as soon as you hit the top. I'm going after Katie."

"I'll go with you." Christian moved to stand in front of him, Shadow at his side.

Hunter shook his head. "I don't think so."

"I know this mountain, you don't. And she's my sister." Determination marched across Christian's face and sunk into his eyes.

"And that's exactly why you're going with Ariel and the others."

"Do you think Katie would lead Jerry up the route she knows we'd take?" Christian snorted and shook his head. "Not hardly. She'll be leading him to the top, but in an abstract way. And you won't be able to figure it out, even if you are FBI."

Hunter hesitated, weighing the information. "Are you sure about that?"

"I know Katie."

"Okay. What way would she go?"

Christian shook his head. "I'll have to track her."

"Track her?" Hunter's veins filled with adrenaline.

"Yeah, track her path."

"Can you do that?"

Christian smiled, even though it didn't reach his eyes. "You betcha." He hauled in a deep breath, letting it hiss back out. "What're we waiting on? Let's go get my sister."

Glancing at the dog's soulful eyes, Hunter looked back to Christian. "The dog has to stay here."

"He'll track her even faster than I can," Christian said with a glance at the Blue Heeler.

"But he's got a broken leg. I can't risk him tipping our hand to Jerry."

Christian nodded. He stared down at the dog, snapped his fingers like Katie did, and pointed to Ariel. "Stay."

The dog whimpered.

"Stay, Shadow." Christian turned back to Hunter. "He'll stay with Ariel now. Let's go get Katie."

Rustling noises reached Katie's ears. She slowly lifted her eyelids. Bright sunlight flooded her vision, sending shots of agony through her head. She pinched her eyes closed. Her head pounded as she tried to remember what happened. In a rush, it all came back to her: Jerry's rage, the sharp pain to her head, the darkness.

She pushed herself into a sitting position. Katie sat on the wet ground, her head against the boulder. Flashes of pain simmered at the base of her skull. She touched the area, then cringed as more powerful waves of throbbing shot through her head. Jerking her hand down, she noticed the red, sticky blood clinging to her fingers. Nausea burned in the back of her throat.

Katie attempted to stand, but white dots merged before her eyes. She slumped to the ground. Her body ached and her spirits sank even lower. Where was Jerry? Would he soon come back to finish her off? She curled into the fetal position, overwhelmed by the torment of the last few days. Resentment assaulted her senses. Her mind defeated, her heart without hope.

Cry out to Me for help, Daughter.

Katie's breath came in gasps and spurts. Did Jerry whisper to her, taunting her before he killed her? Her thoughts tasted bitter on her tongue. She closed her eyes, surrendering to her fate.

From My temple I will hear your voice. Your cry will come before Me, into My ears. Cry out to Me for help, Daughter.

She jerked up her head, sure Jerry would be hovering over her, mocking her with the gun. The movement sent spirals of pain bouncing inside her skull. She flinched, blinking several times, then scanned the area. No sign of Jerry. Once more, she pushed against the boulder, letting hope bolster her strength.

Her energy and strength zapped, Katie lay over the boulder. The exertion of getting off the ground wiped her out. She fought to catch her breath. Laying the side of her face against the rock, she let the coolness seep into her burning head. A pounding, matching the erratic beat of her heart, echoed inside her mind.

The torrents of destruction overwhelm you. Call out to Me, Daughter, and I will hear you.

Katie's heart stilled. She held her breath, allowing the words to sink in. Dawning hit her as hard as the crack on her skull. Her voice croaked shakily as she whispered, "God . . . is that You?"

I am here, Daughter. Call out to Me.

Her teeth chattered, her beaten body trembled. Hot tears trickled down her face. "God, help me. Please."

The crackling of bushes sounded to her right. Her breathing became labored. Her lips moved of their own. "God, I'm sorry I turned away from You. I was wrong. I know that now. I'm so sorry. Please forgive me, God. I call on You now, save me. In the name of Your precious Son, my savior Christ, please help me."

A warming sensation covered her. Peace oozed over her body, drenching her in love and security. She relaxed, relishing the emotions wrapping around her. Katie closed her eyes, moving out of consciousness. Tears of accepted grace streaked down her cheeks. A sentence formed on her lips, barely uttering the words before darkness overtook her. "Thank You, sweet Jesus. Thank You."

Dread and longing filled Hunter with each passing footstep. Fear walked beside him in the woods. Christian led the way, stopping often to inspect bushes and the ground. Impatience boiled in Hunter's chest. The need to see Katie, to hold her and be assured of her safety, drove his every movement. He touched the grip of his firearm, as if to reassure himself the weapon stood at the ready. The black rubber offered him comfort. A constant companion in his line of work, the gun existed as his permanent partner, even closer than Ariel.

Christian led the way up the trail, quickly picking his steps. Hunter's mind wouldn't rest. Memories swarmed his brain, refusing to be placed in a box and ignored. Images of Katie stomped to the forefront of his very being. He relived the physical punch in his gut the first time he'd seen her, so beautiful and intriguing. Hunter recalled the sound of her voice, the curve of her face, the lift of her smile. He groaned.

"They went this way." Christian moved farther to the left. His voice carried a brotherly hope, the belief that he'd find his sister safe and sound. Right around the corners of the mind, logic and reasoning attacked hope. With every passing minute, the odds of recovering Katie alive and unharmed crashed.

Hunter's first case with the bureau had been a stalker-turned-kidnapper. While the young woman had filed charges, they had no proof her ex-boyfriend was the one following her, calling her, sending her dead roses and eventually kidnapping her. Weeks of investigation turned up nothing, not one single shred of physical evidence. The agents in charge backed off from the case. Within a week, they'd found the young woman, dead. It had been Hunter's first casualty. He'd never forgiven himself for not doing more. The woman's name, Misty Mulligan, haunted him to this day.

Hunter followed Christian's quickened pace. Not this time. Hunter wouldn't back down, wouldn't be called off this kidnapping for anything. He'd give Katie everything he had to give.

Or die trying.

"See anything?" He pulled his way by using the oaks lining the hillside.

Christian glanced over his shoulder. "We're on their trail. She's leading him up, but strongly to the left." He smiled. "Katie always was a devious thing."

Hunter hoisted himself beside Christian. "Tell me about her."

"What do you want to know?"

"What kind of woman is she? What does she love?"

Christian continued to keep his stare glued to the surrounding foliage. "Nature . . . the river . . . the trees." He bent to touch a bush, then stepped two paces to the left. "She loves animals and rafting and peace."

Flipping the information around inside his head, Hunter cast a sideways glance to her brother. "And God?"

Christian stopped and met his stare. "What about God?"

"Why doesn't she have faith in Him anymore?"

Christian moved again. "We were all raised in a godly home, Hunter, if that's what you want to know. We were taught Scripture and prayers." His voice barely lifted above the sound of their footsteps on the wet ground.

"So what happened?"

"Mom died. Well, at least that's what everyone assumes. Katie believes Mom just left us. Abandoned the family."

Hunter hesitated, torn by conflicting thoughts. As a man, a son, he understood grief occurred on many levels. As a Federal agent, his mind demanded answers, details. He swallowed as they continued their ascent. "What happened?"

"A typical day, totally average. Mom woke us and got us ready for school. She took us to the bus-stop, kissed us bye, and went to run errands like she always did." Christian let out a heavy sigh. "We never saw her again."

"Man, that's rough." He paused, giving Christian time to recover. "Did anybody ever figure it out?"

"Dad hired private investigators. The police worked the case for months on end. She vanished without a trace."

The trained cop in Hunter tossed ideas through his brain right and left. He bit the inside of his mouth, refusing to press the gentle man beside him.

"We prayed every night, as a family, for God to return our mother to us. Or, at least, to give us some answers." Christian stopped, dropped to a squat and inspected a bush. He stood and brushed his hands off. "God never answered our pleas. Seven years later, my father had her declared legally dead and held a memorial service for her. Katie refused to go."

"She still believed her mother alive?"

Christian shrugged. "Katie never said anything more after Dad petitioned the court. She took it harder than Gabe and I did. I mean, she's a girl and needed Mom." He stopped and stared out into blank space. His eyes shone with tears. "She prayed her heart out. Walked around all the time, uttering prayers." He stared at the ground for a moment, his chest rising and falling rapidly before he looked back at Hunter. "After Mom's memorial service, Katie took all the Bibles in the house and shoved them into our old cedar chest. She clamped it shut and refused to open it again." He climbed farther.

Hunter's mind reeled with the information. Oh, poor Katie. He felt her loss, her grief. "How old was she?"

"Eleven when Mom disappeared, eighteen when Dad had Mom declared dead."

Such a vulnerable age for such an unspeakable loss. His heart ached for the young girl, yet, a pull in the corner of his mind refused to be stilled.

Hunter stole a glance at Christian, who was clearly filled with torment and fear.

Hunter sent up silent prayers for Katie. For Christian.

Lost in his conversation with God, Hunter jumped when Christian laid a hand on his shoulder and pressed a finger over his lips. Like a bird of prey, Hunter froze.

The distant sound of sobbing carried over the breeze.

Twenty-two

A jerk of her hair brought Katie roughly to her feet.

She leaned into the pull, nearly doing a back-bend in the middle of the small clearing as her head yanked back even farther. The force made her eyes water. Fresh, burning pain reverberated around her skull. She cried out and lifted her hands to the strands closest to the scalp.

Spinning her around like a rag doll, Jerry glared. "It's time to go." He pointed the gun at her and jabbed it into her ribs again. "Now!"

Katie limped along and rubbed her throbbing scalp, pushed by the barrel of the unwavering handgun. Devastated by her circumstances, her heart still soared over the treetops. God loved her! Even with all the denials, the accusations, the curses she spewed out at Him in her anger, God still loved her. Unbelievable, but God's assurances stirred within her soul.

"Move it." Jerry's voice came out harsher, meaner. He dug the muzzle of the gun harder into her shoulder blades. Her muscles spasmed in agony.

The pounding in her head split pain all the way down her neck and into her spine, reminding her of Jerry's dark intentions. The clear recollection prompted her to quicken her pace. A breeze blew against her, lifting the hair clinging to the side of her face. Her muscles tensed as she picked her way along. She bit her lip to hold back the retort on her tongue that begged to spurt forth. What-ever she did, Katie needed to remain calm and focused in order to lead Jerry away from the group's access. And not enraging him again would probably be a smart move on her part.

Each step made the soreness in her ankle more unbearable. Several times she faltered, her ankle giving out entirely. She crumbled to the ground, only to have Jerry jerk her up by her hair and shove the gun into her spine again—a bruise in the making. Everything in her wanted to lash out, to turn around and slap Jerry's face, yet she knew doing so would seal her fate. How ironic—

just when she decided to live for God, she'd probably soon be living with God.

Katie gingerly chose her footholds, wary of the rocks jutting up from the squishy ground. The thicket of trees lost some of its density, causing her to rely on bushes and brambles to pull herself along. Prickly branches and thorns dug into her hands, drawing blood. She ignored the pain, choosing to focus on her progress. A few times she ducked clear of a low-lying limb at the last minute, causing it to pop Jerry right in the face. Each time he grunted, her resolve to make the trip as painful on him as possible rising another notch.

A large rock loomed in front of her, directly in their path, protruding out with sharp edges and points, like a mountain breaking through the horizon. She made four steps to the left to move around it, but never recovered back to the right. Jerry blindly followed. Even though the muzzle of the gun tucked hard into her back, Katie tossed her hair over her shoulder, and enjoyed her little acts of defiance. Knowing she thwarted Jerry's plans made her brighten inside.

Her newfound inner strength surprised her. Oh, she'd never been a mealy-mouth, helpless female, not growing up around Gabe and Christian, but the power surging through her now felt unfamiliar —and exhilarating. Or, maybe her will to live had at long last emerged. Either way, her mind and body screamed with a strong sense of survival.

She'd endure and prevail in the end. She had to!

"Stop." The single word barely made it through Jerry's labored breathing.

Katie turned and faced him with a deliberately casual movement.

He bent at the waist, hands propped against his kneecaps, and dropped his head. The gun dangled from his right hand. His breathing came fast and furious. A fine sheen of perspiration dotted his upper lip. Jerry truly was a desk jockey, so out of shape he panted like a backyard dog in the midday sun.

The wind shifted, moving down the mountain, pulling her toward the water. A clean, earthy odor infusing the area, and Katie's heart settled. This was her home turf, and she could beat Jerry at his own game, if she held her cards close to her chest and played them at the right time.

She pressed her lips together and leaned her shoulder against a nearby oak tree. Her breathing remained steady. She hadn't even broken a sweat.

His lack of physical fitness worked well into her plan. Not only did she want to keep the others safe, but she wanted to buy herself some time. Time for Christian to find her. She had no doubt her brother would come for her. He'd be able to track her and find them.

A warming sensation settled over her at the idea. Hunter would come after her as well. The freshness of his deception still ate at her conscious, but he hadn't meant to hurt her. Not intentionally. He should've told her the truth, on that she remained firm, but in all honesty, she hadn't allowed him much opportunity to tell him the truth after they'd kissed.

Kissing. The heat rose up the back of her neck as she replayed their kiss in her mind.

She tilted her head, pushing aside the pain in the back of her neck, and gauged the time from the placement of the sun. By her rough estimations, her rescuers should be storming on the scene any moment. They'd had time to talk with Ariel, and Christian wouldn't wait to track her. The corners of her mouth tickled as they lifted. Her shining white knight to the rescue.

"What're you smiling about?" Jerry's voice came out in bursts. His breathing still wrenched and the flush continued to cover his face.

She met his accusing stare without flinching. "Just enjoying the day."

He charged at her, shoving her against the tree. Bark dug into her back, abrading her sore skin. Katie refused to cower—finding a perverse pleasure in taking back the control he had over her. She wouldn't be put down by this brute any more.

"There's nothing to enjoy." Jerry nudged her sore ankle with the toe of his boot.

"That's where you're wrong." She ran a shaking hand through her hair. "Come on, Jerry, tell me your story. Why are you doing this?"

He glared at her, then his expression softened a slight measure. "You wouldn't understand."

She, too, lowered her tone. "Try me."

"I have no choice. I'm merely the fall guy here."

"Come again? You're the one with the gun."

"Desperate times call for desperate measures." His face took on a thoughtful expression.

"Jerry, tell me what's going on. You can trust me." She chewed her bottom lip. Maybe if she could get him to talking, she could get him to listen to reason.

His eyes lit up, then darkened again. "No, I can't. I have no choice. I never did." His voice lowered until he mumbled. "Now I really don't."

She took a step toward him, her mind racing with possibilities. "Jerry . . ."

He raised the tip of the gun to point at her, the moment of sentiment gone. "Get moving."

"Sure you're up to it?" Blatant defiance hung in her tone, as well as a not-so-subtle challenge.

His eyes, cold and proud, flashed with icy contempt. "Just lead the way," he said.

She turned, using the tree as a hold on her way up the mountainside.

Hunter crouched behind the full shrubbery, his eyes locked onto Katie and Jerry. He kept his finger up to make sure Christian understood to keep quiet. The air hung heavy over the mountain, so thick it pressed down oppressively over the terrain. The wet ground, warming by the sun's peek-a-boo rays, quickly turned to steam, only to be blown away in the arms of the gentle, yet constant, breeze dancing over the landscape.

Jerry and Katie had stopped briefly, making Hunter believe he could make his move. He couldn't hear their conversation, but crept toward the duo with Christian on his heels. Jerry slammed her against the tree. It took everything Hunter had not to rush forward and clobber the man. Yet, years of training and conditioning held him firmly in check. Timing was everything.

Now, as they moved upward again, Hunter led Christian stealthy behind the couple. He reached out for a sapling, pulling himself over the slick ground. Looking over his shoulder, he motioned to Christian that he wanted to speed up, to get ahead of Katie and Jerry. Christian nodded and pointed toward a more level area of ground. Hunter moved in that direction.

Painstakingly slow, Hunter and Christian gained on Jerry and Katie, moving like cats stalking their prey, working in silence to not alert Jerry of their presence. Perspiration dripped down Hunter's face into his eyes, even though the temperature dipped below the warm end of the thermometer. He wiped his vision clean with the back of his hand and continued pushing forward.

At last they moved far enough ahead of Jerry that Hunter felt confident in turning onto their path to wait in ambush. In hushed tones he explained his plan to Christian. "I'm going to hide behind those bushes across the way. You stay here. They'll be trapped between us." He peered into Christian's eyes, seeing the anger and worry lurking in their depths. "You stay out of sight. Let me handle Jerry. Once I have his attention, you pull Katie to safety. Understand?"

"Gotcha."

"Once you have her, turn and head toward the others. Try to catch up with Ariel's group."

"What about you?"

Hunter smiled, excitement coursing through his veins to match the adrenaline already pumping his heart at top speed. "Don't worry about me. I'll catch up with you once I contain Jerry."

Christian hitched his brows. "You be careful."

"I'm trained for this kind of stuff, remember?" His chuckle echoed low and hoarse. His fingers itched to curl into a fist and plow into Jerry's face. Repeatedly.

He winked at Christian, then crept across the way and dodged behind a thicket. He'd barely had time to settle against the oak tree's knotted trunk when the unmistakable sound of thrashing under-brush sounded from below his position. He touched the butt of his gun, but left it jammed into the back of his jeans. He wouldn't need to pull his firearm—he had every intention of taking Jerry Sands down, one-on-one.

• • •

Katie reached another clearing and stopped, leaning against a tree to the left of the path. She slumped to the ground. Immediately, mud saturated her jeans, gluing them to her body.

Behind her, Jerry waved the gun in her direction. "What're you stopping here for?"

"My ankle. It hurts too bad to keep going. I have to rest." She reached down and rubbed her shin. Stabs of pain shot up to her knee.

He moved to stand in front of her, his chest rising and falling quickly as his breathing came in spurts. "Oh. We can take a minute's rest, I guess."

Gingerly touching her ankle, Katie cringed. She needed a peppermint, badly. Since she had none, she bit down on her bottom lip and studied her profusely sweating captor. "Jerry . . ."

He glanced into her eyes. Fear danced in his orbs.

"It's okay. Whatever reason you have for doing this, it's okay. I'd like to know what's going on."

Leaning against an opposite tree, he slumped, gripping his knees with his hands. The gun shifted so it no longer pointed at her. He wiped the sweat from his forehead with his shoulder. "It's complicated. But none of this was my decision. I'm only the patsy."

"Who told you to cut the raft?"

His head jerked up. His stare met hers, questions blinking back at her.

"Come on, surely you didn't think I wouldn't recognize a knife cut, did you?"

He swallowed, his Adam's apple bobbing up and down. "I didn't cut the raft."

"You didn't?" She ran a hand over her bangs, pushing them off her brow. "Then who did?"

"Paul."

She snorted as the ludicrous idea tapped against her brain. Paul? Saboteur? She wanted to laugh, but stopped when Jerry's head snapped up.

He glared at her, fear and loathing shooting from his eyes.

A gust of wind tickled the loose strands of hair against her face. She shoved them away with the back of her hand, then rubbed her cheek against the arm of her sweater to brush off the mud. "He seems so harmless. Why would he cut the raft?"

Jerry snickered. "Harmless? You don't get it, do you? He's really that good. Got you all fooled."

She shook her head as her mind raced over the last two days. Had it only been two days? Katie forced her mind to recall every image she had of Paul, every memory. His quiet, unassuming demeanor made him appear the perfect lap-dog. Could it all be an act? She pressed the palm of her hand against her forehead. "Did you knock Steve into the river?" Her stare penetrated the space between them.

He hesitated, then nodded. "Yeah, but only because I was told to."

"And Orson. Did you trip him?"

Again, he nodded. This time he didn't say anything.

"What about Walter? Did you push him into the water?" She forced her words past the lump in her throat.

"No." He shook his head, but met her stare, never wavering in his eye contact.

"You're saying Paul pushed Walter in?" Holding onto the tree, she pulled to a standing position. "Paul did it?" She wiped her hands against her jeans, flinching as the wet denim rubbed against the cuts and nicks in her palms.

He nodded. "Yeah, because he told me to and I wouldn't." He let out a long breath. "By then, I realized what kind of man he was. It wasn't supposed to be like this." Jerry stared off into the distance. "None of this was supposed to happen."

"What was supposed to happen?" She kept her voice low, soothing almost. She needed to keep him talking, to build his trust in her. Yet, her mind wrapped around his confessions and forced her heart to give him the benefit of the doubt. He admitted to pushing Steve in the river and tripping Orson—why would he bother to lie about Walter? Because Walter had died? Katie flipped the ideas around in her head as he replied.

"Paul said we were supposed to find out who leaked info to the FBI, just get a name so he could tell his boss."

"His boss? Paul is answering to someone else?"

Jerry nodded. "Yeah, the guy we've been laundering the money for." He straightened and leaned against the tree. "Paul had me call Carter and set up the trip, which I did. We were supposed to uncover who had been talking, that's it. Steve was too new of a hire to be the one feeding info to the feds. Besides, can you see that little mousey dude being brave enough to play with the big boys?" He chuckled and shook his head. "The FBI had gotten too close, which meant that someone had tipped them off.

"I figured it wasn't Carter, because, hey, he knew the score. That left Walter, Orson, and Hunter." He lifted his shoulder and rubbed his chin against it. "I didn't think it could be old Walter because he seemed too close to Carter to do anything to hurt the firm. Little brown-noser had dreams of taking over the business when Carter retired."

"So why kill Walter?"

Jerry shook his head. "I don't know. That's when I realized maybe Paul had gotten different instructions from his boss than what he'd told me."

"And Carter?"

"It was Paul. We were making our way back to the lean-to when he appeared from nowhere. He told me to take Orson and get outta there. I thought he intended to have words with Carter, give him some orders or something. Orson and I started moving." He closed his eyes, shook his head, then opened his eyes to stare at the ground. "I heard Carter scream, and I knew. I knew." He let out a long breath and glanced up at Katie. "By the time I got to Carter, Paul had already gone and Hunter, your brother and his girlfriend came crashing in."

Katie closed her eyes, replaying that day. She had rejected his affections and he'd stormed out of the lean-to. They'd heard Carter scream and rushed outside. Paul met her before Christian and the others had returned with Orson. She opened her eyes and stared at Jerry. It could have happened the way he told it.

But, did it?

After all, Jerry's the one who'd kidnapped her and slapped her around.

She opened her mouth to ask another question, when a yell erupted and thrashing bore down on them.

A blur of a man running at full speed toward Jerry gave a guttural groan as he lowered his stance and thrust his shoulder into Jerry's stomach.

Katie covered her mouth and sagged against the tree.

Hunter slammed into Jerry, tackling him. The gun sailed in the air, landing in the mud a good five feet from where the men wrestled.

Jerry made a mad crawl toward the weapon. His fingers grazed the handle of the gun.

Hunter grabbed Jerry's ankle and jerked. Jerry grabbed for a hold, but the mud slid him back toward Hunter.

Shoving to stand, Hunter spit in the mud. His body looked hard, quick, and lethal. Katie gasped as he stalked Jerry.

The men faced each other, keeping a distance of about three feet between them as they circled one another.

"Come on, Sands . . . bring it on."

"Just let me go, Malone. It's none of your business." Jerry spat and wiped his mouth with the back of his hand, inching toward the open area.

"You're scum. Oh, and you're under arrest for the murders of Walter Thompson and Carter James, the attempted murder of Steve Smith, and the assault on Orson Toliver. Not to mention kidnapping charges as well as assaulting a federal agent. And that's all before we get to the money laundering." Hunter's clenched fists raised to a fighting position.

"Hunter, wait," Katie cried.

A strong hand gripped her shoulder and pulled her backward. She screamed as she lost her balance and fell against the person behind her.

Twenty-three

Hunter ignored Katie's heart-wrenching cry—he had to trust Christian would look after his sister. If anything, the desperation in her tone made the adrenaline pump faster through his veins. Right now, he only had one thing on his mind . . . bringing down Jerry Sands, and he didn't want to pull his sidearm to do it.

"Might have guessed you'd come." Jerry grunted as he took a quick glance at the gun.

"You should've killed me when you had the chance." Hunter took a step forward as Jerry took a step back. Every muscle in Hunter's body tweaked into action. His stare never faltered from Jerry's face.

"You still don't get it, do you? I'm not a killer!"

"Tell that to Walter and Carter, man."

"I believe him, Hunter!" Katie's words broke his concentration. Spinning on his heel, he stared at her struggling against her brother's restraint. Hadn't he told Christian to take her back to meet the others?

"He took you hostage, Katie."

Jerry dove for the gun, but Hunter moved faster, grabbing Jerry. His face hit the mud with a splat, but he crawled forward. Hunter sprung to his feet and pounced toward Jerry, who'd almost reached the weapon.

Hunter struck Jerry with the palm of his right hand—short, vicious, hard.

The air filled with smell of blood, sweat, and fury.

Jerry wobbled, then lunged for the gun a final time. He barely missed his target.

Hunter used a knife-edge hand strike that connected with the side of Jerry's head.

Smack!

Hunter straddled Jerry, and slammed his fist into Jerry's nose, then his mouth. He drew his arm again, and again until Hunter felt Jerry's jawbone give.

"Stop, Hunter!"

He didn't bother to glance over his shoulder at Katie. She didn't understand. In unarmed combat, he regaled as a master in the field. He grabbed Jerry's collar and lifted the man off the ground, shaking him.

Blood and saliva trickled down the corner of Jerry's mouth.

Hunter let him fall, then stood. He did his best to wipe the mud off his hands as he turned and retrieved the gun from the ground, then approached Katie.

Christian released his sister when Hunter nodded.

She hobbled to him, wrapping her arms around

his waist. Hunter could feel her body shivering as he held her tightly against his chest. He smoothed down her hair and planted feathery kisses on her head. "Shh. It's okay," he whispered.

Lifting her head, her silvery eyes blinked as she stared at him. His heart broke, seeing the fresh tears streak down her cheeks. He pulled her closer, letting her absorb his strength. The smell of peppermint clung to her, drifting up and sending his senses in turmoil. He tightened his hold on her.

"I don't think he's lying, Hunter. I don't believe he killed Walter or Carter."

"He didn't."

Hunter spun, pulling Katie with him. Christian hovered behind them as they all glared at Paul, who held a gun straight out at them. He recognized Ariel's service weapon. Instinctively, Hunter shoved Katie behind him. He took a few steps toward Paul. "How'd you get out of the handcuffs?"

Paul's smile widened as he lifted a casual shoulder. "Practice makes perfect." He chuckled, the low and menacing range sounding forced to Hunter.

Hunter moved forward, his hand inching for his firearm tucked in the back of his jeans, only to freeze when Paul wiggled the barrel of his gun.

"No, no, no, Mr. FBI Man. You stay right there. And toss your gun out here." Paul made clucking sounds with his tongue, but his eyes appeared as sharp as an eagle's. "You, Christian, step up beside Mister Big-Shot here."

Christian moved to Hunter's left, while Hunter pulled out his Beretta and tossed his sidearm onto the ground.

Jerry hauled himself off the ground, grabbed the guns, and stumbled toward Paul. "Thanks, man. I thought I was a goner for sure."

Hunter's mind raced with options, working to form a plan. He had to get Katie and Christian out of here—get them to safety. "Where's Ariel?"

Paul chuckled again. "She's incapacitated at the moment."

Hunter's eyes narrowed. Christian took a step. Hunter grabbed his forearm and tugged him back in line.

Throwing back his head, Paul laughed. "Good move, Malone. Wouldn't want to have to shoot the girl's nice brother." He bounced from foot to foot. "Especially since I haven't decided which Gallagher I'll take as my guide."

Why hadn't he taken Christian in the first place? Katie was injured, sure to be slower. But she'd be easier to subdue than a man. Hunter's heart found the next gear. He clenched his jaw, forcing his mind to fall back into his training. "Where's Ariel?"

"Katie, dear, step up there in line with the others, won't you?" Paul glared at Hunter, snubbing him in his refusal to answer the question.

She shifted and stood between the two men. Her chin jutted out, her hands clasped in front of her body. "Where are Ariel and Orson?"

Paul smiled. "Nice try." His eyes narrowed into slits as he gawked at her. "You know, I went out of my way to be nice to you, and you blew me off. That wasn't very polite, now was it?"

Katie licked her lips. Hunter could feel her trembling beside him.

"No, not nice at all." Paul took a step back, keeping the gun leveled at them. "So, here's my dilemma—I have to take you, Mr. FBI Man, up to the top. You have company waiting." His eyes darted between Katie and Christian. "But I don't need two guides. See my problem?"

He pointed the gun at Christian. "Do I kill you and take her?" He moved the gun to point at Katie's head. "Or do I kill you and take your brother?" He let out a long sigh. "Decisions, decisions."

"Let's get out of here, Paul." Jerry's face, streaked with mud and blood, turned pale. "The police might know by now. That Roy guy could've called in help."

"Oh, yes, I forgot about you. I have new orders." Paul jerked Hunter's gun from Jerry's shaking hands. "Throw down the other gun."

Jerry did so with hesitation. "N-N-New orders? Since when?"

"Since the raft became indisposed." Paul spoke to Jerry, but kept his gaze, as well as the gun, focused on Hunter. He tucked Ariel's weapon in the waist of his pants, but held onto Hunter's. He kicked Jerry's firearm into the woods.

"What new orders?" Jerry shifted his weight, favoring the right side where Hunter had charged him.

"We're to deliver Mr. Malone topside. Seems this entire operation was set up in order for Mr. King to meet Mr. Malone in person." His gaze drifted up and down Hunter's physique. "It appears they have an old score to settle." A mischievous grin sat on Paul's face. "As for the others, well, Ariel and Orson won't be running to the rescue, I'll tell you that."

Hunter swallowed. Had Paul killed Ariel and the tax attorney? Acid ate at his stomach.

"Come on, man, let's run," Jerry said. "We still have the last load of laundered money and can be in Mexico before Mr. King figures it out."

"To come across so tough, you always were a sniveling punk." Paul sighed. "And now, you no longer serve a purpose."

Jerry's eyes widened. "Huh?"

Hunter moved to react just as Paul spun Hunter's gun toward Jerry and fired, then flipped the gun back at Hunter, who halted.

The sound of the gunshot echoed across the mountain—Katie screamed—Christian sucked in air—Jerry dropped like a rock, both mouth and eyes open wide.

Katie moved forward and buried her head against Hunter's shoulder. He wrapped an arm around her automatically, her sobs tearing into his heart.

Paul glanced at Jerry, then met Hunter's stare. "I believe Jerry told you, Katie, that he was a good shot. I'm even better."

Nausea rose in the back of Katie's throat, the bile burning and searing. She gulped in air and buried her face deeper in Hunter's sweater. As long as she lived, she'd never forget seeing Jerry shot before her eyes. "Is he dead?" she asked, her voice squeaking.

"Yeah, he's dead." Hunter's tone sounded cold . . . distant.

She jerked her head to stare at him. His dark eyes glistened with indescribable emotions. Katie touched the side of his face. "Hunter?"

His jaw clenched, the muscles flickering in his cheek. He continued to stare at Paul, his glare so hot, she could feel the burn.

"Hunter, look at me." Katie gripped his arm tighter. "Hunter."

From the corner of his eye, he glanced at her. "Yes?"

"Let it go."

He stared at her, his eyes wide. "What?"

"Let it go. It's not for you to avenge."

His eyes widened even more.

"How sweet," Paul interrupted as he waved the gun, aiming it at Hunter's head. "Now shut up!"

Katie swallowed and stiffened. *Dear Lord, I know we've just now gotten back on speaking terms, but I could really use some help down here.* She licked her lips, then cleared her throat. "Um, Paul . . ."

"Shut up! You had plenty of chances to talk to me. Wouldn't even give me the time of day." His face twisted into a grotesque display of anger. "I should probably just kill you and get it over with." He raised the gun level to her chest.

Peace rested on her shoulders. She tossed her hair in flagrant defiance and rested her shaking hands on her hips. The feeling liberated her! "That's fine with me, Paul. I'm okay with meeting God face-to-face." She leaned forward and lowered her voice a fraction. "The big question is . . . are you?"

Deep, dark red crept up his neck and into his face, which contorted with expressions of outrage, disbelief, then anger. "H-H-How dare you? I'm the one with the gun." He shook it as he kept it aimed in her direction.

"Because I know where I'm going after I die. Do you?" She tightened her hold on her hips, stiffening each individual finger.

"You're about to find out." Paul leveled the gun to where her heart thudded.

Hunter moved beside Katie, and whispered, "You've turned to God?"

Fresh tears filled her eyes and spilled down her cheeks. She slowly nodded. "Yeah, I did." A little smile tickled the corners of her mouth.

"This is all very moving, but get back in line!"

The muscles in Hunter's arms corded as he clenched his fists. "Don't point that gun at me."

"I'll shoot you where you stand." Paul's jaw muscles jumped.

"Thought you said your boss wanted me alive." He leaned on his right leg. "Now what'd you do with Ariel and Orson?"

"What do you think I did with them?" Paul laughed for a moment before halting the eerie sound as quickly as he'd let it burst forth, then moved the handgun to put Katie in the crosshairs. "And if you don't do as I say, I'll shoot her."

Wild, white fury blinded Hunter. Mechanically, he took a step forward, moving toward Paul, his hands balled into tight fists.

Boom!

It all happened in slow motion to Hunter's eyes: the gunshot's discharge echoed over the mountain, reverberating louder and longer than the shot that'd killed Jerry, smoke drifted out from the barrel of the gun, white spirals wandering upward, Katie screamed, sending tidal waves of fear coursing through Hunter's body.

He spun around.

Christian and Katie were on the ground. Katie sobbed as she clutched her brother's shoulders. Sticky, red blood saturated her hands.

Hunter dropped to his knees. His eyes frantically ran over Katie's face and torso, searching for the point of entry.

Pulling her brother into her lap, Katie's face lost all color. Christian groaned loudly.

Dropping his probing gaze to Christian's face, wrapped in pain, Hunter inspected him. The top of Christian's shirtsleeve dripped blood onto Katie's lap. Leaning over, Hunter felt the wound. A clean, straight-through-the-flesh shot. Painful, but not life-threatening. At least, not at this point.

Katie's stare scorched him. Hunter moved her hands to cover the wound, showing her how much pressure to keep applied to lessen the loss of blood. Her tear-heavy eyes blinked. Worry pulled into each feature on her face.

Heart hammering, Hunter gave her the most assuring smile he could muster. "I'm falling for you, Katie Gallagher," he whispered.

"Come on, come on. Let's get moving." Paul said.

Hunter pushed to his feet and turned to glare at the gun-toting man. "That wasn't necessary." This wasn't a time to expend pain, like he'd fought with Jerry. This was time to let his training work and take Paul down.

Paul shrugged, but kept the gun leveled at Hunter. "Not my fault he wanted to be a hero. He moved into the bullet."

"The bullet meant to kill Katie!" Hunter charged Paul.

Paul pointed the gun and pulled the trigger. Hunter dodged to the right and bent over, rushing ahead in a forward-tackling move.

His body connected, then Paul slammed to the ground.

Hunter used his forearm to wedge between Paul's chin and chest, pressing hard against his throat.

Paul grunted.

Using his other hand, Hunter rammed his fist into Paul's side. Hard, and repeatedly.

Kicking at the ground, Paul scrambled to free himself.

Hunter pressed his forearm harder into Paul's throat.

Paul made a sound like a smoker with emphysema.

Hunter brought his knee up and connected with Paul's groin with all the force of his experience.

Eyes bulging, Paul gasped for air.

Hunter, drawing on his training in martial arts, removed his forearm, and in one fluid motion, put a hold on Paul's neck, causing the man to lose consciousness.

Satisfied he'd rendered Paul incapacitated, Hunter pushed himself to his feet and rushed over to Katie and Christian. He knelt beside them, gently lifting Katie's hand.

Christian moaned. "Ow, man. That stings."

"I know. I'm sorry." Hunter pressed slightly on the surrounding tissue.

"Ouch!"

Hunter pulled his hand back. "It went straight through. We need to stop the bleeding." He pulled his shirt over his head, then ripped one of the sleeves free. He laid the material over the gunshot wound, then stared into Christian's eyes. "This is gonna hurt for a minute, buddy."

Christian closed his eyes and nodded.

Hunter tied the shirt sleeve tight over the wound.

Through clamped lips, Christian uttered guttural shouts.

"There. That'll slow down the bleeding." Hunter rocked back on his heels, peering into Katie's face. "Are you okay?"

Her lips quivered, but she nodded. The chill still hovered in the air, despite the sun peeking through the trees. She wanted to curl up and sleep, escape into the warmth of slumber's embrace, but knew she couldn't. Katie stiffened her back, disregarding the pain and exhaustion pulsating through her muscles.

"Okay, we've got to get a move on." Hunter rose and stalked to Paul. He retrieved the guns, slipping them into the waistband of his jeans. He turned to Katie. "Can you hand me my shirt? I've got to tie up Paul."

She tossed it to him. "Are we leaving him here?"

Hunter caught the shirt deftly and ripped it into strips. "We have to. We need to get Christian to the hospital, but we also need to find Ariel and Orson. In the event Paul lied, we have to stop them before they get to the top and walk into an ambush."

She nodded.

Hunter worked on binding Paul's hands and feet, then glanced over his shoulder. "Get Christian to his feet. We need to hurry."

"And if Paul told the truth about hurting Ariel and Orson?" Her bottom lip quivered.

"We'll find out soon enough."

Twenty-four

Katie hobbled forward, refusing to acknowledge the blinding pain in her ankle and head. She had to help Hunter carry Christian, and find Ariel and Orson. Hunter depended on her. She'd let so many people down, she wouldn't disappoint Hunter again. Not if she could help it.

She cut her gaze across her brother to study Hunter. He hadn't mentioned his declaration of feelings again, yet the sentiment still swarmed around in her mind, soothing her battered heart. Did he see a future with her, or had he blurted out under duress? Katie prayed his emotions were genuine. For her heart had already decided it wanted Hunter. Totally and completely, the traitorous organ.

Christian moaned as she wavered in a step, jostling his shoulder.

Wincing, she grimaced. "Sorry."

"It's okay," her brother ground out.

She steadied her grip around his waist and pressed on. But her mind raced. Paul could've killed Christian. Or Hunter.

Hunter led them back to the right where the others would hike. "If there's a way up, Ariel will keep digging in. She's a determined little thing."

His words bit into her heart. Did he have feelings for his partner? Not just feeling responsible for her as a partner? He reached to help Christian over a rocky step, and she noticed his knuckles were cut—dried blood settled in the grooves and notches.

"Should we call them?" Katie couldn't bear to think two more people could be killed. She stopped, taking all weight off her injured ankle and leaning against a tree for balance.

Hunter's penetrating gaze dropped to her ankle. "It's swelling."

"I'm okay. We need to get Christian to safety." She placed her foot on the ground, refusing to waver in the pain. She tilted her head toward her brother and lowered her voice. "His skin is losing color."

Hunter shot his appraising eye to Christian, then back. His gentle stare caressed her face, causing her heart to flutter. "He's lost a lot of blood."

"We need to hurry." She moved toward Christian.

Hunter took Christian's other side and led them up the path. Suddenly, he stopped. His head jerked around to the right, then the left.

Fear constricted in her chest. "What?"

"I can't tell if we need to move up or down from here." He nudged Christian. "Man, is this the path you and Ariel came down?"

Christian lifted his head, his eyes glassy. "Yeah, this is it." His words shoved from his throat, sounding hoarse and broken.

"Let me see." Katie eased away from her brother and limped up the path a short way.

Bending over, she inspected the mud-caked rocks. Streaking marks littered the rocks. She tugged at the low-lying bush, pulling it closer for inspection. Two leaves ripped and a stem snapped. Straightening, Katie turned back to Hunter. "This is the way they came."

He cocked his head to the side, holding Christian upright. "Are you sure?"

She gave a snort of laughter. "Of course I'm sure. Born and raised on the Gauley, I know how to track. Who do you think taught Christian?" She nodded toward the bushes. "Someone's come through here recently, since the rains stopped."

"Well then, let's go."

Christian didn't look good. Staggering to his feet and then leaning heavily on Katie and Hunter, he kept his eyes closed and his lips pulled into a tight line. Katie worried her bottom lip with her top teeth.

"He's gonna make it, but he may lose consciousness soon." Hunter's words startled her.

She glanced at him, seeing his eyes soften as hers met with his. "But he'll be okay?"

"We need to get him medical attention as soon as possible, but he should be fine. The bullet went straight through his arm. I think it might've nicked an artery."

Remaining silent, Katie nodded and concentrated on the terrain. She picked her steps carefully, avoiding any possible disruption of Christian's injury.

"He'll be all right, Katie."

She jerked her head at the intensity of his words. His stare filled her with happiness, pure unadulterated joy. She smiled at him, feeling the warmth creep up from inside. "I know."

"So . . . tell me when you realized God hadn't abandoned you?" His dark chocolate eyes twinkled. "I imagine you're bursting to share."

"How'd you know?"

"Because I was the same way." He paused. "So, tell me all about it."

"Well," she grinned even as she worked to keep Christian upright, "Jerry knocked me out."

Hunter's eyes clouded over and fury washed across his face.

She shook her head. "No, it's okay." Taking in a deep breath, she let the air out slowly. "I regained consciousness and thought I must have a concussion because I heard a voice. Not like Jerry or anybody talking—the voice came from inside my head."

Hunter nodded and pulled Christian toward him, taking on more of his weight.

"I thought I was going crazy, hearing things and all. Then I realized God spoke to my heart." At the memory, goosebumps prickled her arms, even though she sweated. "And I just knew, deep inside, that He was there, waiting for me to run into His open arms." Katie blinked rapidly, fighting back the tears of joy. They escaped the corners of her eyes despite her attempts.

"Oh, Katie. That's wonderful." Hunter's eyes glistened in the smatterings of sunbeams cutting through the canopy of leaves.

She sniffed back hiccups. "And a feeling of such peace and love came over me. Like, like . . . I can't even describe it."

Behind Christian's back, Hunter squeezed her hand. "I know exactly what you mean."

Smiling, Katie stared at the ground again. Her heart filled with happiness and acceptance. Now, she only had to find the courage to ask Hunter if he'd meant what he'd said.

She hauled in a deep breath, holding it for a few seconds, then let it out in a whoosh. "Hunter?"

"Yeah?"

She really wanted Hunter to want to see about a relationship with her.

"Uh . . . about before . . ."

A dog's high-pitched bark cut off her question.

Hunter narrowed his eyes as thrashing and footfalls slushed up ahead on the path, careening down toward them at a rapid speed. He braced himself as Shadow came into view, obviously moving as fast as he could on his splinted leg. He took Christian's weight off Katie, whose eyes lit up.

The dog barreled straight for them. At least Paul hadn't killed her beloved pet.

Katie cried out and dropped to her knees, holding her arms open wide.

Shadow barreled into her, his entire back end wagging in lieu of a tail.

Burying her face in the dog's fur, Katie crooned and whispered. She finally stood, new tears shining in her eyes. Her happiness could send his spirits soaring high above the treetops. Katie could make him forget about the danger lurking ahead.

Excitement radiating from her like the welcome sun after so much rain, Katie looped her arm around Christian's waist. "Come on, Christian. Not much farther until you can rest for a minute." Her smile widened as she hobbled along, but his heart ached. Would they find Ariel and Orson dead?

Happiness bubbled up in Hunter's throat, and he couldn't explain why. Being in her presence made him content. An emotion he hadn't felt in ages. Now that he enjoyed it, even in these rough circumstances, he realized how much he'd missed it.

Thank You, Lord. Thank You, thank You, thank You.

He opened his mouth, intending to tell her he wanted to get to know her better, like on a real date, when Christian drooped.

Katie gave under his weight, slumping down to land on her knees.

Hunter tightened his grip on Christian's waist, bearing all of his weight. He lowered Katie's brother to the ground, then checked his pulse. Slow and thready, but present.

Shadow barked once, then turned and scampered up the pathway, only slightly dragging his broken leg.

Hunter situated Christian so his head rested in Katie's lap. She wiped at his face with the edge of her sweater, her tears wetting her brother's face. "Oh, Christian, wake up. Come on, it's going to be okay. You need to fight. Come on, open your eyes and look at me."

Hunter stared at them. He swallowed as she looked at him, her eyes pleading for assurances that her brother would live. He pressed his lips together and cleared his throat. "I'll run ahead to find help."

Katie's eyes widened. Wetness cloaked the silvery orbs. Hunter leaned down and pressed his lips to hers. He pulled away, intending to head up the mountain, when he heard Ariel's ear-splitting scream.

"Hunter!"

Relief flooded his system. He sprinted into a run. His knees looked like pistons popping up and down as he built up speed while he climbed.

"Hunter!"

The desperation in his partner's voice propelled him faster. "Ariel!"

Unmindful of the nicks and cuts on his hands, Hunter utilized every tree and shrub he could in his race to reach Ariel. Seconds later, he glanced over his shoulder. He couldn't see Katie and Christian. He had to find his partner. "Ariel, where are you?"

Shadow darted between his legs and barked. The

dog scampered up the path, turned and looked back at Hunter, and whimpered before running out of sight.

Hunter hauled in a big breath, then pushed himself back into a sprint, following the hop-a-long dog. He rounded a curve and tripped over something, sending him sprawling in the mud, face first.

"Hunter!" Ariel's sharp shout caused him to push up on his arms and shake his head, removing the chunks of earth.

Rolling over into a sitting position, he swiped at the remaining mud and glanced around. Orson lay in the middle of the path, the object Hunter had tripped over. Even he, who grimaced off and on from the pain of his leg, chuckled at Hunter. "Son, you look like one of those creatures in a B-grade horror movie."

Ariel laughed so hard, she bent at the waist, holding her sides. She perched on the edge of a large boulder, just off the main path. Her face turned a brighter shade of red as she gulped for air. "You . . . you . . ." Fits of laughter overtook her again. She cackled until tears ran down her cheeks.

Hunter stood, his hands on his hips. "I thought you were calling because you were in trouble."

"I am." She sobered immediately. "I can't pull Orson anymore and Paul got away from me." Her face lost all traces of humor. "He's the real culprit, Hunter, not Jerry. He shot us."

"Shot you? Then . . . how . . ."

She shook her head and lowered her eyes. "When I reloaded after shooting the bear, I must've accidentally put in blanks that I carry for target practice. The shots stunned us, but we're okay. We'll be sporting some seriously nasty bruises tomorrow, but we're alive."

"How'd he get out of the handcuffs, Ariel?" His voice sounded low, but stern, while his heart thumped wildly against his ribs. "Please don't tell me you took them off."

A blush crept over her face. "He conned me."

His heart sank to his knees. He shook his head. "Ariel, you know better. You're trained."

"I know, I know. But he said he needed to go to the bathroom. I didn't think I had a choice."

"You understand procedure."

She pressed her lips together until they turned white. "I'm sorry." Tears welled in her Caribbean-blue eyes. "And when he was done taking care of his personal business, I needed help with Orson." She ran a hand over her hair. "I'm so sorry, Hunter." Her gaze drifted over his face. "Where is he?"

"Tied up with what's left of my shirt about two hundred yards to the left and about four clicks down." Tossing her service firearm to her, he nodded. "I think this belongs to you."

Ariel grabbed her gun and shoved it into her waistband. Her eyes drifted to Shadow, who stood next to Hunter. "Where are Katie and Christian?"

"Down the path. Paul almost shot Katie."

Ariel sucked in air and covered her mouth with her hand again. "She okay?"

He nodded. "She's fine. Christian took the bullet for her." He watched his partner's face to see her reaction. She didn't disappoint.

"No!" She yelled as she rose, hovered for a moment, then slumped back down on the rock. Her face wreathed in misery and tears flowed down her face.

Guilt at not telling her the whole truth knocked him in the gut. "He's okay, Ariel. An in-and-out shot."

She lifted her head to stare at him, not bothering to hide her crying.

"But," he held up a finger, "he's lost a lot of blood and he's unconscious."

Ariel rose again. "Let's go get him."

Hunter nodded, then turned to Orson. "You going to be okay here?"

"Let's see, Jerry's dead and Paul's tied up nice and tight. Yeah, I'll be fine." The older man nodded. "Go get that young man. Ariel brought the first-aid kit with us. I'll get some stuff ready." He nodded at Hunter. "Go."

Shadow rushed down the path, scampering on his broken leg until he hobbled out of view.

Making fast tracks, Ariel at his side, Hunter felt as if a load had settled back over his shoulders. Sure, Paul was contained and Jerry no longer a threat, but what about the kingpin at the top of the mountain waiting on him?

"Are you sure he's okay, Hunter?"

Keeping pace with Ariel's shorter jogging stride, he nodded. "Yeah. You really care a lot about him, huh?"

"Yeah, I guess I do." She sighed and matched his steps. "You know, this started out as a routine assignment, but now . . ."

"Now it's different?"

She nodded. "Yeah."

"I know what you mean."

Ariel cocked her head, staring up at her partner. "You do?"

Hunter smiled as he caught sight of Katie rocking Christian. "Yeah, I do."

Twenty-five

Katie snapped up her head as Hunter and Ariel approached. They had to be close . . . Shadow had returned and still sat with his body pressed against hers. Part of her heart begged her to rush into Hunter's arms while another part held her in place, still cradling Christian's head in her lap. As if she were being ripped in two, Katie let fat tears wash her face.

Ariel ran to her side and dropped to her knees,

her fingers feeling Christian's wrist for a pulse. "Has he regained consciousness?"

Clenching her jaw, Katie shook her head.

Hunter knelt behind Katie, wrapping his arms around her shoulders. His face so close, his breath tickled her ear as he spoke. "Ariel got top scores in emergency first-aid in the field. Let her help."

Tension slid down Katie's spine and she leaned back into Hunter. He tightened his grip and kissed her temple. Even in such a chaotic situation, the thrill of his touch moved her.

Ariel struck Christian's cheek repeatedly with a firm yet gentle slap.

Shadow growled, but didn't move away from Katie, who laid a hand on the dog's neck.

Christian's eyes flickered open, staring up into the leaves of the treetops. He moved his gaze to Ariel's face, blinked several times, then smiled. "Ariel?"

She smiled back, running a caressing finger down the side of his face. "Hey, you. How're you feeling?"

"Like I've been shot."

Everyone laughed. Katie's spirit lifted once more. One thought ran through her mind, like a stuck record player: *Thank You, Lord. Thank You.*

"Let's get you up." Hunter shifted around Katie, hoisting Christian to his feet.

Christian swayed for a moment, gripping Ariel's shoulders, then steadied. He flashed Katie a quick smile as she pushed to her feet, mindful of not tripping on Shadow. "Thought you'd gotten rid of me, Katie-cat?"

Tears burning her eyes, Katie shook her head. "Nah. You're a Gallagher—we're made of stronger stuff than that."

He gave her a slow wink before leaning against Ariel and Hunter, letting them lead him up the path.

Watching her brother walk away with Ariel, Katie's heart quivered. Ariel acted as if she truly cared about Christian, and the secrets she'd buried were no more awful than Hunter's, yet Katie had been able to forgive him. A thought flashed across her mind. If God could forgive her for all the atrocities she'd committed, surely she could forgive Ariel for her deception. Katie swallowed again.

Katie cut her gaze to Hunter. Could he be sincere in his proclamation of his feelings for her? She'd ask him as soon as they were safe— as soon as she could handle the truth.

Katie's ankle throbbed when she took the first step up the path. She cried out, then pressed her lips together. Hot tears scorched her cheeks.

Shadow moved to her side, whimpering.

Hunter released Christian and wrapped his arm around her waist. "How bad is it?"

She swallowed. "It hurts."

He lowered her to the ground, untied her boot,

then whistled under his breath. "Katie, this has swollen almost three times its normal size." His stare stilled her quivering chin. "Why didn't you loosen the laces?"

Lifting a casual shoulder, she closed her eyes, only to snap them open a moment later when he scooped her up into his arms.

Shadow barked and pawed at the ground.

"Put me down, Hunter. I can walk."

"Not well, you can't. I'll carry you." He took steps to follow Ariel and Christian. "Hold on to me."

"This is silly. Put me down."

"Nope." Hunter pulled her tighter against his chest. He leaned forward and planted a kiss on the tip of her upturned nose.

He pulled back and kept walking. She blinked, opened her mouth, then clamped it shut.

Shadow limped alongside them.

Hunter kept marching up the path.

Katie snaked her arm around the back of his neck and let her body relax against him.

They broke into view of Christian, Ariel, and Orson, and her brother let out a whooping sound. Her body stiffened again. From between clenched teeth, she said, "Put me down."

Hunter lowered her to the ground, but kept a supporting arm around her waist. For every step they took, she bit back cries. Shadow paced beside her. At last, Hunter helped her sit on the rock beside Orson. Shadow licked her hand, which dangled limply at her side.

"What's our plan?" Ariel faced Hunter.

Christian moved toward Katie, resting the back of his head against her thigh. The dog shifted to allow Christian more room.

"You guys need to keep moving up," Hunter announced. "With three injured parties . . ." His gaze dropped to Shadow. "Make that four injured parties, progress is going to be slow. I'm going to meet the mastermind of the whole operation."

"Oh, no, you aren't." Ariel cocked out her hip, her fingertips grazing the butt of her handgun. "You aren't going anywhere by yourself."

"Ariel, Paul told me he's been answering to someone else, someone who's been calling all the shots. And it's personal. Between me and whoever it is." He squared his shoulders. "And I can bring back help."

"I'm not buying that." Ariel shook her head. "You need backup and you know it. I'm going with you."

"You can't. Someone needs to stay here with the group. Someone with a gun." He hitched an eyebrow.

She looked at him, over to the others, then back.

Katie watched the interaction with interest. Great interest.

Hunter took a deep breath. "Besides, as senior agent, I'm ordering you to stay here and protect this group." He widened his stance. "Is that understood?"

Ariel's shoulders slumped. "Understood."

"Good." Hunter turned and knelt before Katie. "You're going to be okay. I'll get help down here as soon as I can."

His stare nearly made her knees buckle.

He ran a finger down the side of her face, sending her mercury into the red. "Okay? I'll be back. I promise."

Not trusting herself to speak, she nodded.

"There're radios on the four-wheelers," Christian ground out. "Emergency channel is eight."

Hunter laid a hand on Christian's uninjured shoulder. "Thanks. You're a good man, Christian Gallagher." He rose to his full height, nodded at Ariel, then took off up the trail, heading in the direction of the parking lot.

A little piece of Katie's heart tightened.

As soon as Hunter moved out of sight, Ariel nodded toward Christian. "We need to redress his wound."

"Here's the first-aid kit," Orson mumbled as he tossed the bag to Ariel. It landed in the mud at her feet.

Christian shifted, still leaning on Katie for support. "Let's get it done, then." His voice sounded weak, light.

Ariel untied Hunter's shirt sleeve, while Katie mopped her brother's brow. A fine sheen of sweat dotted his face. She pulled Christian to her, settling his back against her chest. Jaw set, he pinched his eyes shut tightly. Katie held her breath as he shuddered.

Once Ariel replaced the shirt sleeve with gauze and medical wrap, she handed Christian two ibuprofens and a bottle of warm water. "Here, take these. It'll help with the inflammation and the pain." Her eyes stayed glued to his face as he took the pills. Water dribbled down his chin as he swallowed.

Katie propped her brother against the over-sized rock, situating his head against the smooth edge. Using the rock's ridge as leverage, she pulled herself into a standing position.

Ariel, rewrapping Orson's splint, glanced at her. She used a hand to shield her eyes from the sun's hot glare. "Katie, where are you going? I'll wrap your ankle as soon as I finish with Orson."

Pressing her lips together, Katie stared at the woman whose hands cared for Orson's injury. The same woman who'd dressed Christian's wound with gentleness and concern.

A tension-filled haze lingered over the area, appearing to consume all the oxygen on the pathway.

Katie hauled in a deep breath. "I'm going after Hunter."

"No, you aren't." Ariel finished addressing Orson's splint and stood.

"Yes, I am." Katie wouldn't back down . . . couldn't. She had to make sure Hunter stayed safe and sound.

"You heard his orders—we're to stay here until help arrives."

"No, he gave you the order." Katie pulled her spine tight, drawing herself up to her full height.

"You can't go, Katie." Ariel's voice softened. "Look, I know you care about him and all, but by getting involved, you're putting him at risk."

"I don't care what you think is best, Ariel. I'm going." Katie turned from the woman's glare and squatted in front of her brother. "Christian, I need you to keep Shadow here. He shouldn't be running around on a broken leg." Her hands sought Shadow's collar as she pet her best friend.

"You either."

Katie stood and faced Ariel again. "Come again?"

"You said the dog shouldn't be running around on a hurt leg." Ariel nodded toward Katie's ankle. "You either."

"Shadow has a broken leg. I just have a twisted ankle. Big difference."

"Not enough. I'm telling you, stay put." Ariel took a step toward Katie. "If I have to, I'll arrest you for obstruction of justice and handcuff you."

"Like you handcuffed Paul?" The sarcasm burned Katie's tongue, but she had no choice. "We saw how well that worked out."

Ariel's face washed white. Katie hated being mean and cruel, but she had to make sure Hunter was safe—she couldn't risk losing him. "You can't stop me unless you shoot me, and that would really ruin your chances with my brother, now wouldn't it?"

"Just let her go, Ariel." Christian spoke with a soft resignation. "If she's determined, you aren't going to stop her anyway."

Ariel glanced at him, then lifted her stare back to Katie. "You'll distract Hunter. You would just get in the way."

"I'm going." Katie set her feet in a tough stance.

The two women stood face-to-face, an imaginary line drawn in the mud between them. Sun glaring down on them, neither moved a muscle.

"Come on, girl . . . let Katie go get her man." Orson's gruff words tugged a smile out of Katie.

Sighing, Ariel gave a slow nod. Under her breath she mumbled, "Hunter's gonna write me up for sure now."

Katie dropped to her knees, hugged Shadow, and planted a soft kiss on her brother's cheek. "Thank you," she whispered in his ear before she stood.

"Just be careful," he said.

"Here, take this." Ariel pulled the gun from her waistband and offered it to Katie.

Fear and revulsion sparred in her heart. Katie

looked at Ariel and shook her head. "Thanks, but I don't do guns."

"You'll need some protection."

Again, Katie shook her head. "No, thanks." She turned to her brother, then stopped and met Ariel's eyes. She gave a shaky smile. "Thank you."

Ariel nodded, but her smile lifted.

Katie winked at her brother. "I'll radio for help as soon as I get up there. Are the keys under the seats?"

He flashed her a weak grin. "Yeah."

"I'll be back soon." She swallowed back the tears. "I promise."

Sniffing, Katie turned and headed up the path as quickly as her throbbing ankle would allow her.

Hunter crouched in the bushes lining the parking lot. His clasp tightened on his gun. He didn't move a muscle.

Large puddles of water sat on the concrete, reflecting the sun and casting glares dancing on the asphalt. Hunter squinted as he scoped out the area. No sign of anyone.

At the far end of the lot, two oversized Polaris four-wheelers sat parked, side-by-side. Nothing near them.

Like a lion tracking its prey, Hunter moved. Slowly, as to not disturb the low-lying bushes and underbrush, Hunter crept toward the vehicles, keeping inside the tree line for cover. Birds scattered overhead, halting his progress. He held his breath as he cased the lot again.

He continued on his trek—heel first, then pad of the foot, picking his steps carefully, avoiding twigs that could snap. The birds sang their happy tunes above his head. His heart thumped wildly.

Guide me, Lord.

The breeze stirred the air. Hunter froze. He sniffed, but only caught the odor of rain, dirt, and river. The distant hum of the raging water registered only in the back of his mind. He worked to reach the edge of the trees closest to the four-wheelers. Two more steps and he could touch one of the vehicles.

Only the glittering of the sun in the water and the leaves being carried in the wind. Could it be this easy? Had Paul lied about having a boss? Hunter remained still, letting reflexes overtake his awareness of self.

God, I need to radio for help. Please, Father . . . so many are depending on me. I can't let them down.

Propelling himself forward, Hunter crept over the asphalt, his body on full alert.

He reached the four-wheeler and crouched beside it. What channel had Christian told him to use? Eight? He dialed the channel knob. Static spewed from the radio, a squeak and squall right on its heels. Hunter grabbed the volume knob and twisted. Silence prevailed.

Hunter peered over the vehicle's seat. The radio's blast hadn't brought some evil drug lord running. It hadn't brought down a hail of bullets.

Drawing in a deep breath, he pressed the speak button and held the microphone close to his mouth. "Help needed. FBI agent requesting medical and law enforcement assistance immediately."

The radio came alive. "This is Sheriff Towns, who are you, and where are you?"

"This is Special Agent Hunter Malone of the FBI. We're at the top of the mountain by Meadow River, in the parking lot. I need backup and emergency medical personnel."

"Is this a joke?"

Hunter tightened his jaw and shifted, holding his weapon in a death grip. "No. My badge number is 3-9-9-8—you can verify it. I have two members of Gauley Guides by Gallagher here, and one of them has been shot—Christian Gallagher. Just send backup and ambulances."

Rustling from the trees reached Hunter's ears.

He dropped the microphone and turned, ready to shoot. "Freeze! FBI!"

Twenty-six

"Hunter!"

He whipped around, gun drawn, as his heart crashed at the sound of Katie's voice.

Rushing forward, she leaned into his arms. "Where is he?"

"I don't know." He pushed her an arm's length away, even though he wanted nothing more than to hold her forever, and slipped the weapon back into his waistband. He had to make her understand the severity of the situation and the predicament she could've put him in. Gripping her shoulders, Hunter peered into her flashing eyes. "You shouldn't be here. I told you to stay with the others."

"I couldn't let you come alone. It's too dangerous."

For a split second, he wanted to chuckle. "Katie, it's what I do." His eyes drank in the sight of concern in her gaze. "What do you think you could've done?"

Her face flushed, red spreading to the tips of her ears.

Hunter ran his knuckles across her chin. The touch sent sparks off in his heart. "I'm touched you came running to my rescue, really I am, but I don't want you putting yourself in danger."

She smiled. "I don't see anyone."

He sighed. She couldn't even take orders when it came to her life being at stake. "Me either." He ran a hand through his hair. "Paul may have been lying about having a boss." He tweaked her nose. "But you should've stayed where I told you to."

The beginnings of a smile hugged the edge of her mouth. It made his mouth go dry. "Yes, sir," she said as she executed a snappy salute.

"This isn't a game, Katie. I can't afford to be distracted."

"Oh, so I'm a distraction now, am I?" Her eyes turned as cold and deadly as the steel of his Beretta, and she took a step back.

His heart exploded with regret. "That didn't come out right. I didn't mean it like it sounded."

"But that's what you said."

He took a step toward her, but she hobbled back. "I only meant that I have feelings for you, I honestly do, but I have a job to do and it involves protecting you and those you love." He reached out and took her hand, tugging her to him.

Her eyes blinked, filling with moisture. "I have feelings for you, too, Hunter," she murmured.

The knot in his chest loosened as he pulled her into an embrace. His lips covered hers, capturing her mouth in a kiss that should've singed them both. All the emotion and hopes and daring-to-dream thoughts bottled inside him broke forth in his kiss. Her hand tugged at his hair. Her heart pounded between them, his matching its fervor.

"How very touching."

Instinctively, Hunter released Katie, withdrew the gun from the back of his waistband, and spun to face the man who'd spoken.

And stared into the black barrel of a .357 Magnum.

The air left Katie's lungs in one big whoosh. Her knees went weak. "S-S-Steve? But . . . but why?"

"First things first." He pointed his weapon at Hunter's head. "I suggest you drop that gun. Now."

Hunter inched up the end of his pistol, pointing it at Steve's chest, and shook his head. "You first."

The .357's muzzle shifted, drawing Katie into the sights. "Then I'll shoot Ms. Gallagher here." Steve shrugged. "Should have known that moron Jerry couldn't follow orders."

She gasped. *Oh, God, not now. Please, not yet.*

Hunter's body went rigid. His knees locked and his shoulders adjusted. He dropped his gun. It clattered against the gravel. "That moron Jerry is dead."

Steve hitched an eyebrow as he kicked the gun. It skidded to a stop about two feet to Hunter's right. "You're better than I gave you credit for, Master Sleuth."

Hunter crossed his arms over his chest, looking relaxed. "I didn't kill him. Paul did."

"Now I am impressed. Didn't think the weasel had it in him." His eyes narrowed at Katie. "He was too sweet on you, and obviously it was a mistake. Where is Paul?"

"In custody, of course." Hunter jutted out his jaw. "Just as you will be soon."

Steve laughed, the sound dry and callous. "I don't think so. I've been waiting nine years to kill you, Malone. You won't get away." He bobbed his head, motioning Katie to move beside Hunter.

Hobbling forward, Katie grasped Hunter's arm for balance. Just touching him gave her strength. "I don't understand."

The man she'd perceived as weak and skittish transformed. Even his manner of speaking, his pronunciation, the method he articulated his words came out differently. "Poor woman, of course you don't." His eyes slid to Hunter. "Then again, you don't know Super Agent here very well, do you?"

Hunter massaged the bridge of his nose. "What's your beef with me, Steve? I've never been anything but nice to you."

"Nice?" Steve pushed the gun farther, pointing it back at Hunter. His expression of cold amusement shifted to something dark. Sinister.

Katie shivered. How could she have been so wrong about two people?

"And, by the way, my name's not Steve." His voice took on a nasally octave. "Look at me carefully, Agent-Man. I've had some minor alterations made to my facial features, but surely you can recognize me."

Hunter's forehead wrinkled, etching deep lines across his face. He stared hard at Steve, scrutinizing the man's face. No spark of recognition popped into his eyes.

"Look into my eyes," Steve almost shouted.

Hunter still showed no signs of recognition.

Katie let out a pent-up breath. So much for the mystery being solved any time soon. *God please, help us out here.*

Steve chuckled, the sound echoing hauntingly over the space between them. "Not as smart as you thought, huh, Mr. Rocket Scientist? I've been working two cubicles down from you for six months, and you never figured it out. You're not the brightest crayon in the box, are you?" His laughter deepened, prickling the warning hairs on the back of Katie's neck. "But since I'm such a sporting guy, I'll help out by giving you a couple of clues."

Hunter's eyes held that dark, dangerous look. The one he'd worn when fighting with Jerry and Paul. Her breathing hitched and she grasped his forearm tightly. Looking back at Steve, she forced her voice to be firm, steady. "What kind of clues?"

Steve's eyes narrowed before he gave her a crooked smile. "You know what? An ironic opportunity has just dropped into my lap. We'll make it a game. A payback, if you will. A lost love for losing love."

His sneer made her confidence waver. "What kind of game?"

"I'll give Agent-Man here a clue. If he guesses who I am, I'll shoot you, my dear, in the heart, killing you instantly."

Katie's hope deflated like a lead balloon.

"However, for each incorrect guess he delivers, I'll shoot you once. Not enough to kill, mind you, just enough to hurt really bad."

Even the wind stilled as the tension tightened over Hunter like the cranking of a vise.

The acid in Hunter's stomach churned. He stiffened as Katie struggled for breath. Fury lined his muscles. "What kind of sick game is that?"

"The kind of eye-for-an-eye game. You took my love, now I'll take yours. How much she suffers depends entirely on you." Steve's eyes were as cold and lifeless as those of a dead fish.

"This is stupid." Hunter moved to take a step.

Steve lifted the gun, pointing the muzzle at Katie.

Hunter froze.

"That's better." Steve nodded at Katie. "You move about three feet away from him."

Katie hesitated.

Steve waved the weapon at her. "Now!"

Katie hobbled a few feet to the right of Hunter. "That's better."

"I'm not going to play any game with the likes of you." Hunter sucked in air, hoping all the psychological lectures he'd endured were right. Refuse to stoop to the criminal's level, that's what the instructors drilled into every agent's head.

Steve shifted the gun's barrel to Hunter's leg, and pulled the trigger.

Hot pain sliced through Hunter's thigh before the ripples of the boom ended.

Katie screamed, her sobbing louder than the gunshot.

His knees gave out—Hunter crashed to the ground. Colored dots converged before his eyes. He blinked, working to focus through the blinding pain. So much for the psychological training.

Crying out again, Katie made a move to limp to Hunter.

"No, ma'am. You stay right where you are."

Hunter forced himself to look at Katie and gave a slight shake of his head. Even that subtle movement caused the blood rushing to his brain to pound harder.

"I'm sorry, Mr. Malone, have I been unclear? Did you think you had a choice?" Steve's condescending tone salted Hunter's wound. "Stand up, or I shoot her."

Struggling to his feet, Hunter balanced on one leg. The hammering of his heart reverberated against his chest. He took a second to study Steve carefully, taking note of his bone structure and build. Hunter's mind shifted through his mental databank of every criminal he'd put away. His search came up empty.

"Your only option is to guess correctly, and quickly. If you refuse, I'll shoot her in the knee-caps, drawing out her suffering as long as I can. Much like the suffering you caused me. Got it?" Steve's aim never wavered from Katie.

"Why?" Katie cried, her sobs tearing Hunter apart.

"Why?" Steve stomped the ground like a petulant child. Mud shot up the leg of his jeans. "Because he took the woman I loved. Ripped her away from me. Just like that." He snapped his fingers. His face twisted into a frown. "We never had a chance. Just like you two will never have a chance."

Hunter gauged the distance between him and Steve. If he rushed him, would he be able to stop Steve before he got a shot off? He spied his faithful Beretta lying on the pavement, between him and Katie. Could he make it to his firearm in time?

"So, here we go. Okay, hotshot, here's your first clue. Nine years ago you were a rookie agent, fresh into the field. You made a bad call and missed catching your man. I'm that man. Who am I?" Steve glanced at his watch. "You have one minute, starting . . . now!"

Nine years ago. First year in the field. The battery of cases flipped through the Rolodex of Hunter's mind. Drug dealers . . . no, they were busted by DEA. The bombings in New York? No, all the culprits were caught. Kidnappings? Hunter recalled every missing person's case he'd ever worked. Nothing.

"Thirty seconds."

Katie whimpered. Hunter's heart twisted in response. He continued his race down memory lane. Rookie agent, working with Danny. Case he worked with Danny. Hunter stared into Steve's eyes. The man truly enjoyed his game. *Oh, God, help me out. Help me remember.*

"Time's up. Take a guess."

Hunter's mouth went as dry as the Arizona desert, while his mind went blank.

"If you don't take a guess, I'll shoot her anyway."

"Bobby Miller." Hunter studied Steve's expression, which twisted into a wry grin.

"Nope. You cost this Bobby guy his love too? Shame on you, Agent Malone." Steve lifted the .357 and shut an eye. "Wrong guess. That'll cost you. I mean, her."

Please, God, no!

The bullet whipped through the air and landed in Katie's thigh with a nauseating pop. She screamed as she fell.

Instinctively, Hunter moved toward her.

"No, sir. You stay put. We're just getting started with our game."

"You sick, lousy excuse of a human being." His heart thumped erratically. Sweat trickled between his shoulder blades as rage threatened to overtake him. He clenched his jaw, forcing his emotions to still.

Steve laughed. "Now you know how it feels, Malone. It hurts, doesn't it?"

Hunter stared at Katie, hunched over on the ground. Her body shook as she cried. It ripped his heart from his chest. "Steve, this is between you and me. Let her go."

"Now what would be the sport in that?" Steve leaned against the four-wheeler, propping his weight against the back bar. "Ready for your next question?"

"You've shot her, isn't that enough?" Hunter despised the weakness in his voice. He clenched and unclenched his fingers, helplessness encroaching over him.

Lord, please, no more. I beg You, not again.

"Here's your next clue, Malone. Pay attention." Steve crossed one foot over the other. "She was confused, unsure. You turned her against me. Made her afraid of me. It wasn't her fault—she'd have come around in time. But your lies made her scared of me. You thought you were smart, trying to set me up, forcing her to act as if she wanted nothing to do with me." A deep red washed over

347

his face as his jaw muscles popped. "I had no choice. I had to take her. Had to kill her. And it's all your fault. Who am I?" He glanced at his watch again. "You have one minute, starting . . . now."

A girl who died on his watch. Amanda Rails? No, she committed suicide. Or did she? Hunter recounted the facts. No, there'd been no man involved—wrong case. Delaney Mills? She died in an auto accident that her boyfriend swore had been bombed. Hunter glared at Steve. Couldn't be him—too short.

"Thirty seconds."

First year case . . . she died . . . her murderer never captured . . . fearful . . . scared . . . a stalking case! He lifted his gaze to probe Steve's appearance. No way.

Dear God, not him!

But Steve stood about the same height with the same build. His hair looked different—a new color, but that could easily be changed. Clean shaven, again, a minor alteration to appearance. Hunter narrowed his eyes and intensified his scrutiny.

Same cold eyes she'd described. The same aristocratic cheekbones the bureau's sketch artist had drawn in dark charcoals. Same sinister laugh she'd described. But no, he had to be dead. They'd assumed he'd killed himself. Isn't that what the profilers said? That he'd have to kill himself because he'd never be able to live with what he'd done to her.

"Time's up. Who am I, Agent Malone?" Steve's eyes mocked him.

Katie's cries rose. For the rest of his life, her sobs would haunt his mind. Just like Misty's death haunted his soul.

Hunter stared into Steve's eyes. "You're Edward Allistar, Misty Mulligan's stalker, kidnapper, and murderer."

Twenty-seven

Katie held her breath, waiting for the next bullet to slam into her body.

It didn't come.

She lifted her head and stared at the men, now glaring at each other. She kept her hand pressed hard against her thigh, using the same amount of pressure Hunter had shown her when Christian was shot. So much useless violence. Christian, Jerry, Hunter, and herself. Would the insanity never end?

"Very good, Agent Malone. I'm impressed." Steve snickered and straightened. "Took you long enough."

"You stalked that woman, kidnapped, and killed her."

Steve's face puffed and turned red. "I loved

her! And she would have loved me if you . . . you . . ." He pointed at Hunter. "You and the other agents hadn't turned her against me."

"She didn't even know you." Hunter's voice sounded amazingly calm. Like they were having an afternoon chat in the park. She moaned under her breath, wincing from the fresh throbbing in her wound.

Steve's sneer sent a shiver racing up her spine. "In time, she would have realized we were meant to be together. But noooo . . . you couldn't let that happen, right?"

Katie gripped her leg harder as ripples of pain shot throughout her body.

Hunter's gun lay on the concrete, shimmering in the overhead sun, beckoning for her to pick it up and save them. She stole a glance at the men. Both were arguing and scowling at each other, so enthralled in their anger that neither paid any attention to her. Could she get to the weapon before Steve/Edward/whoever saw her intent? Katie swallowed and slid four inches toward the gun. Neither man looked in her direction.

Dear God, let me do this. Help me. I'm not ready to die.

"You ruined my life! I had to have plastic surgery, take on a new identity, move away from my job, family, and friends." His eyes bored into Hunter, pure hatred shooting forth.

Only a couple more inches, God. Don't let that

man—Steve, Edward, whatever his name is—look over and catch me. Please, God.

She pulled herself farther across the asphalt, a smear of blood trailing behind her. Slowly leaning forward, she extended her hand. Her fingertips grazed the metal. The gun moved across the pave-ment, sounding like gravel in a top.

Edward glared at her, pointing his big handgun at her face. "No you don't, you miserable wench." A litany of curses spewed from his mouth.

Katie pulled back, balling herself into the fetal position.

Oh, God, I failed. Help me, Lord. He's going to kill me and Hunter. Save us.

The unmistakable click of the gun's hammer echoed over the still, quiet afternoon.

Katie tensed, waiting for him to deliver the fatal shot. Her thigh quivered as she tightened her muscles.

A deep growl sounded from the trees.

Her heart pounding, Katie snapped to attention.

Shadow raced across the parking lot, faster than she would've imagined he could on a broken leg. Propelling himself through the air, the dog collided with Edward's upper body, knocking him off balance.

The back of the man's heel hit a fallen log, and he crashed to the asphalt.

The gun clattered to the ground.

Hunter dove for the firearm at the same time

Katie's fingers wrapped around Hunter's weapon. Both pulled the handguns up, pointing them at Edward. Only Katie's shook so violently, she had to clasp one hand over the other to steady her aim.

Still lying flat on his back, Edward shoved at Shadow. The dog didn't move. His teeth broke the skin on Steve's neck, little pinpricks of blood trickling down his neck.

"Arrrrgh! Get this dog off of me."

"Shadow!" Katie snapped her fingers twice.

The Blue Heeler rushed to her side, his body panting against her as he whined.

She hugged her dog. "Good boy."

"Freeze! FBI!"

Ariel burst through the trees, her firearm aimed at Edward, who struggled to his feet. Christian and Orson limped up behind her.

Hunter slipped his gun into his waistband and on one leg, hopped to Katie and eased down beside her. "Are you okay?" He pulled her into his arms, planting little kisses on the top of her head.

Tears flowed freely down her face.

In the distance, the whirring of sirens sounded.

She collapsed against Hunter's strong chest.

Hunter's heart tightened as he rocked Katie. His lips pressed against her hair, his thoughts focusing only on praise to God for their safety.

The ambulances whipped into the parking lot, followed by three police cars and a fire truck.

Ariel, roughly dragging the handcuffed Edward, moved to the police officer and spoke with him in low tones. The officer shoved Edward inside his cruiser.

A firm tap on his shoulder jerked Hunter around. "Sir, you need to let her go so we can stabilize you both for the trip to the hospital." The young Emergency Medical Technician nodded at Hunter's wound.

Hunter planted a final kiss on Katie's temple, then released his hold. An older EMT examined and treated Hunter's wounds. Hunter couldn't pull his gaze away from Katie, even as the paramedics moved her to a stretcher. Her eyes were closed and her face drawn, pale. Had he failed another woman? The one he was falling in love with?

"They'll take your statements at the hospital." Ariel hovered over him. She held out her hand. His Beretta laid flat in her palm. "I think this belongs to you." Her voice hitched.

He took the gun and gripped it tightly, staring at its icy steel. He found his voice wavering. "Thanks, partner."

Tears welled in Ariel's eyes. "They're taking all of you to the Emergency Room. I'm riding with that nice Lt. Lyons." She flashed a wry grin. "We get to escort Steve to the local bureau."

"His name is Edward Allistar."

"Huh?"

Hunter grunted as he helped the EMT shift him to the stretcher. "Edward Allistar. Stalker. Kidnapper. Murderer. My first field case."

Ariel's face went as blank as an erased blackboard. "The one you told me about?"

The pain in his chest thumping worse than the gunshot wound to the thigh, Hunter nodded. His throat tightened, making speech impossible.

"Oh!" She cleared her throat. "I'd better make sure I get all the info correct." She turned to head back to the police cruiser.

He forced the words out. "Call Brian back in Virginia and tell him to fax the locals all the paperwork. Paul needs to be picked up. And make sure they send units back to retrieve Jerry's and Carter's bodies and they know Walter's in a death cave." Hunter bit back the pain when the medics pushed him toward the waiting ambulance.

"Will do," Ariel tossed over her shoulder as she jogged away.

Hunter shaded his eyes against the movement under the bright sun. Misty had finally been avenged. Nine years too late to save her, but at least her killer would no longer roam free.

Trust in Me, Son.

Stilling on the rolling stretcher, Hunter gasped.

"Are you okay, sir?"

Be still and know that I am God.

Hunter tightened his hands on the nylon straps holding him on the stretcher. *I'm listening, Father God.*

Let go of the past and move forward.

His heart quickened, then sputtered. Let go?

Lean not unto your own understandings, but trust in My ways.

"This might be bumpy. Hang on, sir." The EMT tightened the strap holding Hunter in place on the stretcher.

I trust You, God.

Let go of the past and move forward.

The medics loaded him into the ambulance alongside Katie.

She turned to look at him. Her silver eyes reflected the flashing lights from the fire truck behind them. Reaching out to him, she smiled.

Hunter stared at her hand.

Let go of the past and move forward.

He closed his eyes. *Good-bye, Misty Mulligan. May your soul rest in peace in our Father's house.*

Opening his eyes, Hunter took Katie's hand and squeezed it.

Let go of the past and move forward.

Dear Reader,

Thank you so much for joining me in the adventure on the Gauley River. This story was inspired after my husband returned from a trip where he and a friend completed a "double upper" on the Gauley. The photos and video he brought home to share spurred my imagination into overdrive.

I originally wrote this novel in 2005, then when it was finished, as writers often do, moved on to other stories. My husband recently asked to read this manuscript again. When he'd finished, he asked why I'd stuck it on a drive and forgot about it. So I reread the story, and fell in love with the Gauley, the Gallaghers, and Hunter Malone all over again. After much revising and editing, I'm so excited to share it with you readers. It is my intention to eventually tell Christian and Gabe's stories . . . as soon as those characters are ready, so stay tuned.

If you are interested in discussion questions for this novel, please visit my website at www. robincaroll.com and click on FOR READERS. You'll find many extras there, just for you, my reader friend.

I'm always delighted to hear from fellow readers. Click here to sign up for my newsletter on my website so we can stay in touch. I'm on Facebook under Author.RobinCaroll on Twitter under RobinCaroll, and you can always reach me via snail mail at PO Box 242091, Little Rock, AR 72223. I'd be honored to hear from you.

Blessings, and keep reading,

Robin

About theAuthor

The best-selling author of more than twenty novels, ROBIN CAROLL writes to entertain. Her books have been recognized by the Carol Award, HOLT Medallion, Dauphe du Maurier, RT Reviewer's Choice Award, and more. She serves the writing community as the Executive/ Conference Director for ACFW. Find out more about Robin at RobinCaroll.com.

Center Point Large Print
600 Brooks Road / PO Box 1
Thorndike, ME 04986-0001 USA

(207) 568-3717

**US & Canada:
1 800 929-9108**
www.centerpointlargeprint.com